PENGUIN BOOKS

THE PRINCESS
AND OTHER STORIES

David Herbert Lawrence was born at Eastwood, Notts, in 1885, the fourth child of a miner. At 13 he won a scholarship to Nottingham High School, which he left for a job with a firm of surgical goods manufacturers at a wage of thirteen shillings a week. He soon abandoned this to become a pupil-teacher at Eastwood.

While attending Nottingham University College for his teacher's certificate, he began his first novel, *The White Peacock*, which was published by Heinemann in 1911. From that time onwards, with the exception of a short period as a schoolmaster in Croydon he lived entirely by his writing. For two years he travelled in Germany and Italy, and, returning to England, was married in July 1914 to Frieda von Richthofen. In 1919 the Lawrences left England and travelled, first in Europe and then in Australia and America.

They settled for a while in New Mexico, but came back finally to Europe in 1925. Four years later Lawrence became seriously ill, and he died of tuberculosis on 2 March 1930.

D. H. LAWRENCE

The Princess

AND OTHER STORIES

Edited by Keith Sagar

PENGUIN BOOKS
in association with William Heinemann Ltd

Penguin Books Ltd, Harmondsworth, Middlesex, England
Penguin Books Australia Ltd, Ringwood, Victoria, Australia

—

'The Princess' was first published in the Calendar of Modern Letters
March/April/May 1925;
'Mercury' in the *Atlantic Monthly* February 1927;
'Things' in *The Bookman* (N.Y.) August 1928;
'Sun' (in this version) by the Black Sun Press in 1928;
'Blue Moccasins' in *Eve* 22 November 1928;
'Mother and Daughter' in the *New Criterion* April 1929;
'The Overtone' in *The Lovely Lady* (Secker, 1932);
'The Flying Fish', 'A Dream of Life' (as Autobiographical Fragment)
and 'The Undying Man' in Phoenix (Heinemann, 1936);
'The Man Who Was Through with the World' in
Essays in Criticism July 1959.
'The Wilful Woman' is here published for the first time.

This collection published in Penguin Books 1971
Reprinted 1972

—

Made and printed in Great Britain by
Cox & Wyman Ltd, London, Reading and Fakenham
Set in Monotype Garamond

*D. H. Lawrence's complete short stories are also
available in Canada in a Viking/Compass edition*

Contents

Introduction

THIS volume and its companion *The Mortal Coil and Other Stories* complete the publication of Lawrence's shorter fiction in Penguin. These twelve stories all date from the last eight years of Lawrence's life.

On 11 September 1922 the Lawrences arrived at Taos, New Mexico, as guests of Mabel Dodge Luhan. Three days later her husband Tony, a Taos Indian, took Lawrence motoring in the Apache country for five days. On the evening of his return Lawrence asked Mabel if she would like to work on a book with him: 'He said he wanted to write an American novel that would express the life, the spirit, of America and he wanted to write it around me – my life from the time I left New York to come out to New Mexico.' Two days later Lawrence sent a note to Mabel: 'I have done your "train" episode and brought you to Lamy at 3 in the morning.' This is possibly the first imaginative writing Lawrence attempted in the new continent, and the style is quite different from anything he had written before, sardonic in tone, with something of the timelessness and hard-edged, spiky character of the landscape. It is a superb opening for a novel, or, better still, a novella like 'The Woman Who Rode Away' (a story more freely based on Mabel Luhan who called it 'that story where Lorenzo thought he finished me up'). Yet it seems Lawrence wrote no more, partly, according to Mabel, because of Frieda's opposition to the close collaboration which would have been involved.

In December the Lawrences moved out to a large ranch, the Del Monte, seventeen miles away in the mountains:

I think New Mexico was the greatest experience from the outside world that I have ever had. It certainly changed me for ever. In the magnificent fierce morning of New Mexico one sprang awake, a new part of the soul woke up suddenly and the old world gave way to a new. All those mornings when I went with a hoe along the ditch to the Cañon, at the ranch, and stood, in the fierce, proud silence of the Rockies, on their foothills, to look far over the desert to the blue mountains away in Arizona, blue as chalcedony, with the sage-brush desert sweeping grey-blue in between, dotted with tiny cube-crystals of houses, the vast amphitheatre of lofty, indomitable desert, sweeping round to the ponderous

Sangre de Cristo mountains on the east, and coming up flush at the pine-dotted foot-hills of the Rockies! What splendour! Only the tawny eagle could really sail out into the splendour of it all.

The spring and summer of 1923 the Lawrences spent in Mexico, where Lawrence began *The Plumed Serpent*. But Frieda was pining to see her children again and wanted to return to Europe. In August they got as far as New York, but there Lawrence dug his heels in and refused to go any further. Frieda left alone. She refused to return alone, so in November Lawrence sailed after her, arriving in London at the beginning of December. There the Lawrences shared a house with Catherine and Donald Carswell, whom they had met before the war. One day Lawrence asked Catherine if she was writing anything, and she told him of a novel she had in mind: 'The theme had been suggested to me by reading of some savages who took a baby girl, and that they might rear her into a goddess for themselves, brought her up on a covered river boat, tending her in all respects, but never letting her mix with her kind and leading her to believe that she was herself no mortal, but a goddess.' Lawrence was fired by the idea and offered to collaborate. Indeed, he sketched an outline the same day (see Carswell, *The Savage Pilgrimage*, 202–4). Catherine felt herself inadequate and left the story to Lawrence who completed it, as 'The Princess', the following autumn, after his return to New Mexico.

The Lawrences stayed in Europe for three months. Lawrence hated it. He tried to persuade several of his friends to return to New Mexico with him to form a little colony at the ranch, but only one, Dorothy Brett, accepted. To amuse himself, he wrote several short stories, one of them 'The Overtone'. In New Mexico Lawrence had found a name for his dark god 'as shaggy as the pine trees and horrible as the lightning'. That name was Pan. The essay 'Pan in America', written immediately after Lawrence's return to the ranch, states his position most fully. Pan figures in many of the stories of the time, not only as an abstract life force and a necessary counterbalance to the Christian ideal, but also as a terrifying supernatural presence like Dionysus in *The Bacchae* or Arthur Machen's Great God Pan, wreaking a terrible vengeance upon those who deny him. 'A man who should see Pan by daylight fell dead, as if blasted by lightning'. (And according to 'Mercury', which Lawrence wrote in Germany two years later, the same applies to other gods.) There is an amusing painting by Dorothy Brett of Lawrence upon a cross. Before him dances a horned and goat-footed figure who also bears the face of Lawrence.

The Lawrences spent the summer of 1924 on their new ranch, the Kiowa, even higher than the Del Monte, then returned to Mexico to finish *The Plumed Serpent*. There, in February 1925, Lawrence contracted malaria, which, on top of his tuberculosis, should have killed him. By the sheer will to live, he survived, and during his convalescence dictated to Frieda the beginning of a story called 'The Flying Fish'. Frieda recorded the wonder of his recuperation: 'How he loved every minute of life at the ranch. The morning, the squirrels, every flower that came in its turn, the big trees, chopping wood, the chickens, making bread, all our hard work, and the people and all assumed the radiance of new life.' Gethin Day, the hero of 'The Flying Fish', is also recovering from a near-fatal illness. We see that radiance through his eyes. Later Lawrence read this fragment to his friends the Brewsters, who pleaded with him to finish it. He replied: 'It was written so near the borderline of death, that I have never been able to carry it through, in the cold light of day.' Lawrence's notes give some indication of how the story was to have ended:

Gethin Day of Daybrook in the Lathkill Dale comes home at forty and marries a girl from the valley; No day in Daybrook Is a bad outlook: weather-vane is a fish, and below, the Zodiac revolves. She causes it to reverse. Though Day be dreary, yet Fish will play. When Fish lie weary Day can be gay. When woman's thoughts turn on herself Fish turns his belly up Beasts walk the other way round Sup sorrow, sorrow sup.

When she reverses the vane, the world looks different. She feels *free*. She thinks she might love the engineer whom she sees stopping his car. She thinks she might have a cap of peacock breastfeathers. She thinks she might rival Lady Diana: and she might.

Husband falls sick – says something is wrong, something is wrong. Finds out at last the vane is reversed, fish belly up. Asks her. She says life feels bigger, freer. She wants freedom. She wants to go up to town.

He takes her to town: her child is born: she adores it, but at the very very centre, is cold about it, and knows it. At the centre, she is cold about everything, but her *will* sparkles.

She is ill – sees in the sky a cloud like a dead fish, belly up: knows the world is widdershins: goes back to Daybrook to try to reverse the vane again: lightning kills her.

Lawrence told the Brewsters: 'The last part will be regenerate man, a real life in this Garden of Eden.' He never finished the story.

Regenerate man appears in 'The Man Who Died', fusing the figures of Christ and Pan.

The Lawrences returned to Europe for good in September 1925 and settled at Spotorno in November. One of the first stories Lawrence wrote there was 'Sun'. It was published a few months later in *New Coterie* and collected in 1928 in *The Woman Who Rode Away*, but in an expurgated version. Harry Crosby was a young American poet and publisher living in Paris for whom the sun was an almost obsessive symbol. His press was The Black Sun Press, his collection of poems for which Lawrence later wrote an introduction was called *Chariot of the Sun*, his racehorse was called Sunstroke. There was no Lawrentian influence here, for Crosby read his first Lawrence novel, *The Plumed Serpent*, in January 1928. He immediately wrote an enthusiastic letter to Lawrence about sun-worship, and asked if Lawrence had any manuscripts to sell. Lawrence sent *The Man Who Loved Islands*, the unexpurgated 'Sun', and several poems: 'I am sending you tomorrow the Mss., bound by the binder in Florence, nothing grand – but with my phoenix rising from the nest in flames. *Sun* is the final Ms., and I wish the story had been printed as it stands there, really complete. One day, when the public is more educated, I shall have the story printed whole, as it is in this Ms.' Harry Crosby paid for the Mss. in twenty-dollar gold pieces, the eagle and the sun. Lawrence wrote: 'How beautiful the gold is! – such a pity it ever became currency. One should love it for its yellow life, answering the sun.' The Black Sun Press published 'Sun' from this Ms. in 1928. It has never been reprinted.

Between finishing the second version of *Lady Chatterley's Lover* in February 1927 and beginning *The Man Who Died* in April, Lawrence began and abandoned a story which John R. Elliott, Jr has called 'The Man Who Was Through with the World'. Lawrence himself was such a man, at times; he felt very strongly the attractions of the hermit life. In 1922 he had written: 'I think one must for the moment withdraw from the world, away towards the inner realities that *are* real: and return, maybe, to the world later, when one is quiet and sure. I am tired of the world, and want the peace like a river: not this whisky and soda, bad whisky, too, of life so-called.' Lawrence has much more sympathy for Henry the Hermit than he had for Cathcart in *The Man Who Loved Islands* a few months earlier. Henry's predicament is the same as that faced by Mellors, by the Man Who Died, and by Lawrence himself. It is a choice between Scylla and Charybdis: to allow oneself to be swallowed by the world, exposing oneself to 'the pollution of people', or to withdraw to the island of oneself and die the spiritual death of solipsism. At best the rejection of the world is a gathering of strength, a preparation for a further effort in the world of man. At worst it nurses and nourishes a jaundiced misanthropy until the hatred extends to the hermit's own life. One cannot tell whether Henry is going to lose his grip on life as the winter advances and die for lack of human contact, or whether the following spring will see him enter the world again, resurrected like the man who died. Either way we have a rejection of the hermit state as a permanent way of life or as an end in itself.

In New Mexico Lawrence had found religion, Pan alive and dancing. But the rhythm was not one the European races could dance to. The joy was 'dark' in a sense which would exclude the kind of joy which belongs to 'the upper world of daylight and fresh air'. In the Etruscan tombs which Lawrence visited in the spring of 1927 with Earl Brewster he discovered 'a living, fresh, jolly people'. As he peered at the flaked and faded frescoes with the aid of a pocket torch in dark underground caverns, he imaginatively recreated the life of these people. It was the Etruscan experience which freed Lawrence from the 'world of care'. He gave up his 'savage pilgrimage', his exhausting quest for a life-mode fully in tune with the elemental sources of life, yet fully human, and, in the finest sense, civilized. He did not find a living embodiment of his desire. Yet what could be more living than these men and women dancing gaily to the double flute. The following October Lawrence began a story (misleadingly called 'Autobiographical Sketch' in *Phoenix*) in which he sleeps for a thousand years in a cavern near Eastwood and wakes to find himself near a handsome town among gentle people who combine the qualities of Etruscan civilization with the best qualities of the mining communities of the Midlands as Lawrence was later to describe them in *Nottingham and the Mining Country* – the 'physical awareness and intimate togetherness', the 'remote sort of contemplation which shows a real awareness of the presence of beauty', the 'instinct of community'. In a thousand years it seems men have at last reached the state of 'swift laughing togetherness' Gethin Day had marvelled at in the dolphins.

At the beginning of October 1927 Lawrence's friend S. S. Koteliansky sent him two stories recorded by his mother which he had translated from the Yiddish, in the hope that Lawrence might remake them. Lawrence replied that he would try to work them up when he had an inspired moment, and, probably shortly afterwards, began the first of them, a tiny story called 'Maimonides and Aristotle', under the new title 'The Undying Man'. His first five paragraphs hardly differ from Koteliansky's version, but once the little vein has been sealed in its jar, Lawrence's imagination begins to take hold, and the whole of the rest of his version is expanded from a mere dozen lines in Koteliansky's. Since Lawrence never finished 'The Undying Man', Koteliansky published his original translation in the *London Mercury* in February 1937. The story ends:

After a time the little vein in the jar began to grow, and Rabbi Moses Maimonides – blessed be his memory! – perceived that the man who was to grow up from the little vein and live eternally, would be made into a God by the people; that the people would abandon the living God and serve the eternal man, whom Aristotle and himself had created. Maimonides felt terribly distressed on that account; but as he had given his hand to Aristotle not to interfere with the growth of the man in the jar, he could not destroy the jar and thus prevent the little vein from becoming an eternal man. The more marked became the signs of the little vein turning into man, the more grieved and distressed Maimonides became for he had no longer any doubt that the people would turn the eternal man into God, and serve him and worship him. After many months of deliberation, prayer, and fasting, Maimonides came to a decision. He told the servants to let into the room, where he prayed and studied, and where on a shelf stood the jar with the little vein, all the chickens and cocks of his household. Maimonides then put on his long praying cloak; and as his habit was to walk about the room while praying, as soon as he began to pray, the chickens and cocks got frightened by the waving cloak, and began to jump and fly about the room. At last a big cock jumped on the shelf where the jar stood, and upset the jar. The jar fell to the ground and broke in pieces. And when Maimonides saw that the tiny little creature pointed a tiny little finger to him as a sign that he had broken his oath to Aristotle, Maimonides wept bitterly, and all the rest of his life prayed for forgiveness.

The next three stories, 'The Blue Moccasins', 'Things' and 'Mother and Daughter', were all written in the latter half of 1928. They are typical of the satirical and often cruel stories of this period. The couple in 'Things' are Earl and Aschah Brewster, who remained loyal to Lawrence despite his ruthless handling of them in his art.

Lawrence died in 1930 at the age of forty-four. The movement of his later fiction away from realism towards myth and fable is evident in this collection.

KEITH SAGAR

THE PRINCESS
AND OTHER STORIES

The Wilful Woman

NOVEMBER of the year 1916. A woman travelling from New York to the South West, by one of the tourist trains. On the third day the train lost time more and more. She raged with painful impatience. No good, at every station the train sat longer. They had passed the prairie lands and entered the mountain and desert region. They ought soon to arrive, soon. This was already the desert of grey-white sage and blue mountains. She ought to be there, soon, soon she ought to be there. This journey alone should be over. But the train comfortably stretched its length in the stations, and would never arrive. There was no end. It could not arrive. She could not bear it.

The woman sat in that cubby-hole at the end of the Pullman which is called in America a Drawing-Room. She had the place to herself and her bags. Volts of distracted impatience and heart-brokenness surged out of her, so that the negro did not dare to come in and sweep her floor with his little brush and dustpan. He left the 'Room' unswept for the afternoon.

Frustration and a painful volcanic pressure of impatience. The train would not arrive, *could* not arrive. That was it.

She was a sturdy woman with a round face, like an obstinate girl of fourteen. Like an obstinate girl of fourteen she sat there devouring her unease, her heavy, muscular fore-arms inert in her lap. So still, yet at such a pressure. So child-like – yet a woman approaching forty. So naïve-looking, softly full and feminine. And curiously heart-broken at being alone, travelling alone. Of course any man might have rushed to save her, and reap the reward of her soft, heavy, grateful magnetism. But wait a bit. Her thick, dark brows like curved horns over the naïve-looking face; and her bright, hazel-grey eyes, clear at the first glance as candour and unquenchable youth, at the second glance made up all of devilish grey and yellow bits, as opals are, and the bright candour of youth resolving into something dangerous as the headlights of a great machine coming full at you in the night. Mr Hercules had better think twice before he rushed to pick up this seductive serpent of loneliness that lay on the western trail. He had picked a snake up long ago, without hurting himself. But that was before Columbus discovered America.

Why did she feel that the train would never arrive, *could* never arrive, with her in it. Who knows? But that was how she did feel. The train would never arrive. Simple fate. Perhaps she felt that some power of her will would at last neutralize altogether the power of the engines, and there would come an end to motion, so there they would sit, forever, the train and she, at a deadlock on the Santa Fe Line. She had left New York in a sort of frenzy. Since they had passed Kansas City, Gate of the West, the thing had been getting unbearable. Since they had passed La Junta and come to the desert and the Rockies, the fatality had as good as happened. Yet she was only a few hours from her destination. And she would never get there. This train would never bring her there. Her head was one mass of thoughts and frenzied ideas almost to madness.

Then she sprang out of her Pullman. It was somewhere after Trinidad, she didn't bother where. 'Put my bags out,' she said to the negro, and he, looking at those serpent-blazing eyes under those eyebrows like thorn bushes, silently obeyed. Yet with her mouth she smiled a little and was cajoling, and his tip was reckless. Man must needs be mollified. She remembered to be just sufficiently soft and feminine. But she was distracted and heart-broken.

Started her next whirl. She must have an automobile, she *would* have an automobile, to be driven this hundred or hundred and fifty miles that remained. Yes, she would have an automobile. But she had got out at a station where, at least that afternoon, there *was* no automobile. Nevertheless, she *would* have an automobile. So at last was produced an old worn-out Dodge with no springs left, belonging to a boy of sixteen. Yes, she would have that. The boy had never travelled that trail, didn't know the way. No matter, she would go. She would get to Lamy in front of that hateful train which she had left. And the boy would get twenty-six dollars. Good enough!

She had never been west before, so she reckoned without her host. She had still to learn what trails round the Rockies and across the desert are like. She imagined roads, or forest tracks. She found what actually is a trail in the south west – a blind squirm up sand-banks, a blind rattle along dry river-beds, a breathless scramble in deep cañons over what look like simple landslides and precipices, the car at an angle of forty-five degrees above a green rocky river, banging itself to bits against boulders, surging through the river then back again through the river and once more swooping through the river with the devil's own scramble up a rocky bank on the other side, and a young boy driving on, driving ahead, without knowing where, or what was happening to him, twenty-six dollars at the end. So out on the lurch and bump of the open white-sage desert once more, to follow the trail by scent rather than by sight, cart-ruts this way, tracks that way, please yourself in the god-forsaken landscape, bolting into a slope of piñon and cedar, dark-green bush-scrub, then dropping down to a wire fence and a gate, a sort of ranch, and a lost village of houses like brown mud boxes plonked down in the grey wilderness, with a bigger mud box, oblong, which the boy told her was the sort of church place where the Penitentes scourge and torture themselves, windowless so that no one shall hear their shrieks and groans.

By nightfall she had had a lot of the nonsense bumped and bruised out of her, knocked about as if she were a penitente herself. Not that she was a *penitente*: not she. But at least here was a country that hit her with hard knuckles, right through to the bone. It was something of a country.

Luckily, she had telegraphed to Mark, who would be waiting for her at Lamy station. Mark was her husband – her third. One dead, one divorced, and Mark alternately torn to atoms and thrown to the four corners of the universe, then rather sketchily gathered up and put together again by a desirous, if still desperate Isis. She had torn him in two and pitched him piecemeal away into the southwestern desert. Now she was after him once more, going to put humpty-dumpty together again with a slam. With a slam that might finally do for him.

Of course he is an artist, a foreigner, a Russian. Of course she is an American woman, several generations of wealth and tradition in various cities of New York state behind her, several generations of visiting Europe and staying in the Meurice and seeing Napoleon III or Gambetta or whoever was figuring on the stage of Paris. She herself had stayed in the old Meurice. She too had had her apartment in a fine old hotel, and if there was no Napoleon III left for her, there had been ex-Princesses of Saxony, d'Annunzio, Duse, Isadora Duncan or Matisse.

These American families do actually tend to cumulate and culminate in one daughter. Not that the family had as yet cumulated in Sybil Mond. She had started as Sybil Hamnett, and had been successively Sybil Thomas and

Sybil Danks before she married the Jewish artist from somewhere Poland way, who was, in her family's eyes, the anti-climax. But she herself admitted no possibility of anti-climax for herself, and kept unpleasant surprises still in store for her family. Her family being her mother and the General, Sybil's second step-father. For she was as well-off for step-fathers as for husbands.

The family had actually culminated in Sybil: all the force of the Hamnetts, on her father's side, and the push of the Wilcoxes, on her mother's, focused into this one highly-explosive daughter. No question of dribbling out. Sybil at forty was heavy with energy like a small bison, and strong and young-looking as if she were thirty, often giving the impression of soft crudeness as if she were sixteen. The old colonial vigour had, we repeat, collected in her as in some final dam, like the buffalo's force in his forehead. But the old colonial riches had not yet descended upon her. She had her own sufficient income, but the mass of the family wealth rested on her mother, who, aided by the General, exemplified it in the correct and magnificent Italian Mansion on Lake Erie.

The rackety machine in which she rode had of course no headlights, and the November night fell. The boy hadn't thought to put the lamps on. No headlights! Frustration, always frustration. Sybil annihilated the boy in her soul, and sat still. Or rather, with her body lashed and bruised, her soul sat crying and ominous. There was nothing to be done but to scramble for the nearest station again.

On then, under the many sharp, small stars of the desert. The air was cold in her nostrils, the desert seemed weird and uncanny. But – it was terra nova. It was a new world, the desert at the foot of the mountains, the high desert above the gorges of the cañons, the world of three altitudes. Strange! – doomful!

Yes, destiny had made her get out of the train and into this rackety machine. Destiny even had made the boy bring no headlights. Her ponderous storm began to evaporate. She looked round the night as they emerged from a dark cañon out onto a high flat bit of vague desert, with mountains guarding the flatness beyond, shadows beyond the shadows.

It impressed her, although she *must* get to her journey end, she *must* arrive. No, it was not like desert. Rather like wilderness, the wilderness of the temptation, for example. Shadowy scrub of pale grey sage, knee-high, waist-high, on the flat of the table land; and on the slopes of the mountains that rose still further, starting off the flat table, scrub of gnarled pine and cedar, still hardly more than bushes, but like those Japanese dwarf-trees, full of age, torture and power. Strange country – weird – frightening too. It would need a battle to gain hold over such a land. It would need a battle. She snuffed the curiously-scented air of the desert. With her tongue almost jerked out of her mouth by the jumping of the car, she sat inwardly motionless, facing destiny again. It was her destiny she should come to this land. It was her destiny she should see it for the first time thus, alone, lost, without light. That was destiny, that threw her naked like the black queen onto this unknown chess-board. She hugged her furs and her fate round her, in the cold, rare air, and was somewhat relieved. Her battle! Her hope!

And thus by eight o'clock the frozen, disappointed, but dogged boy brought her to the railway again, as she bade him. It was impossible for him to get her to Lamy without lights or anything. He must forfeit some of the twenty-six dollars. He was disappointed, but he admitted the truth of her contention.

Wagon-Mound, or some such name. She remembered a

sort of dome of a hill in the night. After which nothing to
be done but to go to the 'hotel', to wait three hours for the
slow train which followed the one she had abandoned way
back at Trinidad.

(Unfinished)

The Princess

To her father, she was The Princess. To her Boston aunts and uncles she was just *Dollie Urquhart, poor little thing*.

Colin Urquhart was just a bit mad. He was of an old Scottish family, and he claimed royal blood. The blood of Scottish kings flowed in his veins. On this point, his American relatives said, he was just a bit 'off'. They could not bear any more to be told *which* royal blood of Scotland blued his veins. The whole thing was rather ridiculous, and a sore point. The only fact they remembered was that it was not Stuart.

He was a handsome man, with a wide-open blue eye that seemed sometimes to be looking at nothing, soft black hair brushed rather low on his low, broad brow, and a very attractive body. Add to this a most beautiful speaking voice, usually rather hushed and diffident, but sometimes resonant and powerful like bronze, and you have the sum of his charms. He looked like some old Celtic hero. He looked as if he should have worn a greyish kilt and a sporran, and shown his knees. His voice came direct out of the hushed Ossianic past.

For the rest, he was one of those gentlemen of sufficient but not excessive means who fifty years ago wandered vaguely about, never arriving anywhere, never doing anything, and never definitely being anything, yet well received and familiar in the good society of more than one country.

He did not marry till he was nearly forty, and then it was a wealthy Miss Prescott, from New England. Hannah Prescott at twenty-two was fascinated by the man with the soft black hair not yet touched by grey, and the wide,

rather vague blue eyes. Many women had been fascinated
before her. But Colin Urquhart, by his very vagueness, had
avoided any decisive connection.

Mrs Urquhart lived three years in the mist and glamour
of her husband's presence. And then it broke her. It was
like living with a fascinating spectre. About most things
he was completely, even ghostly oblivious. He was always
charming, courteous, perfectly gracious in that hushed,
musical voice of his. But absent. When all came to all, he
just wasn't there. 'Not all there,' as the vulgar say.

He was the father of the little girl she bore at the end of
the first year. But this did not substantiate him the more.
His very beauty and his haunting musical quality became
dreadful to her after the first few months. The strange
echo: he was like a living echo! His very flesh, when you
touched it, did not seem quite the flesh of a real man.

Perhaps it was that he was a little bit mad. She thought it
definitely the night her baby was born.

'Ah, so my little princess has come at last!' he said, in his
throaty, singing Celtic voice, like a glad chant, swaying
absorbed.

It was a tiny, frail baby, with wide, amazed blue eyes.
They christened it Mary Henrietta. She called the little
thing *My Dollie*. He called it always *My Princess*.

It was useless to fly at him. He just opened his wide blue
eyes wider, and took a childlike, silent dignity there was
no getting past.

Hannah Prescott had never been robust. She had no
great desire to live. So when the baby was two years old
she suddenly died.

The Prescotts felt a deep but unadmitted resentment
against Colin Urquhart. They said he was selfish. Therefore
they discontinued Hannah's income, a month after her
burial in Florence, after they had urged the father to give

the child over to them, and he had courteously, musically, but quite finally refused. He treated the Prescotts as if they were not of his world, not realities to him: just casual phenomena, or gramophones, talking-machines that had to be answered. He answered them. But of their actual existence he was never once aware.

They debated having him certified unsuitable to be guardian of his own child. But that would have created a scandal. So they did the simplest thing, after all – washed their hands of him. But they wrote scrupulously to the child, and sent her modest presents of money at Christmas, and on the anniversary of the death of her mother.

To The Princess her Boston relatives were for many years just a nominal reality. She lived with her father, and he travelled continually, though in a modest way, living on his moderate income. And never going to America. The child changed nurses all the time. In Italy it was a contadina; in India she had an ayah; in Germany she had a yellow-haired peasant girl.

Father and child were inseparable. He was not a recluse. Wherever he went he was to be seen paying formal calls going out to luncheon or to tea, rarely to dinner. And always with the child. People called her Princess Urquhart, as if that were her christened name.

She was a quick, dainty little thing with dark gold hair that went a soft brown, and wide, slightly prominent blue eyes that were at once so candid and so knowing. She was always grown up; she never really grew up. Always strangely wise, and always childish.

It was her father's fault.

'My little Princess must never take too much notice of people and the things they say and do,' he repeated to her. 'People don't know what they are doing and saying. They chatter-chatter, and they hurt one another, and they hurt themselves very often, till they cry. But don't take any notice, my little Princess. Because it is all nothing. Inside everybody there is another creature, a demon which doesn't care at all. You peel away all the things they say and do and feel, as cook peels away the outside of the onions. And in the middle of everybody there is a green demon which you can't peel away. And this green demon never changes, and it doesn't care at all about all the things that happen to the outside leaves of the person, all the chatter-chatter, and all the husbands and wives and children, and troubles and fusses. You peel everything away from people, and there is a green, upright demon in every man and woman; and this demon is a man's real self, and a woman's real self. It doesn't really care about anybody, it belongs to the demons and the primitive fairies, who never care. But, even so, there are big demons and mean demons, and splendid demonish fairies, and vulgar ones. But there are no royal fairy women left. Only you, my little Princess. You are the last of the royal race of the old people; the last, my Princess. There are no others. You and I are the last. When I am dead there will be only you. And that is why, darling, you will never care for any of the people in the world very much. Because their demons are all dwindled and vulgar. They are not royal. Only you are royal, after me. Always remember that. And always remember, it is a *great secret*. If you tell people, they will try to kill you, because they will envy you for being a Princess. It is our great secret, darling. I am a prince, and you a princess, of the old, old blood. And we keep our secret between us, all alone. And so, darling, you must treat all people very politely, because *noblesse oblige*. But you must never forget that you alone are the last of Princesses, and that all others are less than you are, less noble, more vulgar. Treat them politely and gently and kindly, darling. But you are the Princess, and they are commoners. Never try to think of them as if they were like you. They are not. You will find, always, that they are lacking, lacking in the royal touch, which only you have –'

The Princess learned her lesson early – the first lesson, of absolute reticence, the impossibility of intimacy with any other than her father; the second lesson, of naïve, slightly benevolent politeness. As a small child, something crystallized in her character, making her clear and finished, and as impervious as crystal.

'Dear child!' her hostesses said of her. 'She is so quaint and old-fashioned; such a lady, poor little mite!'

She was erect, and very dainty. Always small, nearly tiny in physique, she seemed like a changeling beside her big, handsome, slightly mad father. She dressed very simply, usually in blue or delicate greys, with little collars of old Milan point, or very finely-worked linen. She had exquisite little hands, that made the piano sound like a spinet when she played. She was rather given to wearing cloaks and capes, instead of coats, out of doors, and little eighteenth-century sort of hats. Her complexion was pure apple-blossom.

She looked as if she had stepped out of a picture. But no one, to her dying day, ever knew exactly the strange picture her father had framed her in and from which she never stepped.

Her grandfather and grandmother and her Aunt Maud demanded twice to see her, once in Rome and once in Paris. Each time they were charmed, piqued, and annoyed. She was so exquisite and such a little virgin. At the same time so knowing and so oddly assured. That odd, assured touch of condescension, and the inward coldness, infuriated her American relations.

Only she really fascinated her grandfather. He was spell-bound; in a way, in love with the little faultless thing. His wife would catch him brooding, musing over his grand-child, long months after the meeting, and craving to see her again. He cherished to the end the fond hope that she might come to live with him and her grandmother.

'Thank you so much, grandfather. You are so very kind. But Papa and I are such an old couple, you see, such a crotchety old couple, living in a world of our own.'

Her father let her see the world – from the outside. And he let her read. When she was in her teens she read Zola and Maupassant, and with the eyes of Zola and Maupassant she looked on Paris. A little later she read Tolstoy and Dostoevsky. The latter confused her. The others, she seemed to understand with a very shrewd, canny under-standing, just as she understood the Decameron stories as she read them in their old Italian, or the Nibelung poems. Strange and *uncanny*, she seemed to understand things in a cold light perfectly, with all the flush of fire absent. She was something like a changeling, not quite human.

This earned her, also, strange antipathies. Cabmen and railway porters, especially in Paris and Rome, would sud-denly treat her with brutal rudeness, when she was alone. They seemed to look on her with sudden violent anti-pathy. They sensed in her curious impertinence, an easy, sterile impertinence towards the things *they* felt most. She was so assured, and her flower of maidenhood was so scentless. She could look at a lusty, sensual Roman cabman as if he were a sort of grotesque, to make her smile. She knew all about him, in Zola. And the peculiar condescen-sion with which she would give him her order, as if she, frail, beautiful thing, were the only reality, and he, coarse monster, were a sort of Caliban floundering in the mud on the margin of the pool of the perfect lotus, would suddenly enrage the fellow, the real Mediterranean who prided himself on his *beauté male*, and to whom the phallic mystery was still the only mystery. And he would turn a terrible face on her, bully her in a brutal, coarse fashion – hideous. For to him she had only the blasphemous impertinence of her own sterility.

Encounters like these made her tremble, and made her know she must have support from the outside. The power of her spirit did not extend to these low people, and they had all the physical power. She realized an implacability of hatred in their turning on her. But she did not lose her head. She quietly paid out money and turned away.

Those were dangerous moments, though, and she learned to be prepared for them. The Princess she was, and the fairy from the North, and could never understand the volcanic phallic rage with which coarse people could turn on her in a paroxysm of hatred. They never turned on her father like that. And quite early she decided it was the New England mother in her whom they hated. Never for one minute could she see with the old Roman eyes, see herself as sterility, the barren flower taking on airs and an intolerable impertinence. This was what the Roman cabman saw in her. And he longed to crush the barren blossom. Its sexless beauty and its authority put him in a passion of brutal revolt.

When she was nineteen her grandfather died, leaving her a considerable fortune in the safe hands of responsible trustees. They would deliver her her income, but only on condition that she resided for six months in the year in the United States.

'Why should they make me conditions?' she said to her father. 'I refuse to be imprisoned six months in the year in the United States. We will tell them to keep their money.'

'Let us be wise, my little Princess, let us be wise. No, we are almost poor, and we are never safe from rudeness. I

cannot allow anybody to be rude to me. I hate it, I hate it!'
His eyes flamed as he said it. 'I could kill any man or woman
who is rude to me. But we are in exile in the world. We are
powerless. If we were really poor, we should be quite
powerless, and then I should die. No, my Princess. Let us
take their money, then they will not dare to be rude to us.
Let us take it, as we put on clothes, to cover ourselves from
their aggressions.'

There began a new phase, when the father and daughter
spent their summers on the Great Lakes or in California, or
in the South-West. The father was something of a poet, the
daughter something of a painter. He wrote poems about
the lakes or the redwood trees, and she made dainty draw-
ings. He was physically a strong man, and he loved the
out-of-doors. He would go off with her for days, paddling
in a canoe and sleeping by a camp-fire. Frail little Princess,
she was always undaunted, always undaunted. She would
ride with him on horseback over the mountain trails till she
was so tired she was nothing but a bodiless consciousness
sitting astride her pony. But she never gave in. And at
night he folded her in her blankets on a bed of balsam pine
twigs, and she lay and looked at the stars unmurmuring.
She was fulfilling her role.

People said to her as the years passed, and she was a
woman of twenty-five, then a woman of thirty, and always
the same virgin dainty Princess, 'knowing' in a dispassionate way, like an old woman, and utterly intact:

'Don't you ever think what you will do when your
father is no longer with you?'

She looked at her interlocutor with that cold, elfin detachment of hers:

'No, I never think of it,' she said.

She had a tiny, but exquisite little house in London, and
another small, perfect house in Connecticut, each with a

faithful housekeeper. Two homes, if she chose. And she knew many interesting literary and artistic people. What more?

So the years passed imperceptibly. And she had that quality of the sexless fairies, she did not change. At thirty-three she looked twenty-three.

Her father, however, was ageing, and becoming more and more queer. It was now her task to be his guardian in his private madness. He spent the last three years of life in the house in Connecticut. He was very much estranged, sometimes had fits of violence which almost killed the little Princess. Physical violence was horrible to her; it seemed to shatter her heart. But she found a woman a few years younger than herself, well-educated and sensitive, to be a sort of nurse-companion to the mad old man. So the fact of madness was never openly admitted. Miss Cummins, the companion, had a passionate loyalty to the Princess, and a curious affection, tinged with love, for the handsome, white-haired, courteous old man, who was never at all aware of his fits of violence once they had passed.

The Princess was thirty-eight years old when her father died. And quite unchanged. She was still tiny, and like a dignified, scentless flower. Her soft brownish hair, almost the colour of beaver fur, was bobbed, and fluffed softly round her apple-blossom face, that was modelled with an arched nose like a proud old Florentine portrait. In her voice, manner and bearing she was exceedingly still, like a flower that has blossomed in a shadowy place. And from her blue eyes looked out the Princess's eternal laconic challenge, that grew almost sardonic as the years passed. She was the Princess, and sardonically she looked out on a princeless world.

She was relieved when her father died, and at the same time, it was as if everything had evaporated around her.

She had lived in a sort of hot-house, in the aura of her father's madness. Suddenly the hot-house had been removed from around her, and she was in the raw, vast, vulgar open air.

Quoi faire? What was she to do? She seemed faced with absolute nothingness. Only she had Miss Cummins, who shared with her the secret, and almost the passion for her father. In fact, the Princess felt that her passion for her mad father had in some curious way transferred itself largely to Charlotte Cummins during the last years. And now Miss Cummins was the vessel that held the passion for the dead man. She herself, the Princess, was an empty vessel.

An empty vessel in the enormous warehouse of the world.

Quoi faire? What was she to do? She felt that, since she could not evaporate into nothingness, like alcohol from an unstoppered bottle, she must *do* something. Never before in her life had she felt the incumbency. Never, never had she felt she must *do* anything. That was left to the vulgar.

Now her father was dead, she found herself on the *fringe* of the vulgar crowd, sharing their necessity to *do* something. It was a little humiliating. She felt herself becoming vulgarized. At the same time she found herself looking at men with a shrewder eye: an eye to marriage. Not that she felt any sudden interest in men, or attraction towards them. No. She was still neither interested nor attracted towards men vitally. But *marriage*, that peculiar abstraction, had imposed a sort of spell on her. She thought that *marriage*, in the blank abstract, was the thing she ought to *do*. That *marriage* implied a man she also knew. She knew all the facts. But the man seemed a property of her own mind rather than a thing in himself, another being.

Her father died in the summer, the month after her thirty-eighth birthday. When all was over, the obvious thing to do, of course, was to travel. With Miss Cummins. The two women knew each other intimately, but they were always Miss Urquhart and Miss Cummins to one another, and a certain distance was instinctively maintained. Miss Cummins, from Philadelphia, of scholastic stock, and intelligent but untravelled, four years younger than the Princess, felt herself immensely the junior of her 'lady'. She had a sort of passionate veneration for the Princess, who seemed to her ageless, timeless. She could not see the rows of tiny, dainty, exquisite shoes in the Princess's cupboard without feeling a stab at the heart, a stab of tenderness and reverence, almost of awe.

Miss Cummins also was virginal, but with a look of puzzled surprise in her brown eyes. Her skin was pale and clear, her features well modelled, but there was a certain blankness in her expression, where the Princess had an odd touch of Renaissance grandeur. Miss Cummins's voice was also hushed almost to a whisper; it was the inevitable effect of Colin Urquhart's room. But the hushedness had a hoarse quality.

The Princess did not want to go to Europe. Her face seemed turned west. Now her father was gone, she felt she would go west, westwards, as if for ever. Following, no doubt, the March of Empire, which is brought up rather short on the Pacific coast, among swarms of wallowing bathers.

No, not the Pacific coast. She would stop short of that. The South-West was less vulgar. She would go to New Mexico.

She and Miss Cummins arrived at the Rancho del Cerro Gordo towards the end of August, when the crowd was beginning to drift back east. The ranch lay by a stream on the desert some four miles from the foot of the mountains, a mile away from the Indian pueblo of San Cristobal. It was a ranch for the rich; the Princess paid thirty dollars a day for herself and Miss Cummins. But then she had a little cottage to herself, among the apple trees of the orchard, with an excellent cook. She and Miss Cummins, however, took dinner at evening in the large guest-house. For the Princess still entertained the idea of *marriage*.

The guests at the Rancho del Cerro Gordo were of all sorts, except the poor sort. They were practically all rich, and many were romantic. Some were charming, others were vulgar, some were movie people, quite quaint and not unattractive in their vulgarity, and many were Jews. The Princess did not care for Jews, though they were usually the most interesting to *talk* to. So she talked a good deal with the Jews, and painted with the artists, and rode with the young men from college, and had altogether quite a good time. And yet she felt something of a fish out of water, or a bird in the wrong forest. And *marriage* remained still completely in the abstract. No connecting it with any of these young men, even the nice ones.

The Princess looked just twenty-five. The freshness of her mouth, the hushed, delicate-complexioned virginity of her face gave her not a day more. Only a certain laconic look in her eyes was disconcerting. When she was *forced* to write her age, she put twenty-eight, making the figure *two* rather badly, so that it just avoided being a three.

Men hinted marriage at her. Especially boys from college suggested it from a distance. But they all failed before the look of sardonic ridicule in the Princess's eyes. It always seemed to her rather preposterous, quite ridiculous, and a tiny bit impertinent on their part.

The only man that intrigued her at all was one of the guides, a man called Romero – Domingo Romero. It was he who had sold the ranch itself to the Wilkiesons, ten years before, for two thousand dollars. He had gone away, then reappeared at the old place. For he was the son of the old Romero, the last of the Spanish family that had owned miles of land around San Cristobal. But the coming of the white man and the failure of the vast flocks of sheep, and the fatal inertia which overcomes all men, at last, on the desert near the mountains, had finished the Romero family. The last descendants were just Mexican peasants.

Domingo, the heir, had spent his two thousand dollars, and was working for white people. He was now about thirty years old, a tall, silent fellow, with a heavy closed mouth and black eyes that looked across at one almost sullenly. From behind he was handsome, with a strong, natural body, and the back of his neck very dark and well-shapen, strong with life. But his dark face was long and heavy, almost sinister, with that peculiar heavy meaninglessness in it, characteristic of the Mexicans of his own locality. They are strong, they seem healthy. They laugh and joke with one another. But their physique and their natures seem static, as if there were nowhere, nowhere at all for their energies to go, and their faces, degenerating to misshapen heaviness, seem to have no *raison d'être*, no radical meaning. Waiting either to die or to be aroused into passion and hope. In some of the black eyes a queer, haunting mystic quality, sombre and a bit gruesome, the skull-and-cross-bones look of the Penitentes. They had found their *raison d'être* in self-torture and death-worship. Unable to wrest a *positive* significance for themselves from the vast, beautiful, but vindictive landscape they were born into, they turned on their own selves, and worshipped death through self-torture. The mystic gloom of this showed in their eyes.

But as a rule the dark eyes of the Mexicans were heavy and half-alive, sometimes hostile, sometimes kindly, often with the fatal Indian glaze on them, or the fatal Indian glint.

Domingo Romero was *almost* a typical Mexican to look

at, with the typical heavy, dark, long face, clean-shaven, with an almost brutally heavy mouth. His eyes were black and Indian-looking. Only, at the centre of their hopelessness was a spark of pride, or self-confidence, or dauntlessness. Just a spark in the midst of the blackness of static despair.

But this spark was the difference between him and the mass of men. It gave a certain alert sensitiveness to his bearing and a certain beauty to his appearance. He wore a low-crowned black hat, instead of the ponderous headgear of the usual Mexican, and his clothes were thinnish and graceful. Silent, aloof, almost imperceptible in the landscape, he was an admirable guide, with a startling quick intelligence that anticipated difficulties about to rise. He could cook, too, crouching over the camp-fire and moving his lean deft brown hands. The only fault he had was that he was not forthcoming, he wasn't chatty and cosy.

'Oh, don't send Romero with us,' the Jews would say. 'One can't get any response from him.'

Tourists come and go, but they rarely *see* anything, inwardly. None of them ever saw the spark at the middle of Romero's eye; they were not alive enough to see it.

The Princess caught it one day, when she had him for a guide. She was fishing for trout in the canyon, Miss Cummins was reading a book, the horses were tied under the trees, Romero was fixing a proper fly on her line. He fixed the fly and handed her the line, looking up at her. And at that moment she caught the spark in his eye. And instantly she knew that he was a gentleman, that his 'demon', as her father would have said, was a fine demon. And instantly her manner towards him changed.

He had perched her on a rock over a quiet pool, beyond the cottonwood trees. It was early September, and the canyon already cool, but the leaves of the cotton-woods were still green. The Princess stood on her rock, a small but perfectly-formed figure, wearing a soft, close grey sweater and neatly-cut grey riding-breeches, with tall black boots, her fluffy brown hair straggling from under a little grey felt hat. A woman? Not quite. A changeling of some sort, perched in outline there on the rock, in the bristling wild canyon. She knew perfectly well how to handle a line. Her father had made a fisherman of her.

Romero, in a black shirt and with loose black trousers pushed into wide black riding-boots, was fishing a little farther down. He had put his hat on a rock behind him; his dark head was bent a little forward, watching the water. He had caught three trout. From time to time he glanced up-stream at the Princess, perched there so daintily. He saw she had caught nothing.

Soon he quietly drew in his line and came up to her. His keen eye watched her line, watched her position. Then, quietly, he suggested certain changes to her, putting his sensitive brown hand before her. And he withdrew a little, and stood in silence, leaning against a tree, watching her. He was helping her across the distance. She knew it, and thrilled. And in a moment she had a bite. In two minutes she had landed a good trout. She looked round at him quickly, her eyes sparkling, the colour heightened in her cheeks. And as she met his eyes a smile of greeting went over his dark face, very sudden, with an odd sweetness.

She knew he was helping her. And she felt in his presence a subtle, insidious male *kindliness* she had never known before waiting upon her. Her cheek flushed, and her blue eyes darkened.

After this, she always looked for him, and for that curious dark beam of a man's kindliness which he could give her, as it were, from his chest, from his heart. It was something she had never known before.

A vague, unspoken intimacy grew up between them. She liked his voice, his appearance, his presence. His natural language was Spanish; he spoke English like a foreign language, rather slow, with a slight hesitation, but with a sad, plangent sonority lingering over from his Spanish. There was a certain subtle correctness in his appearance; he was always perfectly shaved; his hair was thick and rather long on top, but always carefully groomed behind. And his fine black cashmere shirt, his wide leather belt, his well-cut, wide black trousers going into the embroidered cowboy boots had a certain inextinguishable elegance. He wore no silver rings or buckles. Only his boots were embroidered and decorated at the top with an inlay of white suède. He seemed elegant, slender, yet he was very strong.

And at the same time, curiously, he gave her the feeling that death was not far from him. Perhaps he too was half in love with death. However that may be, the sense she had that death was not far from him made him 'possible' to her.

Small as she was, she was quite a good horsewoman. They gave her at the ranch a sorrel mare, very lovely in colour, and well-made, with a powerful broad neck and the hollow back that betokens a swift runner. Tansy, she was called. Her only fault was the usual mare's failing, she was inclined to be hysterical.

So that every day the Princess set off with Miss Cummins and Romero, on horseback, riding into the mountains. Once they went camping for several days, with two more friends in the party.

'I think I like it better,' the Princess said to Romero, 'when we three go alone.'

And he gave her one of his quick, transfiguring smiles. It was curious no white man had ever showed her this capacity for subtle gentleness, this power to *help* her in silence across a distance, if she were fishing without success, or tired of her horse, or if Tansy suddenly got scared. It was as if Romero could send her *from his heart* a dark beam of succour and sustaining. She had never known this before, and it was very thrilling.

Then the smile that suddenly creased his dark face, showing the strong white teeth. It creased his face almost into a savage grotesque. And at the same time there was in it something so warm, such a dark flame of kindliness for her, she was elated into her true Princess self.

Then that vivid, latent spark in his eye, which she had seen, and which she knew he was aware she had seen. It made an inter-recognition between them, silent and delicate. Here he was delicate as a woman in this subtle inter-recognition.

And yet his presence only put to flight in her the *idée fixe* of 'marriage'. For some reason, in her strange little brain, the idea of *marrying* him could not enter. Not for any definite reason. He was in himself a gentleman, and she had plenty of money for two. There was no actual obstacle. Nor was she conventional.

No, now she came down to it, it was as if their two 'daemons' could marry, were perhaps married. Only their two *selves*, Miss Urquhart and Señor Domingo Romero, were for some reason incompatible. There was a peculiar subtle intimacy of inter-recognition between them. But she did not see in the least how it would lead to marriage. Almost she could more easily marry one of the nice boys from Harvard or Yale.

The time passed, and she let it pass. The end of September came, with aspens going yellow on the mountain heights, and oak-scrub going red. But as yet the cotton-woods in the valley and canyons had not changed.

'When will you go away?' Romero asked her, looking at her fixedly, with a blank black eye.

'By the end of October,' she said. 'I have promised to be in Santa Barbara at the beginning of November.'

He was hiding the spark in his eye from her. But she saw the peculiar sullen thickening of his heavy mouth.

She had complained to him many times that one never saw any wild animals, except chipmunks and squirrels, and perhaps a skunk and a porcupine. Never a deer, or a bear, or a mountain lion.

'Are there no bigger animals in these mountains?' she asked, dissatisfied.

'Yes,' he said. 'There are deer – I see their tracks. And I saw the tracks of a bear.'

'But why can one never see the animals themselves?' She looked dissatisfied and wistful like a child.

'Why, it's pretty hard for you to see them. They won't let you come close. You have to keep still, in a place where they come. Or else you have to follow their tracks a long way.'

'I can't bear to go away till I've seen them: a bear, or a deer –'

The smile came suddenly on his face, indulgent.

'Well, what do you want? Do you want to go up into the mountains to some place, to wait till they come?'

'Yes,' she said, looking up at him with a sudden naïve impulse of recklessness.

And immediately his face became sombre again, responsible.

'Well,' he said, with slight irony, a touch of mockery of her. 'You will have to find a house. It's very cold at night now. You would have to stay all night in a house.'

'And there are no houses up there?' she said.

'Yes,' he replied. 'There is a little shack that belongs to

me, that a miner built a long time ago, looking for gold. You can go there and stay one night, and maybe you see something. Maybe! I don't know. Maybe nothing come.'

'How much chance is there?'

'Well, I don't know. Last time when I was there I see three deer come down to drink at the water, and I shot two raccoons. But maybe this time we don't see anything.'

'Is there water there?' she asked.

'Yes, there is a little round pond, you know, below the spruce trees. And the water from the snow runs into it.'

'Is it far away?' she asked.

'Yes, pretty far. You see that ridge there' – and turning to the mountains he lifted his arm in the gesture which is somehow so moving, out in the West, pointing to the distance – 'that ridge where there are no trees, only rock' – his black eyes were focused on the distance, his face impassive, but as if in pain – 'you go round that ridge, and along, then you come down through the spruce trees to where that cabin is. My father bought that placer claim from a miner who was broke, but nobody ever found any gold or anything, and nobody ever goes there. Too lonesome!'

The Princess watched the massive, heavy-sitting, beautiful bulk of the Rocky Mountains. It was early in October, and the aspens were already losing their gold leaves; high up, the spruce and pine seemed to be growing darker; the great flat patches of oak scrub on the heights were red like gore.

'Can I go over there?' she asked, turning to him and meeting the spark in his eye.

His face was heavy with responsibility.

'Yes,' he said, 'you can go. But there'll be snow over the ridge, and it's awful cold, and awful lonesome.'

'I should like to go,' she said, persistent.

'All right,' he said. 'You can go if you want to.'

She doubted, though, if the Wilkiesons would let her go; at least alone with Romero and Miss Cummins.

Yet an obstinacy characteristic of her nature, an obstinacy tinged perhaps with madness, had taken hold of her. She wanted to look over the mountains into their secret heart. She wanted to descend to the cabin below the spruce trees, near the tarn of bright green water. She wanted to see the wild animals move about in their wild unconsciousness.

'Let us say to the Wilkiesons that we want to make the trip round the Frijoles canyon,' she said.

The trip round the Frijoles canyon was a usual thing. It would not be strenuous, nor cold, nor lonely: they could sleep in the log house that was called an hotel.

Romero looked at her quickly.

'If you want to say that,' he replied, 'you can tell Mrs Wilkieson. Only I know she'll be mad with me if I take you up in the mountains to that place. And I've got to go there first with a pack-horse, to take lots of blankets and some bread. Maybe Miss Cummins can't stand it. Maybe not. It's a hard trip.'

He was speaking, and thinking, in the heavy, disconnected Mexican fashion.

'Never mind!' The Princess was suddenly very decisive and stiff with authority. 'I want to do it. I will arrange with Mrs Wilkieson. And we'll go on Saturday.'

He shook his head slowly.

'I've got to go up on Sunday with a pack-horse and blankets,' he said. 'Can't do it before.'

'Very well!' she said, rather piqued. 'Then we'll start on Monday.'

She hated being thwarted even the tiniest bit.

He knew that if he started with the pack on Sunday at

dawn he would not be back until late at night. But he consented that they should start on Monday morning at seven. The obedient Miss Cummins was told to prepare for the Frijoles trip. On Sunday Romero had his day off. He had not put in an appearance when the Princess retired on Sunday night, but on Monday morning, as she was dressing, she saw him bringing in the three horses from the corral. She was in high spirits.

The night had been cold. There was ice at the edges of the irrigation ditch, and the chipmunks crawled into the sun and lay with wide, dumb, anxious eyes, almost too numb to run.

'We may be away two or three days,' said the Princess.

'Very well. We won't begin to be anxious about you before Thursday, then,' said Mrs Wilkieson, who was young and capable: from Chicago. 'Anyway,' she added, 'Romero will see you through. He's so trustworthy.'

The sun was already on the desert as they set off towards the mountains, making the greasewood and the sage pale as pale-grey sands, luminous the great level around them. To the right glinted the shadows of the adobe pueblo, flat and almost invisible on the plain, earth of its earth. Behind lay the ranch and the tufts of tall, plumy cotton-woods, whose summits were yellowing under the perfect blue sky.

Autumn breaking into colour in the great spaces of the South-West.

But the three trotted gently along the trail, towards the sun that sparkled yellow just above the dark bulk of the ponderous mountains. Side-slopes were already gleaming yellow, flaming with a second light, under the coldish blue of the pale sky. The front slopes were in shadow, with submerged lustre of red oak scrub and dull-gold aspens, blue-black pines and grey-blue rock. While the canyon was full of a deep blueness.

They rode single file, Romero first, on a black horse. Himself in black, made a flickering black spot in the delicate pallor of the great landscape, where even pine trees at a distance take a film of blue paler than their green. Romero rode on in silence past the tufts of furry greasewood. The Princess came next, on her sorrel mare. And Miss Cummins, who was not quite happy on horseback, came last, in the pale dust that the others kicked up. Sometimes her horse sneezed, and she started.

But on they went at a gentle trot. Romero never looked round. He could hear the sound of the hoofs following, and that was all he wanted.

For the rest, he held ahead. And the Princess, with that black, unheeding figure always travelling away from her, felt strangely helpless, withal elated.

They neared the pale, round foot-hills, dotted with the round dark piñon and cedar shrubs. The horses clinked and clattered among stones. Occasionally a big round greasewood held out fleecy tufts of flowers, pure gold. They wound into blue shadow, then up a steep stony slope, with the world lying pallid away behind and below. Then they dropped into the shadow of the San Cristobal canyon.

The stream was running full and swift. Occasionally the horses snatched at a tuft of grass. The trail narrowed and became rocky; the rocks closed in; it was dark and cool as the horses climbed and climbed upwards, and the tree trunks crowded in in the shadowy, silent tightness of the canyon. They were among cottonwood trees that ran up straight and smooth and round to an extraordinary height. Above, the tips were gold, and it was sun. But away below, where the horses struggled up the rocks and wound among the trunks, there was still blue shadow by the sound of waters and an occasional grey festoon of old man's beard, and here and there a pale, dipping cranes-bill flower among the tangle and the débris of the virgin place. And again the chill entered the Princess's heart as she realized what a tangle of decay and despair lay in the virgin forests.

They scrambled downwards, splashed across stream, up rocks and along the trail of the other side. Romero's black horse stopped, looked down quizzically at the fallen trees, then stepped over lightly. The Princess's sorrel followed, carefully. But Miss Cummins's buckskin made a fuss, and had to be got round.

In the same silence, save for the clinking of the horses and the splashing as the trail crossed stream, they worked their way upwards in the tight, tangled shadow of the canyon. Sometimes, crossing stream, the Princess would glance upwards, and then always her heart caught in her breast. For high up, away in heaven, the mountain heights shone yellow, dappled with dark spruce firs, clear almost as speckled daffodils against the pale turquoise blue lying high and serene above the dark-blue shadow where the Princess was. And she would snatch at the blood-red leaves of the oak as her horse crossed a more open slope, not knowing what she felt.

They were getting fairly high, occasionally lifted above the canyon itself, in the low groove below the speckled, gold-sparkling heights which towered beyond. Then again they dipped and crossed stream, the horses stepping gingerly across a tangle of fallen, frail aspen stems, then suddenly floundering in a mass of rocks. The black emerged ahead, his black tail waving. The Princess let her mare find her own footing; then she too emerged from the clatter. She rode on after the black. Then came a great frantic rattle of the buckskin behind. The Princess was aware of Romero's dark face looking round, with a strange, demon-like watchfulness, before she herself looked round, to see the buckskin scrambling rather lamely beyond the rocks, with one of his pale buff knees already red with blood.

'He almost went down!' called Miss Cummins.

But Romero was already out of the saddle and hastening down the path. He made quiet little noises to the buckskin, and began examining the cut knee.

'Is he hurt?' cried Miss Cummins anxiously, and she climbed hastily down.

'Oh, my goodness!' she cried, as she saw the blood running down the slender buff leg of the horse in a thin trickle. 'Isn't that *awful*?' She spoke in a stricken voice, and her face was white.

Romero was still carefully feeling the knee of the buckskin. Then he made him walk a few paces. And at last he stood up straight and shook his head.

'Not very bad!' he said. 'Nothing broken.'

Again he bent and worked at the knees. Then he looked up at the Princess.

'He can go on,' he said. 'It's not bad.'

The Princess looked down at the dark face in silence.

'What, go on right up here?' cried Miss Cummins. 'How many hours?'

'About five!' said Romero simply.

'Five hours!' cried Miss Cummins. 'A horse with a lame knee! And a steep mountain! Why-y!'

'Yes, it's pretty steep up there,' said Romero, pushing back his hat and staring fixedly at the bleeding knee. The buckskin stood in a stricken sort of dejection. 'But I think he'll make it all right,' the man added.

'Oh!' cried Miss Cummins, her eyes bright with sudden passion of unshed tears. 'I wouldn't think of it. I wouldn't ride him up there, not for any money.'

'Why wouldn't you?' asked Romero.

'It *hurts* him.'

Romero bent down again to the horse's knee.

'Maybe it hurts him a little,' he said. 'But he can make it all right, and his leg won't get stiff.'

'What! Ride him five hours up the steep mountains?' cried Miss Cummins. 'I couldn't. I just couldn't do it. I'll lead him a little way and see if he can go. But I *couldn't* ride him again. I couldn't. Let me walk.'

'But Miss Cummins, dear, if Romero says he'll be all right?' said the Princess.

'I know it hurts him. Oh, I just couldn't bear it.'

There was no doing anything with Miss Cummins. The thought of a hurt animal always put her into a sort of hysterics.

They walked forward a little, leading the buckskin. He limped rather badly. Miss Cummins sat on a rock.

'Why, it's agony to see him!' she cried. 'It's *cruel*!'

'He won't limp after a bit, if you take no notice of him,' said Romero. 'Now he plays up, and limps very much, because he wants to make you see.'

'I don't think there can be much playing up,' said Miss Cummins bitterly. 'We can *see* how it must hurt him.'

'It don't hurt much,' said Romero.

But now Miss Cummins was silent with antipathy.

It was a deadlock. The party remained motionless on the trail, the Princess in the saddle, Miss Cummins seated on a rock, Romero standing black and remote near the drooping buckskin.

'Well!' said the man suddenly at last. 'I guess we go back, then.'

And he looked up swiftly at his horse, which was cropping at the mountain herbage and treading on the trailing reins.

'No!' cried the Princess. 'Oh no!' Her voice rang with

a great wail of disappointment and anger. Then she checked herself.

Miss Cummins rose with energy.

'Let me lead the buckskin home,' she said, with cold dignity, 'and you two go on.'

This was received in silence. The Princess was looking down at her with a sardonic, almost cruel gaze.

'We've only come about two hours,' said Miss Cummins. 'I don't mind a bit leading him home. But I *couldn't* ride him. I *couldn't* have him ridden with that knee.'

This again was received in dead silence. Romero remained impassive, almost inert.

'Very well, then,' said the Princess. 'You lead him home. You'll be quite all right. Nothing can happen to you, possibly. And say to them that we have gone on and shall be home tomorrow – or the day after.'

She spoke coldly and distinctly. For she could not bear to be thwarted.

'Better all go back, and come again another day,' said Romero – non-committal.

'There will never *be* another day,' cried the Princess. 'I want to go on.'

She looked at him square in the eyes, and met the spark in his eye.

He raised his shoulders slightly.

'If you want it,' he said. 'I'll go on with you. But Miss Cummins can ride my horse to the end of the canyon, and I lead the buckskin. Then I come back to you.'

It was arranged so. Miss Cummins had her saddle put on Romero's black horse, Romero took the buckskin's bridle, and they started back. The Princess rode very slowly on, upwards, alone. She was at first so angry with Miss Cummins that she was blind to everything else. She just let her mare follow her own inclinations.

The peculiar spell of anger carried the Princess on, almost unconscious, for an hour or so. And by this time she was beginning to climb pretty high. Her horse walked steadily all the time. They emerged on a bare slope, and the trail wound through frail aspen stems. Here a wind swept, and some of the aspens were already bare. Others were fluttering their discs of pure, solid yellow leaves, so *nearly* like petals, while the slope ahead was one soft, glowing fleece of daffodil yellow; fleecy like a golden foxskin, and yellow as daffodils alive in the wind and the high mountain sun.

She paused and looked back. The near great slopes were mottled with gold and the dark hue of spruce, like some unsinged eagle, and the light lay gleaming upon them. Away through the gap of the canyon she could see the pale blue of the egg-like desert, with the crumpled dark crack of the Rio Grande Canyon. And far, far off, the blue mountains like a fence of angels on the horizon.

And she thought of her adventure. She was going on alone with Romero. But then she was very sure of herself, and Romero was not the kind of man to do anything to her against her will. This was her first thought. And she just had a fixed desire to go over the brim of the mountains, to look into the inner chaos of the Rockies. And she wanted to go with Romero, because he had some peculiar kinship with her; there was some peculiar link between the two of them. Miss Cummins anyhow would have been only a discordant note.

She rode on, and emerged at length in the lap of the summit. Beyond her was a great concave of stone and stark, dead-grey trees, where the mountain ended against the sky. But nearer was the dense black, bristling spruce, and at her feet was the lap of the summit, a flat little valley of sere grass and quiet-standing yellow aspens, the stream trickling like a thread across.

It was a little valley or shell from which the stream was gently poured into the lower rocks and trees of the canyon. Around her was a fairy-like gentleness, the delicate sere grass, the groves of delicate-stemmed aspens dropping their flakes of bright yellow. And the delicate, quick little stream threading through the wild, sere grass.

Here one might expect deer and fawns and wild things, as in a little paradise. Here she was to wait for Romero, and they were to have lunch.

She unfastened her saddle and pulled it to the ground with a crash, letting her horse wander with a long rope. How beautiful Tansy looked, sorrel, among the yellow leaves that lay like a patina on the sere ground. The Princess herself wore a fleecy sweater of a pale, sere buff, like the grass, and riding-breeches of a pure orange-tawny colour. She felt quite in the picture.

From her saddle-pouches she took the packages of lunch, spread a little cloth, and sat to wait for Romero. Then she made a little fire. Then she ate a devilled egg. Then she ran after Tansy, who was straying across-stream. Then she sat in the sun, in the stillness near the aspens, and waited.

The sky was blue. Her little alp was soft and delicate as fairy-land. But beyond and up jutted the great slopes, dark with the pointed feathers of spruce, bristling with grey dead trees among grey rock, or dappled with dark and gold. The beautiful, but fierce, heavy cruel mountains, with their moments of tenderness.

She saw Tansy start, and begin to run. Two ghost-like figures on horseback emerged from the black of the spruce across the stream. It was two Indians on horseback, swathed like seated mummies in their pale-grey cotton blankets. Their guns jutted beyond the saddles. They rode straight towards her, to her thread of smoke.

As they came near, they unswathed themselves and greeted her, looking at her curiously from their dark eyes. Their black hair was somewhat untidy, the long rolled plaits on their shoulders were soiled. They looked tired.

They got down from their horses near her little fire – a camp was a camp – swathed their blankets round their hips, pulled the saddles from their ponies and turned them loose, then sat down. One was a young Indian whom she had met before, the other was an older man.

'You all alone?' said the younger man.

'Romero will be here in a minute,' she said, glancing back along the trail.

'Ah, Romero! You with him? Where are you going?'

'Round the ridge,' she said. 'Where are you going?'

'We going down to Pueblo.'

'Been out hunting? How long have you been out?'

'Yes. Been out five days.' The young Indian gave a little meaningless laugh.

'Got anything?'

'No. We see tracks of two deer – but not got nothing.'

The Princess noticed a suspicious-looking bulk under one of the saddles – surely a folded-up deer. But she said nothing.

'You must have been cold,' she said.

'Yes, very cold in the night. And hungry. Got nothing to eat since yesterday. Eat it all up.' And again he laughed his little meaningless laugh. Under their dark skins, the two men looked peaked and hungry. The Princess rummaged for food among the saddle-bags. There was a lump of bacon – the regular stand-back – and some bread. She gave them this, and they began toasting slices of it on long sticks at the fire. Such was the little camp Romero saw as he rode down the slope: the Princess in her orange breeches, her head tied in a blue-and-brown silk kerchief, sitting opposite the two dark-headed Indians across the camp-fire, while one of the Indians was leaning forward toasting bacon, his two plaits of braid-swathed hair dangling as if wearily.

Romero rode up, his face expressionless. The Indians greeted him in Spanish. He unsaddled his horse, took food from the bags, and sat down at the camp to eat. The Princess went to the stream for water, and to wash her hands.

'Got coffee?' asked the Indians.

'No coffee this outfit,' said Romero.

They lingered an hour or more in the warm midday sun. Then Romero saddled the horses. The Indians still squatted by the fire. Romero and the Princess rode away, calling *Adios!* to the Indians over the stream and into the dense spruce whence two strange figures had emerged.

When they were alone, Romero turned and looked at her curiously, in a way she could not understand, with such a hard glint in his eyes. And for the first time she wondered if she was rash.

'I hope you don't mind going alone with me,' she said.

'If you want it,' he replied.

They emerged at the foot of the great bare slope of rocky summit, where dead spruce trees stood sparse and bristling like bristles on a grey dead hog. Romero said the Mexicans, twenty years back, had fired the mountains, to drive out the white. This grey concave slope of summit was corpse-like.

The trail was almost invisible. Romero watched for the trees which the Forest Service had blazed. And they climbed the stark corpse slope, among dead spruce, fallen and ash-grey, into the wind. The wind came rushing from the west, up the funnel of the canyon, from the desert. And there was the desert, like a vast mirage tilting slowly upwards towards the west, immense and pallid, away beyond the funnel of the canyon. The Princess could hardly look.

For an hour their horses rushed the slope, hastening with a great working of the haunches upwards, and halting to breathe, scrambling again, and rowing their way up length by length, on the livid, slanting wall. While the wind blew like some vast machine.

After an hour they were working their way on the incline, no longer forcing straight up. All was grey and dead around them; the horses picked their way over the silver-grey corpses of the spruce. But they were near the top, near the ridge.

Even the horses made a rush for the last bit. They had worked round to a scrap of spruce forest near the very top. They hurried in, out of the huge, monstrous, mechanical wind, that whistled inhumanly and was palely cold. So, stepping through the dark screen of trees, they emerged over the crest.

In front now was nothing but mountains, ponderous, massive, down-sitting mountains, in a huge and intricate knot, empty of life or soul. Under the bristling black feathers of spruce near by lay patches of white snow. The lifeless valleys were concaves of rock and spruce, the rounded summits and the hog-backed summits of grey rock crowded one behind the other like some monstrous herd in arrest.

It frightened the Princess, it was *so* inhuman. She had not thought it could be so inhuman, so, as it were, anti-life. And yet now one of her desires was fulfilled. She had seen it, the massive, gruesome, repellent core of the Rockies. She saw it there beneath her eyes, in its gigantic, heavy gruesomeness.

And she wanted to go back. At this moment she wanted

to turn back. She had looked down into the intestinal knot of these mountains. She was frightened. She wanted to go back.

But Romero was riding on, on the lee side of the spruce forest, above the concaves of the inner mountains. He turned round to her and pointed at the slope with a dark hand.

'Here a miner has been trying for gold,' he said. It was a grey scratched-out heap near a hole – like a great badger hole. And it looked quite fresh.

'Quite lately?' said the Princess.

'No, long ago – twenty, thirty years.' He had reined in his horse and was looking at the mountains. 'Look!' he said. 'There goes the Forest Service trail – along those ridges, on the top, way over there till it comes to Lucy-town, where is the Government road. We go down there – no trail – see behind that mountain – you see the top, no trees, and some grass?'

His arm was lifted, his brown hand pointing, his dark eyes piercing into the distance, as he sat on his black horse twisting round to her. Strange and ominous, only the demon of himself, he seemed to her. She was dazed and a little sick, at that height, and she could not see any more. Only she saw an eagle turning in the air beyond, and the light from the west showed the pattern on him underneath.

'Shall I ever be able to go so far?' asked the Princess faintly, petulantly.

'Oh yes! All easy now. No more hard places.'

They worked along the ridge, up and down, keeping on the lee side, the inner side, in the dark shadow. It was cold. Then the trail laddered up again, and they emerged on a narrow ridge-track, with the mountain slipping away enormously on either side. The Princess was afraid. For one moment she looked out, and saw the desert, the desert ridges, more desert, more blue ridges, shining pale and very vast, far below, vastly palely tilting to the western horizon. It was ethereal and terrifying in its gleaming, pale, half-burnished immensity, tilted at the west. She could not bear it. To the left was the ponderous, involved mass of mountains all kneeling heavily.

She closed her eyes and let her consciousness evaporate away. The mare followed the trail. So on and on, in the wind again.

They turned their backs to the wind, facing inwards to the mountains. She thought they had left the trail; it was quite invisible.

'No,' he said, lifting his hand and pointing. 'Don't you see the blazed trees?'

And making an effort of consciousness, she was able to perceive on a pale-grey dead spruce stem the old marks where an axe had chipped a piece away. But with the height, the cold, the wind, her brain was numb.

They turned again and began to descend; he told her they had left the trail. The horses slithered in the loose stones, picking their way downward. It was afternoon, the sun stood obtrusive and gleaming in the lower heavens – about four o'clock. The horses went steadily, slowly, but obstinately onwards. The air was getting colder. They were in among the lumpish peaks and steep concave valleys. She was barely conscious at all of Romero.

He dismounted and came to help her from her saddle. She tottered, but would not betray her feebleness.

'We must slide down here,' he said. 'I can lead the horses.'

They were on a ridge, and facing a steep bare slope of pallid, tawny mountain grass on which the western sun shone full. It was steep and concave. The Princess felt she might start slipping, and go down like a toboggan into the great hollow.

But she pulled herself together. Her eye blazed up again with excitement and determination. A wind rushed past her; she could hear the shriek of spruce trees far below. Bright spots came on her cheeks as her hair blew across. She looked a wild, fairy-like little thing.

'No,' she said. 'I will take my horse.'

'Then mind she doesn't slip down on top of you,' said Romero. And away he went, nimbly dropping down the pale, steep incline, making from rock to rock, down the grass, and following any little slanting groove. His horse hopped and slithered after him, and sometimes stopped dead, with forefeet pressed back, refusing to go farther. He, below his horse, looked up and pulled the reins gently, and encouraged the creature. Then the horse once more dropped his forefeet with a jerk, and the descent continued.

The Princess set off in blind, reckless pursuit, tottering and yet nimble. And Romero, looking constantly back to see how she was faring, saw her fluttering down like some queer little bird, her orange breeches twinkling like the legs of some duck, and her head, tied in the blue and buff kerchief, bound round and round like the head of some blue-topped bird. The sorrel mare rocked and slipped behind her. But down came the Princess in a reckless intensity, a tiny, vivid spot on the great hollow flank of the tawny mountain. So tiny! Tiny as a frail bird's egg. It made Romero's mind go blank with wonder.

But they had to get down, out of that cold and dragging wind. The spruce trees stood below, where a tiny stream emerged in stones. Away plunged Romero, zigzagging down. And away behind, up the slope, fluttered the tiny, bright-coloured Princess, holding the end of the long reins, and leading the lumbering, four-footed, sliding mare.

At last they were down. Romero sat in the sun, below the wind, beside some squaw-berry bushes. The Princess came near, the colour flaming in her cheeks, her eyes dark blue, much darker than the kerchief on her head, and glowing unnaturally.

'We made it,' said Romero.

'Yes,' said the Princess, dropping the reins and subsiding on to the grass, unable to speak, unable to think.

But, thank heaven, they were out of the wind and in the sun.

In a few minutes her consciousness and her control began to come back. She drank a little water. Romero was attending to the saddles. Then they set off again, leading the horses still a little farther down the tiny stream-bed. Then they could mount.

They rode down a bank and into a valley grove dense with aspens. Winding through the thin, crowding, pale-smooth stems, the sun shone flickering beyond them, and the disc-like aspen leaves, waving queer mechanical signals, seemed to be splashing the gold light before her eyes. She rode on in a splashing dazzle of gold.

Then they entered shadow and the dark, resinous spruce trees. The fierce boughs always wanted to sweep her off her horse. She had to twist and squirm past.

But there was a semblance of an old trail. And all at once they emerged in the sun on the edge of the spruce grove, and there was a little cabin, and the bottom of a small, naked valley with a grey rock and heaps of stones, and a round pool of intense green water, dark green. The sun was just about to leave it.

Indeed, as she stood, the shadow came over the cabin and over herself; they were in the lower gloom, a twilight. Above, the heights still blazed.

It was a little hole of a cabin, near the spruce trees, with an earthen floor and an unhinged door. There was a wooden bed-bunk, three old sawn-off log-lengths to sit on as stools, and a sort of fireplace; no room for anything else. The little hole would hardly contain two people. The roof had gone – but Romero had laid on thick spruce boughs.

The strange squalor of the primitive forest pervaded the place, the squalor of animals and their droppings, the squalor of the wild. The Princess knew the peculiar repulsiveness of it. She was tired and faint.

Romero hastily got a handful of twigs, set a little fire going in the stove grate, and went out to attend to the horses. The Princess vaguely, mechanically, put sticks on the fire, in a sort of stupor, watching the blaze, stupefied and fascinated. She could not make much fire – it would set the whole cabin alight. And smoke oozed out of the dilapidated mud-and-stone chimney.

When Romero came in with the saddle-pouches and saddles, hanging the saddles on the wall, there sat the little Princess on her stump of wood in front of the dilapidated fire-grate, warming her tiny hands at the blaze, while her orange breeches glowed almost like another fire. She was in a sort of stupor.

'You have some whisky now, or some tea? Or wait for some soup?' he asked.

She rose and looked at him with bright, dazed eyes, half comprehending; the colour glowing hectic in her cheeks.

'Some tea,' she said, 'with a little whisky in it. Where's the kettle?'

'Wait,' he said. 'I'll bring the things.'

She took her cloak from the back of her saddle, and followed him into the open. It was a deep cup of shadow. But above the sky was still shining, and the heights of the mountains were blazing with aspen like fire blazing.

Their horses were cropping the grass among the stones.

Romero clambered up a heap of grey stones and began lifting away logs and rocks, till he had opened the mouth of one of the miner's little old workings. This was his cache. He brought out bundles of blankets, pans for cooking, a little petrol camp-stove, an axe, the regular camp outfit. He seemed so quick and energetic and full of force. This quick force dismayed the Princess a little.

She took a saucepan and went down the stones to the water. It was very still and mysterious, and of a deep green colour, yet pure, transparent as glass. How cold the place was! How mysterious and fearful.

She crouched in her dark cloak by the water, rinsing the saucepan, feeling the cold heavy above her, the shadow like a vast weight upon her, bowing her down. The sun was leaving the mountain-tops, departing, leaving her under profound shadow. Soon it would crush her down completely.

Sparks? – or eyes looking at her across the water? She gazed, hypnotized. And with her sharp eyes she made out in the·dusk the pale form of a bob-cat crouching by the water's edge, pale as the stones among which it crouched, opposite. And it was watching her with cold, electric eyes of strange intentness, a sort of cold, icy wonder and fearlessness. She saw its *museau* pushed forward, its tufted ears pricking intensely up. It was watching her with cold, animal curiosity, something demonish and conscienceless.

She made a swift movement, spilling her water. And in a flash the creature was gone, leaping like a cat that is escaping; but strange and soft in its motion, with its little bob-tail. Rather fascinating. Yet that cold, intent, demonish watching! She shivered with cold and fear. She knew well enough the dread and repulsiveness of the wild.

Romero carried in the bundles of bedding and the camp outfit. The windowless cabin was already dark inside. He lit a lantern, and then went out again with the axe. She heard him chopping wood as she fed sticks to the fire under her water. When he came in with an armful of oak-scrub faggots, she had just thrown the tea into the water.

'Sit down,' she said, 'and drink tea.'

He poured a little bootleg whisky into the enamel cups, and in the silence the two sat on the log-ends, sipping the hot liquid and coughing occasionally from the smoke.

'We burn these oak sticks,' he said. 'They don't make hardly any smoke.'

Curious and remote he was, saying nothing except what had to be said. And she, for her part, was as remote from him. They seemed far, far apart, worlds apart, now they were so near.

He unwrapped one bundle of bedding, and spread the blankets and the sheepskin in the wooden bunk.

'You lie down and rest,' he said, 'and I make the supper.'

She decided to do so. Wrapping her cloak round her, she lay down in the bunk, turning her face to the wall. She could hear him preparing supper over the little petrol stove. Soon she could smell the soup he was heating; and soon she heard the hissing of fried chicken in a pan.

'You eat your supper now?' he said.

With a jerky, despairing movement, she sat up in the bunk, tossing back her hair. She felt concerned.

'Give it me here,' she said.

He handed her first the cupful of soup. She sat among the blankets, eating it slowly. She was hungry. Then he gave her an enamel plate with pieces of fried chicken and currant jelly, butter and bread. It was very good. As they ate the chicken he made the coffee. She said never a word. A certain resentment filled her. She was cornered.

When supper was over he washed the dishes, dried them, and put everything away carefully, else there would have been no room to move in the hole of a cabin. The oak-wood gave out a good bright heat.

He stood for a few moments at a loss. Then he asked her:

'You want to go to bed soon?'

'Soon,' she said. 'Where are you going to sleep?'

'I make my bed here –' he pointed to the floor along the wall. 'Too cold out of doors.'

'Yes,' she said. 'I suppose it is.'

She sat immobile, her cheeks hot, full of conflicting thoughts. And she watched him while he folded the blankets on the floor, a sheepskin underneath. Then she went out into night.

The stars were big. Mars sat on the edge of a mountain, for all the world like the blazing eye of a crouching mountain lion. But she herself was deep, deep below in a pit of shadow. In the intense silence she seemed to hear the spruce forest crackling with electricity and cold. Strange, foreign stars floated on that unmoving water. The night was going to freeze. Over the hills came the far sobbing-singing howling of the coyotes. She wondered how the horses would be.

Shuddering a little, she turned to the cabin. Warm light showed through its chinks. She pushed at the rickety, half-opened door.

'What about the horses?' she said.

'My black, he won't go away. And your mare will stay with him. You want to go to bed now?'

'I think I do.'

'All right. I feed the horses some oats.'

And he went out into the night.

He did not come back for some time. She was lying wrapped up tight in the bunk.

He blew out the lantern, and sat down on his bedding to take off his clothes. She lay with her back turned. And soon, in the silence, she was asleep.

She dreamed it was snowing, and the snow was falling on her through the roof, softly, softly, helplessly, and she was going to be buried alive. She was growing colder and colder, the snow was weighing down on her. The snow was going to absorb her.

She awoke with a sudden convulsion, like pain. She was really very cold; perhaps the heavy blankets had numbed her. Her heart seemed unable to beat, she felt she could not move.

With another convulsion she sat up. It was intensely dark. There was not even a spark of fire, the light wood had burned right away. She sat in thick oblivious darkness. Only through a chink she could see a star.

What did she want? Oh, what did she want? She sat in bed and rocked herself woefully. She could hear the steady breathing of the sleeping man. She was shivering with cold; her heart seemed as if it could not beat. She wanted warmth, protection, she wanted to be taken away from herself. And at the same time, perhaps more deeply than anything, she wanted to keep herself intact, intact, untouched, that no one should have any power over her, or rights to her. It was a wild necessity in her that no one, particularly no man, should have any rights or power over her, that no one and nothing should possess her.

Yet that other thing! And she was so cold, so shivering, and her heart could not beat. Oh, would not someone help her heart to beat?

She tried to speak, and could not. Then she cleared her throat.

'Romero,' she said strangely, 'it is so cold.'

Where did her voice come from, and whose voice was it, in the dark?

She heard him at once sit up, and his voice, startled, with a resonance that seemed to vibrate against her, saying:

'You want me to make you warm?'

'Yes.'

As soon as he had lifted her in his arms, she wanted to scream to him not to touch her. She stiffened herself. Yet she was dumb.

And he was warm, but with a terrible animal warmth that seemed to annihilate her. He panted like an animal with desire. And she was given over to this thing.

She had never, never wanted to be given over to this. But she had *willed* that it should happen to her. And according to her will, she lay and let it happen. But she never wanted it. She never wanted to be thus assailed and handled, and mauled. She wanted to keep herself to herself.

However, she had willed it to happen, and it had happened. She panted with relief when it was over.

Yet even now she had to lie within the hard, powerful clasp of this other creature, this man. She dreaded to struggle to go away. She dreaded almost too much the icy cold of that other bunk.

'Do you want to go away from me?' asked his strange voice. Oh, if it could only have been a thousand miles away from her! Yet she had willed to have it thus close.

'No,' she said.

And she could feel a curious joy and pride surging up again in him: at her expense. Because he had got her. She felt like a victim there. And he was exulting in his power over her, his possession, his pleasure.

When dawn came, he was fast asleep. She sat up suddenly.

'I want a fire,' she said.

He opened his brown eyes wide, and smiled with a curious tender luxuriousness.

'I want you to make a fire,' she said.

He glanced at the chinks of light. His brown face hardened to the day.

'All right,' he said. 'I'll make it.'

She did her face while he dressed. She could not bear to look at him. He was so suffused with pride and luxury. She hid her face almost in despair. But feeling the cold blast of air as he opened the door, she wriggled down into the warm place where he had been. How soon the warmth ebbed, when he had gone!

He made a fire and went out, returning after a while with water.

'You stay in bed till the sun comes,' he said. 'It's very cold.'

'Hand me my cloak.'

She wrapped the cloak fast round her, and sat up among the blankets. The warmth was already spreading from the fire.

'I suppose we will start back as soon as we've had breakfast?'

He was crouching at his camp-stove making scrambled eggs. He looked up suddenly, transfixed, and his brown eyes, so soft and luxuriously widened, looked straight at her.

'You want to?' he said.

'We'd better get back as soon as possible,' she said, turning aside from his eyes.

'You want to get away from me?' he asked, repeating the question of the night in a sort of dread.

'I want to get away from here,' she said decisively. And it was true. She wanted supremely to get away, back to the world of people.

He rose slowly to his feet, holding the aluminium frying-pan.

'Don't you like last night?' he asked.

'Not really,' she said. 'Why? Do you?'

He put down the frying-pan and stood staring at the wall. She could see she had given him a cruel blow. But she did not relent. She was getting her own back. She wanted to regain possession of all herself, and in some mysterious way she felt that he possessed some part of her still.

He looked round at her slowly, his face greyish and heavy.

'You Americans,' he said, 'you always want to do a man down.'

'I am not American,' she said. 'I am British. And I don't want to do any man down. I only want to go back, now.'

'And what will you say about me, down there?'

'That you were very kind to me, and very good.'

He crouched down again, and went on turning the eggs. He gave her her plate, and her coffee, and sat down to his own food.

But again he seemed not to be able to swallow. He looked up at her.

'You don't like last night?' he asked.

'Not really,' she said, though with some difficulty. 'I don't care for that kind of thing.'

A blank sort of wonder spread over his face at these words, followed immediately by a black look of anger, and then a stony, sinister depair.

'You don't?' he said, looking her in the eyes.

'Not really,' she replied, looking back with steady hostility into his eyes.

Then a dark flame seemed to come from his face.

'I make you,' he said, as if to himself.

He rose and reached her clothes, that hung on a peg: the fine linen underwear, the orange breeches, the fleecy jumper, the blue-and-buff kerchief; then he took up her riding-boots and her bead moccasins. Crushing everything in his arms, he opened the door. Sitting up, she saw him stride down to the dark-green pool in the frozen shadow of that deep cup of a valley. He tossed the clothing and the boots out on the pool. Ice had formed. And on the pure, dark green mirror, in the slaty shadow, the Princess saw her things lying, the white linen, the orange breeches, the black boots, the blue moccasins, a tangled heap of colour. Romero picked up rocks and heaved them out at the ice. till the surface broke and the fluttering clothing disappeared in the rattling water, while the valley echoed and shouted again with the sound.

She sat in despair among the blankets, hugging tight her pale-blue cloak. Romero strode straight back to the cabin.

'Now you stay here with me,' he said.

She was furious. Her blue eyes met his. They were like two demons watching one another. In his face, beyond a sort of unrelieved gloom, was a demonish desire for death.

He saw her looking round the cabin, scheming. He saw her eyes on his rifle. He took the gun and went out with it. Returning, he pulled out her saddle, carried it to the tarn, and threw it in. Then he fetched his own saddle, and did the same.

'Now will you go away?' he said, looking at her with a smile.

She debated within herself whether to coax him and wheedle him. But she knew he was already beyond it. She sat among her blankets in a frozen sort of despair, hard as hard ice with anger.

He did the chores, and disappeared with the gun. She got up in her blue pyjamas, huddled in her cloak, and stood in the doorway. The dark-green pool was motionless again, the stony slopes were pallid and frozen. Shadow still lay, like an after-death, deep in this valley. Always in the distance she saw the horses feeding. If she could catch one!

The brilliant yellow sun was half-way down the mountain. It was nine o'clock.

All day she was alone, and she was frightened. What she was frightened of she didn't know. Perhaps the crackling in the dark spruce wood. Perhaps just the savage, heartless wildness of the mountains. But all day she sat in the sun in the doorway of the cabin, watching, watching for hope. And all the time her bowels were cramped with fear.

She saw a dark spot that probably was a bear, roving across the pale grassy slope in the far distance, in the sun.

When, in the afternoon, she saw Romero approaching, with silent suddenness, carrying his gun and a dead deer, the cramp in her bowels relaxed, then became colder. She dreaded him with a cold dread.

'There is deer-meat,' he said, throwing the dead doe at her feet.

'You don't want to go away from here,' he said. 'This is a nice place.'

She shrank into the cabin.

'Come into the sun,' he said, following her. She looked up at him with hostile, frightened eyes.

'Come into the sun,' he repeated, taking her gently by the arm, in a powerful grasp.

She knew it was useless to rebel. Quietly he led her out, and seated himself in the doorway, holding her still by the arm.

'In the sun it is warm,' he said. 'Look, this is a nice place. You are such a pretty white woman, why do you want to act mean to me? Isn't this a nice place? Come! Come here! It is sure warm here.'

He drew her to him, and in spite of her stony resistance, he took her cloak from her, holding her in her thin blue pyjamas.

'You sure are a pretty little white woman, small and

pretty,' he said. 'You sure won't act mean to me – you don't want to, I know you don't.'

She, stony and powerless, had to submit to him. The sun shone on her white, delicate skin.

'I sure don't mind hell fire,' he said. 'After this.'

A queer, luxurious good humour seemed to possess him again. But though outwardly she was powerless, inwardly she resisted him, absolutely and stonily.

When later he was leaving her again, she said to him suddenly:

'You think you can conquer me this way. But you can't. You can never conquer me.'

He stood arrested, looking back at her, with many emotions conflicting in his face – wonder, surprise, a touch of horror, and an unconscious pain that crumpled his face till it was like a mask. Then he went out without saying a word, hung the dead deer on a bough, and started to flay it. While he was at this butcher's work, the sun sank and cold night came on again.

'You see,' he said to her as he crouched, cooking the supper, 'I ain't going to let you go. I reckon you called to me in the night, and I've some right. If you want to fix it up right now with me, and say you want to be with me, we'll fix it up now and go down to the ranch tomorrow and get married or whatever you want. But you've got to say you want to be with me. Else I shall stay right here, till something happens.'

She waited a while before she answered:

'I don't want to be with anybody against my will. I don't dislike you; at least, I didn't, till you tried to put your will over mine. I won't have anybody's will put over me. You can't succeed. Nobody could. You can never get me under your will. And you won't have long to try, because soon they will send someone to look for me.'

He pondered this last, and she regretted having said it. Then, sombre, he bent to the cooking again.

He could not conquer her, however much he violated her. Because her spirit was hard and flawless as a diamond. But he could shatter her. This she knew. Much more, and she would be shattered.

In a sombre, violent excess he tried to expend his desire for her. And she was racked with an agony, and felt each time she would die. Because, in some peculiar way, he had got hold of her, some unrealized part of her which she never wished to realize. Racked with a burning, tearing anguish, she felt that the thread of her being would break, and she would die. The burning heat that racked her inwardly.

If only, only she could be alone again, cool and intact! If only she could recover herself again, cool and intact! Would she ever, ever, ever be able to bear herself again?

Even now she did not hate him. It was beyond that. Like some racking, hot doom. Personally he hardly existed.

The next day he would not let her have any fire, because of attracting attention with the smoke. It was a grey day, and she was cold. He stayed round, and heated soup on the petrol stove. She lay motionless in the blankets.

And in the afternoon she pulled the clothes over her head and broke into tears. She had never really cried in her life. He dragged the blankets away and looked to see what was shaking her. She sobbed in helpless hysterics. He covered her over again and went outside, looking at the mountains, where clouds were dragging and leaving a little snow. It was a violent, windy, horrible day, the evil of winter rushing down.

She cried for hours. And after this a great silence came between them. They were two people who had died. He did not touch her any more. In the night she lay and shivered like a dying dog. She felt that her very shivering would rupture something in her body, and she would die.

At last she had to speak.

'Could you make a fire? I am so cold,' she said, with chattering teeth.

'Want to come over here?' came his voice.

'I would rather you made me a fire,' she said, her teeth knocking together and chopping the words in two.

He got up and kindled a fire. At last the warmth spread, and she could sleep.

The next day was still chilly, with some wind. But the sun shone. He went about in silence, with a dead-looking face. It was now so dreary and so like death she wished he would do anything rather than continue in this negation. If now he asked her to go down with him to the world and marry him, she would do it. What did it matter? Nothing mattered any more.

But he would not ask her. His desire was dead and heavy like ice within him. He kept watch around the house.

On the fourth day as she sat huddled in the doorway in the sun, hugged in a blanket, she saw two horsemen come over the crest of the grassy slope – small figures. She gave a cry. He looked up quickly and saw the figures. The men had dismounted. They were looking for the trail.

'They are looking for me,' she said.

'Muy bien,' he answered in Spanish.

He went and fetched his gun, and sat with it across his knees.

'Oh!' she said. 'Don't shoot!'

He looked across at her.

'Why?' he said. 'You like staying with me?'

'No,' she said. 'But don't shoot.'

'I ain't going to Pen,' he said.

'You won't have to go to Pen,' she said. 'Don't shoot!'

'I'm going to shoot,' he muttered.

And straightaway he kneeled and took very careful aim. The Princess sat on in an agony of helplessness and hopelessness.

The shot rang out. In an instant she saw one of the horses on the pale grassy slope rear and go rolling down. The man had dropped in the grass, and was invisible. The second man clambered on his horse, and on that precipitous place went at a gallop in a long swerve towards the nearest spruce tree cover. Bang! Bang! went Romero's shots. But each time he missed, and the running horse leaped like a kangaroo towards cover.

It was hidden. Romero now got behind a rock; tense silence, in the brilliant sunshine. The Princess sat on the bunk inside the cabin, crouching, paralysed. For hours, it seemed, Romero knelt behind this rock, in his black shirt, bare-headed, watching. He had a beautiful, alert figure. The Princess wondered why she did not feel sorry for him. But her spirit was hard and cold, her heart could not melt. Though now she would have called him to her, with love.

But no, she did not love him. She would never love any man. Never! It was fixed and sealed in her, almost vindictively.

Suddenly she was so startled she almost fell from the bunk. A shot rang out quite close from behind the cabin. Romero leaped straight into the air, his arms fell outstretched, turning as he leaped. And even while he was in the air, a second shot rang out, and he fell with a crash, squirming, his hands clutching the earth towards the cabin door.

The Princess sat absolutely motionless, transfixed, staring at the prostrate figure. In a few moments the figure of a man in the Forest Service appeared close to the house; a young man in a broad-brimmed Stetson hat, dark flannel shirt, and riding-boots, carrying a gun. He strode over to the prostrate figure.

'Got you, Romero!' he said aloud. And he turned the dead man over. There was already a little pool of blood where Romero's breast had been.

'H'm!' said the Forest Service man. 'Guess I got you nearer than I thought.'

And he squatted there, staring at the dead man.

The distant calling of his comrade aroused him. He stood up.

'Hullo, Bill!' he shouted. 'Yep! Got him! Yep! Done him in, apparently.'

The second man rode out of the forest on a grey horse. He had a ruddy, kind face, and round brown eyes, dilated with dismay.

'He's not passed out?' he asked anxiously.

'Looks like it,' said the first young man coolly.

The second dismounted and bent over the body. Then he stood up again, and nodded.

'Yea-a!' he said. 'He's done in all right. It's him all right, boy! It's Domingo Romero.'

'Yep! I know it!' replied the other.

Then in perplexity he turned and looked into the cabin, where the Princess squatted, staring with big owl eyes from her red blanket.

'Hello!' he said, coming towards the hut. And he took his hat off. Oh, the sense of ridicule she felt! Though he did not mean any.

But she could not speak, no matter what she felt.

'What'd this man start firing for?' he asked.

She fumbled for words, with numb lips.

'He had gone out of his mind!' she said, with solemn, stammering conviction.

'Good Lord! You mean to say he'd gone out of his

mind? Whew! That's pretty awful! That explains it then. H'm!'

He accepted the explanation without more ado.

With some difficulty they succeeded in getting the Princess down to the ranch. But she, too, was not a little mad.

'I'm not quite sure where I am,' she said to Mrs Wilkieson, as she lay in bed. 'Do you mind explaining?'

Mrs Wilkieson explained tactfully.

'Oh yes!' said the Princess. 'I remember. And I had an accident in the mountains, didn't I? Didn't we meet a man who'd gone mad, and who shot my horse from under me?'

'Yes, you met a man who had gone out of his mind.'

The real affair was hushed up. The Princess departed east in a fortnight's time, in Miss Cummins's care. Apparently she had recovered herself entirely. She was the Princess, and a virgin intact.

But her bobbed hair was grey at the temples, and her eyes were a little mad. She was slightly crazy.

'Since my accident in the mountains, when a man went mad and shot my horse from under me, and my guide had to shoot him dead, I have never felt quite myself.'

So she put it.

Later, she married an elderly man, and seemed pleased.

The Overtone

HIS wife was talking to two other women. He lay on the lounge pretending to read. The lamps shed a golden light, and through the open door, the night was lustrous, and a white moon went like a woman, unashamed and naked across the sky. His wife, her dark hair tinged with grey looped low on her white neck, fingered as she talked the pearl that hung in a heavy, naked drop against the bosom of her dress. She was still a beautiful woman, and one who dressed like the night, for harmony. Her gown was of silk lace, all in flakes, as if the fallen, pressed petals of black and faded-red poppies were netted together with gossamer about her. She was fifty-one, and he was fifty-two. It seemed impossible. He felt his love cling round her like her dress, like a garment of dead leaves. She was talking to a quiet woman about the suffrage. The other girl, tall, rather aloof, sat listening in her chair, with the posture of one who neither accepts nor rejects, but who allows things to go on around her, and will know what she thinks only when she must act. She seemed to be looking away into the night. A scent of honeysuckle came through the open door. Then a large grey moth blundered into the light.

It was very still, almost too silent, inside the room. Mrs Renshaw's quiet, musical voice continued:

'But think of a case like Mrs Mann's now. She is a clever woman. If she had slept in my cradle, and I in hers, she would have looked a greater lady than I do at this minute. But she married Mann, and she has seven children by him, and goes out charring. Her children she can never leave. So she must stay with a dirty, drunken brute like Mann. If she had an income of two pounds a week, she could say to

73

him: 'Sir, good-bye to you,' and she would be well rid. But no, she is tied to him for ever.'

They were discussing the State-endowment of mothers. She and Mrs Hankin were bitterly keen upon it. Elsa Laskell sat and accepted their talk as she did the scent of the honeysuckle or the blundering adventure of the moth round the silk: it came burdened, not with the meaning of the words, but with the feeling of the woman's heart as she spoke. Perhaps she heard a nightingale in the park outside – perhaps she did. And then this talk inside drifted also to the girl's heart, like a sort of inarticulate music. Then she was vaguely aware of the man sprawled in his homespun suit upon the lounge. He had not changed for dinner: he was called unconventional.

She knew he was old enough to be her father, and yet he looked young enough to be her lover. They all seemed young, the beautiful hostess, too, but with a meaningless youth that cannot ripen, like an unfertilized flower which lasts a long time. He was a man she classed as a Dane – with fair, almost sandy hair, blue eyes, long loose limbs, and a boyish activity. But he was fifty-two – and he lay looking out on the night, with one of his hands swollen from hanging so long inert, silent. The women bored him.

Elsa Laskell sat in a sort of dreamy state, and the feelings of her hostess, and the feeling of her host drifted like iridescence upon the quick of her soul, among the white touch of that moon out there, and the exotic heaviness of the honeysuckle, and the strange flapping of the moth. So still, it was, behind the murmur of talk: a silence of being. Of the third woman, Mrs Hankin, the girl had no sensibility. But the night and the moon, the moth, Will Renshaw and Edith Renshaw and herself were all in full being, a harmony.

To him it was six months after his marriage, and the sky

was the same, and the honeysuckle in the air. He was living again his crisis, as we all must, fretting and fretting against our failure, till we have worn away the thread of our life. It was six months after his marriage, and they were down at the little bungalow on the bank of the Soar. They were comparatively poor, though her father was rich, and his was well-to-do. And they were alone in the little two-roomed bungalow that stood on its wild bank over the river, among the honeysuckle bushes. He had cooked the evening meal, they had eaten the omelette and drank the coffee, and all was settling into stillness.

He sat outside, by the remnants of the fire, looking at the country lying level and lustrous grey opposite him. Trees hung like vapour in a perfect calm under the moonlight. And that was the moon so perfectly naked and unfaltering, going her errand simply through the night. And that was the river faintly rustling. And there, down the darkness, he saw a flashing of activity white betwixt black twigs. It was the water mingling and thrilling with the moon. So! It made him quiver, and reminded him of the starlit rush of a hare. There was vividness then in all this lucid night, things flashing and quivering with being, almost as the soul quivers in the darkness of the eye. He could feel it. The night's great circle was the pupil of an eye, full of the mystery, and the unknown fire of life, that does not burn away, but flickers unquenchable.

So he rose, and went to look for his wife. She sat with her dark head bent into the light of a reading-lamp, in the little hut. She wore a white dress, and he could see her shoulders' softness and curve through the lawn. Yet she did not look up when he moved. He stood in the doorway, knowing that she felt his presence. Yet she gave no sign.

'Will you come out?' he asked.

She looked up at him as if to find out what he wanted,

and she was rather cold to him. But when he had repeated his request, she had risen slowly to acquiesce, and a tiny shiver had passed down her shoulders. So he unhung from its peg her beautiful Paisley shawl, with its tempered colours that looked as if they had faltered through the years and now were here in their essence, and put it round her. They sat again outside the little hut, under the moonlight. He held both her hands. They were heavy with rings. But one ring was his wedding ring. He had married her, and there was nothing more to own. He owned her, and the night was the pupil of her eye, in which was everything. He kissed her fingers, but she sat and made no sign. It was as he wished. He kissed her fingers again.

Then a corncrake began to call in the meadow across the river, a strange, dispassionate sound, that made him feel not quite satisfied, not quite sure. It was not all achieved. The moon, in her white and naked candour, was beyond him. He felt a little numbness, as one who has gloves on. He could not feel that clear, clean moon. There was something betwixt him and her, as if he had gloves on. Yet he ached for the clear touch, skin to skin – even of the moonlight. He wanted a further purity, a newer cleanness and nakedness. The corncrake cried too. And he watched the moon, and he watched her light on his hands. It was like a butterfly on his glove, that he could see, but not feel. And he wanted to unglove himself. Quite clear, quite, quite bare to the moon, the touch of everything, he wanted to be. And after all, his wife was everything – moon, vapour of trees, trickling water and drift of perfume – it was all his wife. The moon glistened on her finger-tips as he cherished them, and a flash came out of a diamond, among the darkness. So, even here in the quiet harmony, life was at a flash with itself.

'Come with me to the top of the red hill,' he said to his wife quietly.

'But why?' she asked.

'Do come.'

And dumbly, she acquiesced, and her shawl hung gleaming above the white flash of her skirt. He wanted to hold her hand, but she was walking apart from him, in her long shawl. So he went to her side, humbly. And he was humble, but he felt it was great. He had looked into the whole of the night, as into the pupil of an eye. And now, he would come perfectly clear out of all his embarrassments of shame and darkness, clean as the moon who walked naked across the night, so that the whole night was as an effluence from her, the whole of it was hers, held in her effluence of moonlight, which was her perfect nakedness, uniting her to everything. Covering was barrier, like cloud across the moon.

The red hill was steep, but there was a tiny path from the bungalow, which he had worn himself. And in the effort of climbing, he felt he was struggling nearer and nearer to himself. Always he looked half round, where, just behind him, she followed, in the lustrous obscurity of her shawl. Her steps came with a little effort up the steep hill, and he loved her feet, he wanted to kiss them as they strove upwards in the gloom. He put aside the twigs and branches. There was a strong scent of honeysuckle like a thick strand of gossamer over his mouth.

He knew a place on the ledge of the hill, on the lip of the cliff, where the trees stood back and left a little dancing-green, high up above the water, there in the midst of miles of moonlit, lonely country. He parted the boughs, sure as a fox that runs to its lair. And they stood together on this little dancing-green presented towards the moon, with the red cliff cumbered with bushes going down to the river below, and the haze of moon-dust on the meadows, and the trees behind them, and only the moon could look straight into the place he had chosen.

She stood always a little way behind him. He saw her face all compounded of shadows and moonlight, and he dared not kiss her yet.

'Will you,' he said, 'will you take off your things and love me here?'

'I can't,' she said.

He looked away to the moon. It was difficult to ask her again, yet it meant so much to him. There was not a sound in the night. He put his hand to his throat and began to unfasten his collar.

'Take off all your things and love me,' he pleaded.

For a moment she was silent.

'I can't,' she said.

Mechanically, he had taken off his flannel collar and pushed it into his pocket. Then he stood on the edge of the land, looking down into all that gleam, as into the living pupil of an eye. He was bareheaded to the moon. Not a breath of air ruffled his bare throat. Still, in the dropping folds of her shawl, she stood, a thing of dusk and moonlight, a little back. He ached with the earnestness of his desire. All he wanted was to give himself, clean and clear into this night, this time. Of which she was all, she was everything. He could go to her now, under the white candour of the moon, without shame or shadow, but in his completeness loving her completeness, without a stain, without a shadow between them such as even a flower could cast. For this he yearned as never in his life he could yearn more deeply.

'Do take me,' he said, gently parting the shawl on her breast. But she held it close, and her voice went hard.

'No – I can't,' she said.

'Why?'

'I can't – let us go back.'

He looked again over the countryside of dimness, saying in a low tone, his back towards her:

'But I love you – and I want you so much – like that, here and now. I'll never ask you anything again,' he said quickly, passionately, as he turned to her. 'Do this for me,' he said. 'I'll never trouble you for anything again. I promise.'

'I can't,' she said stubbornly, with some hopelessness in her voice.

'Yes,' he said. 'Yes. You trust me, don't you?'

'I don't want it. Not here – not now,' she said.

'Do,' he said. 'Yes.'

'You can have me in the bungalow. Why do you want me here?' she asked.

'But I do. Have me, Edith. Have me now.'

'No,' she said, turning away. 'I want to go down.'

'And you won't?'

'No – I can't.'

There was something like fear in her voice. They went down the hill together. And he did not know how he hated her, as if she had kept him out of the promised land that was justly his. He thought he was too generous to bear her a grudge. So he had always held himself deferential to her. And later that evening he had loved her. But she hated it, it had been really his hate ravaging her. Why had he lied, calling it love? Ever since, it had seemed the same, more or less. So that he had ceased to come to her, gradually. For one night she had said: 'I think a man's body is ugly – all in parts with mechanical joints.' And now he had scarcely had her for some years. For she thought him an ugliness. And there were no children.

Now that everything was essentially over, for both of them, they lived on the surface, and had good times. He drove to all kinds of unexpected places in his motor-car, bathed where he liked, said what he liked, and did what he liked. But nobody minded very much his often aggressive unconventionality. It was only fencing with the foils. There was no danger in his thrusts. He was a castrated bear. So he prided himself on being a bear, on being known as an uncouth bear.

It was not often he lay and let himself drift. But always when he did, he held it against her that on the night when they climbed the red bank, she refused to have him. There were perhaps many things he might have held against her, but this was the only one that remained: his real charge against her on the Judgement Day. Why had she done it? It had been, he might almost say, a holy desire on his part. It had been almost like taking off his shoes before God. Yet she refused him, she who was his religion to him. Perhaps she had been afraid, she who was so good – afraid of the big righteousness of it – as if she could not trust herself so near the Burning Bush, dared not go near for transfiguration, afraid of herself.

It was a thought he could not bear. Rising softly, because she was still talking, he went out into the night.

Elsa Laskell stirred uneasily in her chair. Mrs Renshaw went on talking like a somnambule, not because she really had anything to say about the State-endowment of mothers, but because she had a weight on her heart that she wanted to talk away. The girl heard, and lifted her hand, and stirred her fingers uneasily in the dark-purple porphyry bowl, where pink rose-leaves and crimson, thrown this morning from the stem, lay gently shrivelling. There came a slight acrid scent of new rose-petals. And still the girl lifted her long white fingers among the red and pink in the dark bowl, as if they stirred in blood.

And she felt the nights behind like a purple bowl into which the woman's heart-beats were shed, like rose-leaves fallen and left to wither and go brown. For Mrs Renshaw had waited for him. During happy days of stillness and blueness she had moved, while the sunshine glancing through her blood made flowers in her heart, like blossoms underground thrilling with expectancy, lovely fragrant things that would have delight to appear. And all day long she had gone secretly and quietly saying, saying: 'Tonight – tonight they will blossom for him. Tonight I shall be a bed of blossom for him, all narcissi and fresh fragrant things shaking for joy, when he comes with his deeper sunshine, when he turns the darkness like mould, and brings them forth with his sunshine for spade. Yea, there are two suns; him in the sky and that other, warmer one whose beams are our radiant bodies. He is a sun to me, shining full on my heart when he comes, and everything stirs.' But he had come like a bitter morning. He had never bared the sun of himself to her – a sullen day he had been on her heart, covered with cloud impenetrable. She had waited so heavy anxious, with such a wealth of possibility. And he in his blindness had never known. He could never let the real rays of his love through the cloud of fear and mistrust. For once she had denied him. And all her flowers had been shed inwards, so that her heart was like a heap of leaves, brown, withered, almost scentless petals that had never given joy to anyone. And yet again she had come to him pregnant with beauty and love, but he had been afraid. When she lifted her eyes to him, he had looked aside. The kisses she needed like warm raindrops he dared not give, till she was parched and gone hard, and did not want them. Then he gave kisses enough. But he never trusted himself. When she was open and eager to him, he was afraid. When she was shut, it was like playing at pride, to pull her petals apart, a game that gave him pleasure.

So they had been mutually afraid of each other, but he

most often. Whenever she had needed him at some mystery of love, he had overturned her censers and her sacraments, and made profane love in her sacred place. Which was why at last, she had hated his body; but perhaps she had hated it at first, or feared it so much, that it was hate.

And he had said to her: 'If *we* don't have children, you might have them by another man –' which was surely one of the cruellest things a woman ever heard from her husband. For so little was she his, that he would give her a caller and not mind. This was all the wife she was to him. He was a free and easy man, and brought home to dinner any man who pleased him, from a beggar upwards. And his wife was to be as public as his board.

Nay, to the very bowl of her heart, any man might put his lips and he would not mind. And so, she sadly set down the bowl from between her two hands of offering, and went always empty, and aloof.

Yet they were married, they were good friends. It was said they were the most friendly married couple in the county. And this was it. And all the while, like a scent, the bitter psalm of the woman filled the room.

'Like a garden in winter, I was full of bulbs and roots, I was full of little flowers, all conceived inside me.

'And they were all shed away unborn, little abortions of flowers.

'Every day I went like a bee gathering honey from the sky and among the stars I rummaged for yellow honey, filling it in my comb.

'Then I broke the comb, and put it to your lips. But you turned your mouth aside, and said, "You have made my face unclean, and smeared my mouth."

'And week after week my body was a vineyard, my veins were vines. And as the grapes, the purple drops grew full and sweet, I crushed them in a bowl, I treasured the wine.

'Then when the bowl was full I came with joy to you. But you in fear started away, and the bowl was thrown from my hands, and broke in pieces at my feet.

'Many times, and many times, I said, "The hour is striking," but he answered, "Not yet."

'Many times and many times he has heard the cock crow, and gone out and wept, he knew not why.

'I was a garden and he ran in me as in the grass.

'I was a stream, and he threw his waste in me.

'I held the rainbow balanced on my outspread hands, and he said, "You open your hands and give me nothing."

'What am I now but a bowl of withered leaves, but a kaleidoscope of broken beauties, but an empty bee-hive, yea, a rich garment rusted that no one has worn, a dumb singer, with the voice of a nightingale yet making discord.

'And it was over with me, and my hour is gone. And soon like a barren sea-shell on the strand, I shall be crushed underfoot to dust.

'But meanwhile I sing to those that listen with their ear against me, of the sea that gave me form and being, the everlasting sea, and in my song is nothing but bitterness, for of the fluid life of the sea I have no more, but I am to be dust, that powdery stuff the sea knows not. I am to be dead, who was born of life, silent who was made a mouth, formless who was all of beauty. Yea, I was a seed that held the heavens lapped up in bud, with a whirl of stars and a steady moon.

'And the seed is crushed that never sprouted, there is a heaven lost, and stars and a moon that never came forth.

'I was a bud that never was discovered, and in my shut chalice, skies and lake water and brooks lie crumbling, and stars and the sun are smeared out, and birds are a little powdery dust, and their singing is dry air, and I am a dark chalice.'

And the girl, hearing the hostess talk, still talk, and yet her voice like the sound of a sea-shell whispering hoarsely of despair, rose and went out into the garden, timidly, beginning to cry. For what should she do for herself?

Renshaw, leaning on the wicket that led to the paddock, called:

'Come on, don't be alarmed – Pan is dead.'

And then she bit back her tears. For when he said, 'Pan is dead,' he meant Pan was dead in his own long, loose Dane's body. Yet she was a nymph still, and if Pan were dead, she ought to die. So with tears she went up to him.

'It's all right out here,' he said. 'By Jove, when you see a night like this, how can you say that life's tragedy – or death either, for that matter?'

'What is it, then?' she asked.

'Nay, that's one too many – a joke, eh?'

'I think,' she said, 'one has no business to be irreverent.'

'Who?' he asked.

'You,' she said, 'and me, and all of us.'

Then he leaned on the wicket, thinking till he laughed.

'Life's a real good thing,' he said.

'But why protest it?' she answered.

And again he was silent.

'If the moon came nearer and nearer,' she said, 'and were a naked woman, what would you do?'

'Fetch a wrap, probably,' he said.

'Yes – you would do that,' she answered.

'And if he were a man, ditto?' he teased.

'If a star came nearer and were a naked man, I should look at him.'

'That is surely very improper,' he mocked, with still a tinge of yearning.

'If he were a star come near –' she answered.

Again he was silent.

'You are a queer fish of a girl,' he said.

They stood at the gate, facing the silver-grey paddock. Presently their hostess came out, a long shawl hanging from her shoulders.

'So you are here,' she said. 'Were you bored?'

'I was,' he replied amiably. 'But there, you know I always am.'

'And I forgot,' replied the girl.

'What were you talking about?' asked Mrs Renshaw, simply curious. She was not afraid of her husband's running loose.

'We were just saying "Pan is dead",' said the girl.

'Isn't that rather trite?' asked the hostess.

'Some of us miss him fearfully,' said the girl.

'For what reason?' asked Mrs Renshaw.

'Those of us who are nymphs – just lost nymphs among farm-lands and suburbs. I wish Pan were alive.'

'Did he die of old age?' mocked the hostess.

'Don't they say, when Christ was born, a voice was heard in the air saying "Pan is dead." I wish Christ needn't have killed Pan.'

'I wonder how He managed it,' said Renshaw.

'By disapproving of him, I suppose,' replied his wife. And her retort cut herself, and gave her a sort of fakir pleasure.

'The men are all women now,' she said, 'since the fauns died in a frost one night.'

'A frost of disapproval,' said the girl.

'A frost of fear,' said Renshaw.

There was a silence.

'Why was Christ afraid of Pan?' said the girl suddenly.

'Why was Pan so much afraid of Christ, that he died?' asked Mrs Renshaw bitterly.

'And all his fauns in a frost one night,' mocked Renshaw.

Then a light dawned on him. 'Christ was woman, and Pan was man,' he said. It gave him real joy to say this bitterly, keenly – a thrust into himself, and into his wife. 'But the fauns and satyrs are there – you have only to remove the surplices that all men wear nowadays.'

'Nay,' said Mrs Renshaw, 'it is not true – the surplices have grown into their limbs, like Hercules's garment.'

'That his wife put on him,' said Renshaw.

'Because she was afraid of him – not because she loved him,' said the girl.

'She imagined that all her lonely wasted hours wove him a robe of love,' said Mrs Renshaw. 'It was to her horror she was mistaken. You can't weave love out of waste.'

'When I meet a man,' said the girl, 'I shall look down the pupil of his eye, for a faun. And after a while it will come, skipping –'

'Perhaps a satyr,' said Mrs Renshaw bitterly.

'No,' said the girl, 'because satyrs are old, and I have seen some fearfully young men.'

'Will is young even now – quite a boy,' said his wife.

'Oh no!' cried the girl. 'He says that neither life nor death is a tragedy. Only somebody very old could say that.'

There was a tension in the night. The man felt something give way inside him.

'Yes, Edith,' he said, with a quiet, bitter joy of cruelty, 'I am old.'

The wife was frightened.

'You are always preposterous,' she said quickly, crying inside herself. She knew she herself had been never young.

'I shall look in the eyes of my man for the faun,' the girl continued in a sing-song, 'and I shall find him. Then I shall pretend to run away from him. And both our surplices, and all the crucifix, will be outside the wood. Inside nymph and faun, Pan and his satyrs – ah, yes: for Christ and the Cross is only for day-time, and bargaining, Christ came to make us deal honourably.

'But love is no deal, nor merchant's bargaining, and Christ neither spoke of it nor forbade it. He was afraid of it. If once His faun, the faun of the young Jesus had run free, seen one white nymph's brief breast, He would not have been content to die on a Cross – and then the men would have gone on cheating the women in life's business, all the time. Christ made one bargain in mankind's business – and He made it for the women's sake – I suppose for His mother's, since He was fatherless. And Christ made a bargain for me, and I shall avail myself of it. I won't be cheated by my man. When between my still hands I weave silk out of the air, like a cocoon, He shall not take it to pelt me with. He shall draw it forth and weave it up. For I want to finger the sunshine I have drawn through my body, stroke it, and have joy of the fabric.

'And when I run wild on the hills with Dionysus, and shall come home like a bee that has rolled in floury crocuses, he must see the wonder on me, and make bread of it.

'And when I say to him, "It is harvest in my soul", he shall look in my eyes and lower his nets where the shoal moves in a throng in the dark, and lift out the living blue silver for me to see, and know, and taste.

'All this, my faun in commerce, my faun at traffic with me.

'And if he cheat me, he must take his chance.

'But I will not cheat him, in his hour, when he runs like a faun after me. I shall flee, but only to be overtaken. I shall flee, but never out of the wood to the crucifix. For that is to deny I am a nymph; since how can a nymph cling at the crucifix? Nay, the cross is the sign I have on my money, for honesty.

'In the morning, when we come out of the wood, I shall

say to him: "Touch the cross, and prove you will deal fairly," and if he will not, I will set the dogs of anger and judgement on him, and they shall chase him. But if, perchance, some night he contrive to crawl back into the wood, beyond the crucifix, he will be faun and I nymph, and I shall have no knowledge what happened outside, in the realm of the crucifix. But in the morning, I shall say: "Touch the cross, and prove you will deal fairly." And being renewed, he will touch the cross.

'Many a dead faun I have seen, like dead rabbits poisoned lying about the paths, and many a dead nymph, like swans that could not fly and the dogs destroyed.

'But I am a nymph and a woman, and Pan is for me, and Christ is for me.

'For Christ I cover myself in my robe, and weep, and vow my vow of honesty.

'For Pan I throw my coverings down and run headlong through the leaves, because of the joy of running.

'And Pan will give me my children and joy, and Christ will give me my pride.

'And Pan will give me my man, and Christ my husband.

'To Pan I am nymph, to Christ I am woman.

'And Pan is in the darkness, and Christ in the pale light.

'And night shall never be day, and day shall never be night.

'But side by side they shall go, day and night, night and day, for ever apart, for ever together.

'Pan and Christ, Christ and Pan.

'Both moving over me, so when in the sunshine I go in my robes among my neighbours, I am a Christian. But when I run robeless through the dark-scented woods alone, I am Pan's nymph.

'Now I must go, for I want to run away. Not run away from myself, but to myself.

'For neither am I a lamp that stands in the way in the sunshine.

'Now am I a sundial foolish at night.

'I am myself, running through light and shadow for ever, a nymph and a Christian; I, not two things, but an apple with a gold side and a red, a freckled deer, a stream that tinkles and a pool where light is drowned; I, no fragment, no half-thing like the day, but a blackbird with a white breast and underwings, a peewit, a wild thing, beyond understanding.'

'I wonder if we shall hear the nightingale tonight,' said Mrs Renshaw.

'He's a gurgling fowl – I'd rather hear a linnet,' said Renshaw. 'Come a drive with me tomorrow, Miss Laskell.'

And the three went walking back to the house. And Elsa Laskell was glad to get away from them.

The Flying Fish

1 *Departure from Mexico*

'COME home else no Day in Daybrook.' This cablegram was the first thing Gethin Day read of the pile of mail which he found at the hotel in the lost town of South Mexico, when he returned from his trip to the coast. Though the message was not signed, he knew whom it came from and what it meant.

He lay in his bed in the hot October evening, still sick with malaria. In the flush of fever he saw yet the parched, stark mountains of the south, the villages of reed huts lurking among trees, the black-eyed natives with the lethargy, the ennui, the pathos, the beauty of an exhausted race; and above all he saw the weird, uncanny flowers, which he had hunted from the high plateaux, through the valleys, and down to the steaming crocodile heat of the *tierra caliente*, towards the sandy, burning, intolerable shores. For he was fascinated by the mysterious green blood that runs in the veins of plants, and the purple and yellow and red blood that colours the faces of flowers. Especially the unknown flora of South Mexico attracted him, and above all he wanted to trace to the living plant the mysterious essences and toxins known with such strange elaboration to the Mayas, the Zapotecas, and the Aztecs.

His head was humming like a mosquito, his legs were paralysed for the moment by the heavy quinine injection the doctor had injected into them, and his soul was as good as dead with the malaria; so he threw all his letters un-opened on the floor, hoping never to see them again. He lay with the pale yellow cablegram in his hand: 'Come home else no Day in Daybrook.' Through the open doors from the patio of the hotel came the heavy scent of that invisible green night-flower the natives call *Buena de Noche*. The little Mexican servant-girl strode in barefoot with a cup of tea, her flounced cotton skirt swinging, her long black hair down her back. She asked him in her birdlike Spanish if he wanted nothing more. '*Nada más*,' he said. 'Nothing more; leave me and shut the door.'

He wanted to shut out the scent of that powerful green inconspicuous night-flower he knew so well.

> No Day in Daybrook;
> For the Vale a bad outlook.

No Day in Daybrook! There had been Days in Daybrook since time began: at least, so he imagined.

Daybrook was a sixteenth-century stone house, among the hills in the middle of England. It stood where Crichdale bends to the south and where Ashleydale joins in. 'Daybrook standeth at the junction of the ways and at the centre of the trefoil. Even it rides within the Vale as an ark between three seas; being indeed the ark of these vales, if not of all England.' So had written Sir Gilbert Day, he who built the present Daybrook in the sixteenth century. Sir Gilbert's *Book of Days*, so beautifully written out on vellum and illuminated by his own hand, was one of the treasures of the family.

Sir Gilbert had sailed the Spanish seas in his day, and had come home rich enough to rebuild the old house of Daybrook according to his own fancy. He had made it a beautiful pointed house, rather small, standing upon a knoll above the river Ashe, where the valley narrowed and the woods rose steep behind. 'Nay,' wrote this quaint Elizabethan, 'though I say that Daybrook is the ark of the

Vale, I mean not the house itself, but He that Day, that lives in the house in his day. While Day there be in Daybrook, the floods shall not cover the Vale nor shall they ride over England completely.'

Gethin Day was nearing forty, and he had not spent much of his time in Daybrook. He had been a soldier and had wandered in many countries. At home his sister Lydia, twenty years older than himself, had been the Day in Daybrook. Now from her cablegram he knew she was either ill or already dead.

She had been rather hard and grey like the rock of Crichdale, but faithful and a pillar of strength. She had let him go his own way, but always when he came home, she would look into his blue eyes with her searching uncanny grey look and ask: 'Well, have you come, or are you still wandering?' 'Still wandering, I think,' he said. 'Mind you don't wander into a cage one of these days,' she replied; 'you would find far more room for yourself in Daybrook than in these foreign parts, if you knew how to come into your own.'

This had always been the burden of her song to him: *if you knew how to come into your own*. And it had always exasperated him with a sense of futility; though whether his own futility or Lydia's, he had never made out.

Lydia was wrapt up in old Sir Gilbert's *Book of Days*; she had written out for her brother a fair copy, neatly bound in green leather, and had given it him without a word when he came of age, merely looking at him with that uncanny look of her grey eyes, expecting something of him, which always made him start away from her.

The *Book of Days* was a sort of secret family bible at Daybrook. It was never shown to strangers, nor ever mentioned outside the immediate family. Indeed in the family it was never openly alluded to. Only on solemn occasions, or on rare evenings, at twilight, when the evening star shone, had the father, now dead, occasionally read aloud to the two children from the nameless work.

In the copy she had written out for Gethin, Lydia had used different coloured inks in different places. Gethin imagined that her favourite passages were those in the royal-blue ink, where the page was almost as blue as the cornflowers that grew tall beside the walks in the garden at Daybrook.

'Beauteous is the day of the yellow sun which is the common day of men; but even as the winds roll unceasing above the trees of the world, so doth that Greater Day, which is the Uncommon Day, roll over the unclipt bushes of our little daytime. Even also as the morning sun shakes his yellow wings on the horizon and rises up, so the great bird beyond him spreads out his dark blue feathers, and beats his wings in the tremor of the Greater Day.'

Gethin knew a great deal of his *Book of Days* by heart. In a dilettante fashion, he had always liked rather highflown poetry, but in the last years, something in the hard, fierce, finite sun of Mexico, in the dry terrible land, and in the black staring eyes of the suspicious natives, had made the ordinary day lose its reality to him. It had cracked like some great bubble, and to his uneasiness and terror, he had seemed to see through the fissures the deeper blue of that other Greater Day where moved the other sun shaking its dark blue wings. Perhaps it was the malaria; perhaps it was his own inevitable development; perhaps it was the presence of those handsome, dangerous, wide-eyed men left over from the ages before the flood in Mexico, which caused his old connections and his accustomed world to break for him. He was ill, and he felt as if at the very middle of him, beneath his navel, some membrane were torn, some membrane which had connected him with the world and its day. The natives who attended him, quiet, soft, heavy, and rather helpless, seemed, he realized, to be gazing from their wide black eyes always into that greater day whence they had come and where they wished to return. Men of a dying race, to whom the busy sphere of the common day is a cracked and leaking shell.

He wanted to go home. He didn't care now whether England was tight and little and over-crowded and far too full of furniture. He no longer minded the curious quiet atmosphere of Daybrook in which he had felt he would stifle as a young man. He no longer resented the weight of family tradition, nor the peculiar sense of authority which the house seemed to have over him. Now he was sick from the soul outwards, and the common day had cracked for him, and the uncommon day was showing him its immensity, he felt that home was the place. It did not matter that England was small and tight and over-furnished, if the Greater Day were round about. He wanted to go home, away from these big wild countries where men were dying back into the Greater Day, home where he dare face the sun behind the sun, and come into his own in the Greater Day.

But he was as yet too ill to go. He lay in the nausea of the tropics, and let the days pass over him. The door of his room stood open on to the patio where green banana trees and high strange-sapped flowering shrubs rose from the water-sprinkled earth towards that strange rage of blue which was the sky over the shadow-heavy, perfume-soggy air of the closed-in courtyard. Dark-blue shadows moved from the side of the patio, disappeared, then appeared on the other side. Evening had come, and the barefoot natives in white calico flitted with silent rapidity across, and across, for ever going, yet mysteriously going nowhere, threading the timelessness with their transit, like swallows of darkness.

The window of the room, opposite the door, opened on to the tropical parched street. It was a big window, came nearly down to the floor, and was heavily barred with upright and horizontal bars. Past the window went the natives, with the soft, light rustle of their sandals. Big straw hats balanced, dark cheeks, calico shoulders brushed with the silent swiftness of the Indian past the barred window-space. Sometimes children clutched the bars and gazed in, with great shining eyes and straight blue-black hair, to see the Americano lying in the majesty of a white bed. Sometimes a beggar stood there, sticking a skinny hand through the iron grille and whimpering the strange, endless, pullulating whimper of the beggar – '*por amor de Dios!*' – on and on and on, as it seemed for an eternity. But the sick man on the bed endured it with the same endless endurance in resistance, endurance in resistance which he had learned in the Indian countries. Aztec or Mixtec, Zapotec or Maya, always the same power of serpent-like torpor of resistance.

The doctor came – an educated Indian: though he could do nothing but inject quinine and give a dose of calomel. But he was lost between the two days, the fatal greater day of the Indians, the fussy, busy lesser day of the white people.

'How is it going to finish?' he said to the sick man, seeking a word. 'How is it going to finish with the Indians, with the Mexicans? Now the soldiers are all taking *marihuana* – hashish!'

'They are all going to die. They are all going to kill themselves – all – all,' said the Englishman, in the faint permanent delirium of his malaria. 'After all, beautiful it is to be dead, and quite departed.'

The doctor looked at him in silence, understanding only too well. 'Beautiful it is to be dead!' It is the refrain which hums at the centre of every Indian heart, where the greater day is hemmed in by the lesser. The despair that comes when the lesser day hems in the greater. Yet the doctor looked at the gaunt white man in malice: – 'What, would you have us quite gone, you Americans?'

At last, Gethin Day crawled out into the plaza. The square was like a great low fountain of green and of dark shade, now it was autumn and the rains were over. Scarlet craters rose the canna flowers, licking great red tongues, and tropical yellow. Scarlet, yellow, green, blue-green, sunshine intense and invisible, deep indigo shade! and small, white-clad natives pass, passing, across the square, through the green lawns, under the indigo shade, and across the hollow sunshine of the road into the arched arcades of the low Spanish buildings, where the shops were. The low, baroque Spanish buildings stood back with a heavy, sick look, as if they too felt the endless malaria in their bowels, the greater day of the stony Indian crushing the more jaunty, lean European day which they represented. The yellow cathedral leaned its squat, earthquake-shaken towers, the bells sounded hollow. Earth-coloured tiny soldiers lay and stood around the entrance to the municipal palace, which was so baroque and Spanish, but which now belonged to the natives. Heavy as a strange bell of shadow-coloured glass, the shadow of the greater day hung over this coloured plaza which the Europeans had created, like an oasis, in the lost depths of Mexico. Gethin Day sat half lying on one of the broken benches, while tropical birds flew and twittered in the great trees, and natives twittered or flitted in silence, and he knew that here, the European day was annulled again. His body was sick with the poison that lurks in all tropical air, his soul was sick with that other day, that rather awful greater day which permeates the little days of the old races. He wanted to get out, to get out of this ghastly tropical void into which he had fallen.

Yet it was the end of November before he could go. Little revolutions had again broken the thread of railway at the end of which the southern town hung revolving like a spider. It was a narrow-gauge railway, one single narrow little track which ran over the plateau, then slipped down, down the long *barranca*, descending five thousand feet down to the valley which was a cleft in the plateau, then up again seven thousand feet, to the higher plateau to the north. How easy to break the thread! One of the innumerable little wooden bridges destroyed, and it was done. The three hundred miles to the north were impassable wilderness, like the hundred and fifty miles through the low-lying jungle to the south.

At last however he could crawl away. The train came again. He had cabled to England, and had received the answer that his sister was dead. It seemed so natural, there under the powerful November sun of southern Mexico, in the drugging powerful odours of the night-flowers, that Lydia should be dead. She seemed so much more *real*, shall we say actually vital, in death. Dead, he could think of her as quite near and comforting and real, whereas while she was alive, she was so utterly alien, remote and fussy, ghost-like in her petty Derbyshire day.

'For the little day is like a house with the family round the hearth, and the door shut. Yet outside whispers the Greater Day, wall-less, and hearthless. And the time will come at last when the walls of the little day shall fall, and what is left of the family of men shall find themselves out-doors in the Greater Day, houseless and abroad, even here between the knees of the Vales, even in Crichdale. It is a doom that will come upon tall men. And then they will breathe deep, and be breathless in the great air, and salt sweat will stand on their brow, thick as buds on sloe-bushes when the sun comes back. And little men will shudder and die out, like clouds of grasshoppers falling in the sea. Then tall men will remain alone in the land, moving deeper in the Greater Day, and moving deeper. Even as the flying fish, when he leaves the air and recovereth his element in the depth, plunges and invisibly rejoices. So will tall men rejoice, after their flight of fear, through the thin air, pursued by death. For it is on wings of fear, sped from the mouth of death, that the flying fish riseth twinkling in the air, and rustles in astonishment silvery through the thin small day. But he dives again into the great peace of the deeper day, and under the belly of death, and passes into his own.'

Gethin read again his *Book of Days*, in the twilight of his last evening. Personally, he resented the symbolism and mysticism of his Elizabethan ancestor. But it was in his veins. And he was going home, back, back to the house with the flying fish on the roof. He felt an immense doom over everything, still the same next morning, when, an hour after dawn, the little train ran out from the doomed little town, on to the plateau, where the cactus thrust up its fluted tubes, and where the mountains stood back, blue, cornflower-blue, so dark and pure in form, in the land of the Greater Day, the day of demons. The little train, with two coaches, one full of natives, the other with four or five 'white' Mexicans, ran fussily on, in the little day of toys and men's machines. On the roof sat tiny, earthy-looking soldiers, faces burnt black, with cartridge-belts and rifles. They clung on tight, not to be shaken off. And away went this weird toy, this crazy little caravan, over the great lost land of cacti and mountains standing back, on to the shut-in defile where the long descent began.

At half-past ten, at a station some distance down the

barranca, a station connected with old silver mines, the train stood, and all descended to eat: the eternal turkey with black sauce, potatoes, salad, and apple pie – the American apple pie, which is a sandwich of cooked apple between two layers of pie-crust. And also beer, from Puebla. Two Chinamen administered the dinner, in all the decency, cleanness and well-cookedness of the little day of the white men, which they reproduce so well. There it was, the little day of our civilization. Outside, the little train waited. The little black-faced soldiers sharpened their knives. The vast, varying declivity of the *barranca* stood in sun and shadow as on the day of doom, untouched.

On again, winding, descending the huge and savage gully or crack in the plateau-edge, where no men lived. Bushes trailed with elegant pink creeper, such as is seen in hothouses, enormous blue convolvuluses opened out, and in the unseemly tangle of growth, bulbous orchids jutted out from trees, and let hang a trail of white or yellow flower. The strange, entangled squalor of the jungle.

Gethin Day looked down the ravine, where water was running. He saw four small deer lifting their heads from drinking, to look at the train. '*Los venados*! *los venados*!' he heard the soldiers softly calling. As if knowing they were safe, the deer stood and wondered, away there in the Greater Day, in the manless space, while the train curled round a sharp jutting rock.

They came at last to the bottom, where it was very hot, and a few wild men hung round with the sword-like knives of the sugar-cane. The train seemed to tremble with fear all the time, as if its thread might be cut. So frail, so thin the thread of the lesser day, threading with its business the great reckless heat of the savage land. So frail a thread, so easily snapped!

But the train crept on, northwards, upwards. And as the

stupor of heat began to pass, in the later afternoon, the sick man saw among mango trees, beyond the bright green stretches of sugar-cane, white clusters of a village, with the coloured dome of a church all yellow and blue with shiny majolica tiles. Spain putting the bubbles of her little day among the blackish trees of the unconquerable.

He came at nightfall to a small square town, more in touch with civilization, where the train ended its frightened run. He slept there. And next day he took another scrap of a train across to the edge of the main plateau. The country was wild, but more populous. An occasional big *hacienda* with sugar-mills stood back among the hills. But it was silent. Spain had spent the energy of her little day here, now the silence, the terror of the Greater Day, mysterious with death, was filling in again.

On the train a native, a big, handsome man, wandered back and forth among the uneasy Mexican travellers with a tray of glasses of ice-cream. He was no doubt of the Tlascala tribe. Gethin Day looked at him and met his glistening dark eyes. '*Quiere helados, Señor?*' said the Indian, reaching a glass with his dark, subtle-skinned, workless hand. And in the soft, secret tones of his voice, Gethin Day heard the sound of the Greater Day. '*Gracias!*'

'*Padrón! Padrón!*' moaned a woman at the station. '*Por amor de Dios, Padrón!*' and she held out her hand for a few centavos. And in the moaning croon of her Indian voice the Englishman heard again the fathomless crooning appeal of the Indian women, moaning stranger, more terrible than the ring-dove, with a sadness that had no horizon, and a rocking, moaning appeal that drew out the very marrow of the soul of a man. Over the door of her womb was written not only: '*Lasciate ogni speranza, voi ch'entrate,*' but: '*Perdite ogni pianto, voi ch'uscite.*' For the men who had known these women were beyond weeping and beyond even despair, mute in the timeless compulsion of the Greater Day. Big, proud men could sell glasses of ice-cream at twenty-five centavos, and not really know they were doing it. They were elsewhere, beyond despair. Only sometimes the last passion of the death-lust would sweep them, shut up as they were in the white man's lesser day, belonging as they did to the greater day.

The little train ran on to the main plateau, and to the junction with the main-line railway called the Queen's Own, a railway that still belongs to the English, and that joins Mexico City with the Gulf of Mexico. Here, in the big but forlorn railway restaurant the Englishman ordered the regular meal, that came with American mechanical take-it-or-leave-it flatness. He ate what he could, and went out again. There the vast plains were level and bare, under the blue winter sky, so pure, and not too hot, and in the distance the white cone of the volcano of Orizaba stood perfect in the middle air.

'There is no help. O man. Fear gives thee wings like a bird, death comes after thee open-mouthed, and thou soarest on the wind like a fly. But thy flight is not far, and thy flying is not long. Thou art a fish of the timeless Ocean, and must needs fall back. Take heed lest thou break thyself in the fall! For death is not in dying, but in the fear. Cease then the struggle of thy flight, and fall back into the deep element where death is and is not, and life is not a fleeing away. It is a beauteous thing to live and to be alive. Live then in the Greater Day, and let the waters carry thee, and the flood bear thee along, and live, only live, no more of this hurrying away.'

'No more of this hurrying away.' Even the Elizabethans had known it, the restlessness, the 'hurrying away'. Gethin Day knew he had been hurrying away. He had hurried perhaps a little too far, just over the edge. Now, try as he might, he was aware of a gap in his time-space *continuum*; he was, in the words of his ancestor, aware of the Greater Day showing through the cracks in the ordinary day. And it was useless trying to fill up the cracks. The little day was destined to crumble away, as far as he was concerned, and he would *have* to inhabit the greater day. The very sight of the volcano cone in mid-air made him know it. His little self was used up, worn out. He felt sick and frail, facing this change of life.

'Be still, then, be still! Wrap thyself in patience, shroud thyself in peace, as the tall volcano clothes himself in snow. Yet he looks down in him, and sees wet sun in him molten and of great force, stirring with the scald sperm of life. Be still, above the sperm of life, which spills alone in its hour. Be still, as an apple on its core, as a nightingale in winter, as a long-waiting mountain upon its fire. Be still, upon thine own sun.

'For thou hast a sun in thee. Thou hast a sun in thee, and it is not timed. Therefore wait. Wait, and be at peace with thine own sun, which is thy sperm of life. Be at peace with thy sun in thee, as the volcano is, and the dark holly-bush before berry-time, and the long hours of night. Abide by thy sun in thee, even the onion doth so, though you see it not. Yet peel her, and her sun in thine eyes maketh tears. Each thing hath its little sun, even in the wicked house-fly something twinkleth.'

Standing there on the platform of the station open to the great plains of the plateau, Gethin Day said to himself: My old ancestor is more real to me than the restaurant, and the dinner I have eaten, after all. The train still did not come. He turned to another page of cornflower-blue writing, hoping to find something amusing.

'When earth inert lieth too heavy, then Vesuvius spitteth out fire. And if a nightingale would not sing, his song unsung in him would slay him. For to the nightingale his song is Nemesis, and unsung songs are the Erinyes, the impure Furies of vengeance. And thy sun in thee is thy all in all, so be patient, and take no care. Take no care, for what thou knowest is ever less than what thou art. The full fire even of thine own sun in thine own body, thou canst never know. So how shouldst thou load care upon thy sun? Take heed, take thought, take pleasure, take pain, take all things as thy sun stirs. Only fasten not thyself in care about anything, for care is impiety, it spits upon the sun.'

It was the white and still volcano, visionary across the swept plain, that looked back at him as he glanced up from his *Book of Days*. But there the train came, thundering, with all the mock majesty of great equipage, and the Englishman entered the Pullman car, and sat with his book in his pocket.

The train, almost with the splendour of the Greater Day, yet rickety and foolish at last, raced on the level, entered the defile, and crept, cautiously twining round and round, down the cliff-face of the plateau, with the low lands lying thousands of feet below, specked with a village or two like fine specks. Yet the low lands drew up, and the pine trees were gone far above, and at last the thick trees crowded the line, and dark-faced natives ran beside the train selling gardenias, gardenia perfume heavy in all the air. But the train nearly empty.

Veracruz at night-fall was a modern stone port, but disheartened and tropical, mostly shut up, abandoned, as if life had quietly left it. Great customs buildings, unworking, acres of pianofortes in packing-cases, all the endless jetsam of the little day of commerce flung up here and waiting, acres of goods unattended to, waiting till the labour of Veracruz should cease to be on strike. A town, a port struck numb, the inner sun striking vengefully at the little life of commerce. The day's sun set, there was a heavy orange light over the waters, something sinister, a gloom, a deep resentment in nature, even in the washing of the warm sea. In these salt waters natives were still baptized to Christianity, and the socialists, in mockery perhaps, baptized themselves into the mystery of frustration and revenge. The port was in the hands of strikers and wild out-of-workers, and was blank. Officials had almost disappeared. Even here, a woman, a 'lady' examined the passports.

But the ship rode at the end of the jetty: the one lonely passenger ship. There was one other steamer – from Sweden, a cargo boat. For the rest, the port was deserted. It was a point where the wild primeval day of this continent met the busy white man's day, and the two annulled one another. The result was a port of nullity, nihilism concrete and actual, calling itself the city of the True Cross.

2 The Gulf

In the morning they sailed off, away from the hot shores, from the high land hanging up inwards. And world gives place to world. In an hour, it was only ship and ocean, the world of land and affairs was gone.

There were few people on board. In the second-class saloon only seventeen souls. Gethin Day was travelling second. It was a German boat, he knew it would be clean and comfortable. The second-class fare was already forty-five pounds. And a man who is not rich, and who would live his life under as little compulsion as possible, must calculate keenly with money and its power. For the lesser day of money and the mealy-mouthed Mammon is always ready for a victim, and a man who has glimpsed the Greater Day, and the inward sun, will not fall into the clutches of

Mammon's mean day, if he can help it. Gethin Day had a moderate income, and he looked on this as his bulwark against Mammon's despicable authority. The thought of earning a living was repulsive and humiliating to him.

In the first-class saloon were only four persons: two Danish merchants, stout and wealthy, who had been part of a bunch of Danish business men invited by the Mexican government to look at the business resources of the land. They had been fêted and feasted, and shown what they were meant to see, so now, fuller of business than ever, they were going back to Copenhagen to hatch the eggs they had conceived. But they had also eaten oysters in Veracruz, and the oysters also were inside them. They fell sick of poison, and lay deathly ill all the voyage, leaving the only other first-class passengers, an English knight and his son, alone in their glory. Gethin Day was sincerely glad he had escaped the first class, for the voyage was twenty days

The seventeen souls of the second class were four of them English, two Danish, five Spaniards, five Germans, and a Cuban. They all sat at one long table in the dining saloon, the Cuban at one end of the table, flanked by four English on his left, facing the five Spaniards across the table. Then came the two Danes, facing one another, and being buffer-state between the rest and the five Germans, who occupied the far end of the table. It was a German boat, so the Germans were very noisy, and the stewards served them first. The Spaniards and the Cuban were mum, the English were stiff, the Danes were uneasy, the Germans were boisterous, and so the first luncheon passed. It was the lesser day of the ship, and small enough. The menu being in correct German and doubtful Spanish, the Englishwoman on Gethin Day's right put up a lorgnette and stared at it. She was unable to stare it out of countenance, so she put it down and ate uninformed as to what she was eating. The Spaniard opposite Gethin Day had come to table without collar or tie, doing the bluff, go-to-hell colonial touch, almost in his shirt-sleeves. He was a man of about thirty-two. He brayed at the steward in strange, harsh Galician Spanish, the steward grinned somewhat sneeringly and answered in German, having failed to understand, and not prepared to exert himself to try. Down the table a blonde horse of a woman was shouting at the top of her voice, in harsh North-German, to a Herr Doktor with turned-up moustaches who presided at the German head of the table. The Spaniards bent forward in a row to look with a sort of silent horror at the yelling woman, then they looked at one another with a faint grimace of mocking repulsion. The Galician banged the table with the empty wine-decanter: wine was 'included'. The steward, with a sneering little grin at such table-manners, brought a decanter half full. Wine was not *ad lib.*, but *à discrétion*. The Spaniards, having realized this, henceforth snatched it quickly and pretty well emptied the decanter before the English got a shot at it. Which somewhat amused the table-stewards, who wanted to see the two foreign lots fight it out. But Gethin Day solved this problem by holding out his hand to the fat, clean-shaven Basque, as soon as the decanter reached that gentleman, and saying: 'May I serve the lady?' Whereupon the Basque handed over the decanter, and Gethin helped the two ladies and himself, before handing back the decanter to the Spaniards. – Man wants but little here below, but he's damn well got to see he gets it. – All this is part of the little day, which has to be seen to. Whether it is interesting or not depends on one's state of soul.

Bristling with all the bristles of offence and defence which a man has to put up the first days in such a company, Gethin Day would go off down the narrow gangway of the bottom deck, down into the steerage, where the few passengers lay about in shirt and trousers, on to the very front tip of the boat.

She was a long, narrow, old ship, long like a cigar, and not much space in her. Yet she was pleasant, and had a certain grace of her own, was a real ship, not merely a 'liner'. She seemed to travel swift and clean, piercing away into the Gulf.

Gethin Day would sit for hours at the very tip of the ship, on the bowsprit, looking out into the whitish sunshine of the hot Gulf of Mexico. Here he was alone, and the world was all strange white sunshine, candid, and water, warm, bright water, perfectly pure beneath him, of an exquisite frail green. It lifted vivid wings from the running tip of the ship, and threw white pinion-spray from its green edges. And always, always, always it was in the two-winged fountain, as the ship came like life between, and always the spray fell swishing, pattering from the green arch of the water-wings. And below, as yet untouched, a moment ahead, always a moment ahead, and perfectly untouched, was the lovely green depth of the water, depth, deep, shallow-pale emerald above an under sapphire-green, dark and pale, blue and shimmer-green, two waters, many waters, one water, perfect in unison, one moment ahead of the ship's bows, so serene, fathomless and pure and free of time. It was very lovely, and on the softly-lifting bowsprit of the long, swift ship the body was cradled in the sway of timeless life, the soul lay in the jewel-coloured moment, the jewel-pure eternity of this gulf of nowhere.

And always, always, like a dream, the flocks of flying fish swept into the air, from nowhere, and went brilliantly twinkling in their flight of silvery watery wings rapidly fluttering, away, low as swallows over the smooth curved surface of the sea, then gone again, vanished, without splash or evidence, gone. One alone like a little silver twinkle. Gone! The sea was still and silky-surfaced, blue and softly heaving, empty, purity itself, sea, sea, sea.

Then suddenly the faint whispering crackle, and a cloud of silver on webs of pure, fluttering water was soaring low over the surface of the sea, at an angle from the ship, as if jetted away from the cut-water soaring in a low arc, fluttering with the wild emphasis of grasshoppers or locusts suddenly burst out of the grass, in a wild rush to make away, make away, and making it, away, away, then suddenly gone, like a lot of lights blown out in one breath. And still the ship did not pause, any more than the moon pauses, neither to look nor catch breath. But the soul pauses and holds its breath, for wonder, wonder, which is the very breath of the soul.

All the long morning he would be there curled in the wonder of this gulf of creation, where the flying fishes on translucent wings swept in their ecstatic clouds out of the water, in a terror that was brilliant as joy, in a joy brilliant with terror, with wings made of pure water flapping with great speed, and long-shafted bodies of translucent silver like squirts of living water, there in air, brilliant in air, before suddenly they had disappeared, and the blue sea was trembling with a delicate frail surface of green, the still sea lay one moment ahead, untouched, untouched since time began, in its watery loveliness.

Sometimes a ship's officer would come and peer over the edge, and look at him lying there. But nothing was said. People didn't like looking over the edge. It was too beautiful, too pure and lovely, the Greater Day. They shoved their snouts a moment over the rail, then withdrew, faintly abashed, faintly sneering, faintly humiliated. After all, they showed snouts, nothing but snouts, to the unbegotten morning, so they might well be humiliated.

Sometimes an island, two islands, three, would show up, dismal and small, with the peculiar American gloom. No land! The soul wanted to see the land. Only the uninterrupted water was purely lovely, pristine.

And the third morning there was a school of porpoises leading the ship. They stayed below surface all the time, so there was no hullabaloo of human staring. Only Gethin Day saw them. And what joy! what joy of life! what marvellous pure joy of being a porpoise within the great sea, of being many porpoises heading and mocking in translucent onrush the menacing, yet futile onrush of a vast ship!

It was a spectacle of the purest and most perfected joy in life that Gethin Day ever saw. The porpoises were ten or a dozen, round-bodied torpedo fish, and they stayed there as if they were not moving, always there, with no motion apparent, under the purely pellucid water, yet speeding on at just the speed of the ship, without the faintest show of movement, yet speeding on in the most miraculous precision of speed. It seemed as if the tail-flukes of the last fish exactly touched the ship's bows, under-water, with the frailest, yet precise and permanent touch. It seemed as if nothing moved, yet fish and ship swept on through the tropical ocean. And the fish moved, they changed places all the time. They moved in a little cloud, and with the most wonderful sport they were above, they were below, they were to the fore, yet all the time the same one speed, the same one speed, and the last fish just touching with his tail-flukes the iron cut-water of the ship. Some would be down in the blue, shadowy, but horizontally motionless in the same speed. Then with a strange revolution, these would be up in pale green water, and others would be down. Even the toucher, who touched the ship, would in a twinkling be changed. And ever, ever the same pure horizontal speed, sometimes a dark back skimming the water's surface light, from beneath, but never the surface broken. And ever the last fish touching the ship, and ever the others speeding in motionless, effortless speed, and intertwining with strange silkiness as they sped, intertwining among one another, fading down to the dark blue shadow, and strangely emerging again among the silent, swift others, in pale green water. All the time, so swift, they seemed to be laughing.

Gethin Day watched spell-bound, minute after minute, an hour, two hours, and still it was the same, the ship speeding, cutting the water, and the strong-bodied fish heading in perfect balance of speed underneath, mingling among themselves in some strange single laughter of multiple consciousness, giving off the joy of life, sheer joy of life, togetherness in pure complete motion, many lusty-bodied fish enjoying one laugh of life, sheer togetherness, perfect as passion. They gave off into the water their marvellous joy of life, such as the man had never met before. And it left him wonderstruck.

'But they know joy, they know pure joy!' he said to himself in amazement. 'This is the most laughing joy I have ever seen, pure and unmixed. I always thought flowers had brought themselves to the most beautiful perfection in nature. But these fish, these fleshy, warm-bodied fish achieve more than flowers, heading along. This is the purest achievement of joy I have seen in all life: these strong, careless fish. Men have not got in them that secret to be alive together and make one like a single laugh, yet each fish going his own gait. This is sheer joy – and men have lost it, or never accomplished it. The cleverest sportsmen in the world are owls beside these fish. And the togetherness of love is nothing to the spinning unison of dolphins playing under-sea. It would be wonderful to know joy as these fish know it. The life of the deep waters is ahead of us, it contains sheer togetherness and sheer joy. We have never got there.'

There as he leaned over the bowsprit he was mesmerized by one thing only, by joy, by joy of life, fish speeding in water with playful joy. No wonder Ocean was still mysterious, when such red hearts beat in it! No wonder man, with his tragedy, was a pale and sickly thing in comparison! What civilization will bring us to such a pitch of swift laughing togetherness, as these fish have reached?

3 *The Atlantic*

The ship came in the night to Cuba, to Havana. When she became still, Gethin Day looked out of his port-hole and saw little lights on upreared darkness. Havana!

They went on shore next morning, through the narrow dock-streets near the wharf, to the great boulevard. It was a lovely warm morning, already early December, and the town was in the streets, going to mass, or coming out of the big, unpleasant old churches. The Englishman wandered with the two Danes for an hour or so, in the not very exciting city. Many Americans were wandering around, and nearly all wore badges of some sort. The city seemed, on the surface at least, very American. And underneath, it did not seem to have any very deep character of its own left.

The three men hired a car to drive out and about. The elder of the Danes, a man of about forty-five, spoke fluent colloquial Spanish, learned on the oil-fields of Tampico. 'Tell me,' he said to the chauffeur, 'why do all these *americanos*, these Yankees, wear badges on themselves?'

He spoke, as foreigners nearly always do speak of the Yankees, in a tone of half-spiteful jeering.

'Ah, Señor,' said the driver, with a Cuban grin. 'You know they all come here to drink. They drink so much that they all get lost at night, so they all wear a badge: name, name of hotel, place where it is. Then our policemen find them in the night, turn them over as they lie on the pavement, read name, name of hotel, and place, and so they are put on a cart and carted to home. Ah, the season is only just beginning. Wait a week or two, and they will lie in the streets at night like a battle, and the police doing Red Cross work, carting them to their hotels. Ah, *los americanos!* They are so good. You know they own us now. Yes, they own us. They own Havana. We are a Republic owned by the Americans. *Muy bien*, we give them drink, they give us money. Bah!'

And he grinned with a kind of acrid indifference. He sneered at the whole show, but he wasn't going to do anything about it.

The car drove out to the famous beer-gardens, where all drank beer – then to the inevitable cemetery, which almost rivalled that of New Orleans. 'Every person buried in this cemetery guarantees to put up a tomb-monument costing not less than fifty-thousand dollars.' Then they drove past the new suburb of villas, springing up neat and tidy, spick-and-span, same all the world over. Then they drove out into the country, past the old sugar *haciendas* and to the hills.

And to Gethin Day it was all merely depressing and void of real interest. The Yankees owned it all. It had not much character of its own. And what character it had was the peculiar, dreary character of all America wherever it is a little abandoned. The peculiar gloom of Connecticut or New Jersey, Louisiana or Georgia, a sort of dreariness in the very bones of the land, that shows through immediately the human effort sinks. How quickly the gloom and the inner dreariness of Cuba must have affected the spirit of the Conquistadores, even Columbus!

They drove back to town and ate a really good meal, and watched a stout American couple, apparently man and wife, lunching with a bottle of champagne, a bottle of hock, and a bottle of Burgundy for the two of them, and apparently drinking them all at once. It made one's head reel.

The bright, sunny afternoon they spent on the esplanade by the sea. There the great hotels were still shut. But they had, so to speak, half an eye open: a tea-room going, for example.

And Day thought again, how tedious the little day can be! How difficult to spend even one Sunday looking at a city like Havana, even if one has spent the morning driving into the country. The infinite tedium of looking at things! the infinite boredom of things anyhow. Only the rippling, bright, pale-blue sea, and the old fort, gave one the feeling of life. The rest, the great esplanade, the great boulevard, the great hotels, all seemed what they were, dead, dried concrete, concrete, dried deadness.

Everybody was thankful to be back on the ship for dinner, in the dark loneliness of the wharves. See Naples and die. Go seeing any place, and you'll be half dead of exhaustion and tedium by dinner time.

So! good-bye, Havana! The engines were going before breakfast time. It was a bright blue morning. Wharves and harbour slid past, the high bows moved backwards. Then the ship deliberately turned her back on Cuba and the sombre shore, and began to move north, through the blue day, which passed like a sleep. They were moving now into wide space.

The next morning they woke to greyness, grey low sky, and

hideous low grey water, and a still air. Sandwiched between two greynesses, the long, wicked old ship sped on, as unto death.

'What has happened?' Day asked of one of the officers.

'We have come north, to get into the current running east. We come north about the latitude of New York, then we run due east with the stream.'

'What a wicked shame!'

And indeed it was. The sun was gone, the blueness was gone, life was gone. The Atlantic was like a cemetery, an endless, infinite cemetery of greyness, where the bright, lost world of Atlantis is buried. It was December, grey, dark December on a waste of ugly, dead-grey water, under a dead-grey sky.

And so they ran into a swell, a long swell whose oily, sickly waves seemed hundreds of miles long, and travelling in the same direction as the ship's course. The narrow cigar of a ship heaved up the upslope with a nauseating heave, up, up, up, till she righted for a second sickeningly on the top, then tilted, and her screw raced like a dentist's burr in a hollow tooth. Then down she slid, down the long, shivering downslope, leaving all her guts behind her, and the guts of all the passengers too. In an hour, everybody was deathly white, and sicklily grinning, thinking it a sort of joke that would soon be over. Then everybody disappeared, and the game went on: up, up, up, heavingly up, till a pause, ah! – then burr-rr-rr! as the screw came out of water and shattered every nerve. Then whoooosh! the long and awful downrush, leaving the entrails behind.

She was like a plague-ship, everybody disappeared, stewards and everybody. Gethin Day felt as if he had taken poison: and he slept – slept, slept, slept, and yet was all the time aware of the ghastly motion – up, up, up, heavingly up, then ah! one moment, followed by the shattering burr-rr-rr! and the unspeakable ghastliness of the downhill slither, where death seemed inside the entrails, and water chattered like the after-death. He was aware of the hour-long moaning, moaning of the Spanish doctor's fat, pale Mexican wife, two cabins away. It went on for ever. Everything went on for ever. Everything was like this for ever, for ever. And he slept, slept, slept, for thirty hours, yet knowing it all, registering just the endless repetition of the motion, the ship's loud squeaking and chirruping, and the ceaseless moaning of the woman.

Suddenly at tea-time the second day he felt better. He got up. The ship was empty. A ghastly steward gave him a ghastly cup of tea, then disappeared. He dozed again, but came to dinner.

They were three people at the long table, in the horribly travelling grey silence: himself, a young Dane, and the elderly, dried Englishwoman. She talked, talked. The three looked in terror at *Sauerkraut* and smoked loin of pork. But they ate a little. Then they looked out on the utterly repulsive, grey, oily, windless night. Then they went to bed again.

The third evening it began to rain, and the motion was subsiding. They were running out of the swell. But it was an experience to remember.

(*Unfinished*)

Sun

I

'TAKE her away, into the sun,' the doctor said.

She herself was sceptical of the sun, but she permitted herself to be carried away, with her child, and a nurse, and her mother, over the sea.

The ship sailed at midnight. And for two hours her husband stayed with her, while the child was put to bed, and the passengers came on board. It was a black night, the Hudson swayed with heavy blackness, shaken over with spilled dribbles of light. She leaned over the rail, and looking down thought: this is the sea; it is deeper than one imagines, and fuller of memories. At that moment the sea seemed to heave like the serpent of chaos that has lived for ever.

'These partings are no good, you know,' her husband was saying, at her side. 'They're no good. I don't like them.'

His tone was full of apprehension, misgiving, and there was a certain clinging to the last straw of hope.

'No, neither do I,' she responded in a flat voice.

She remembered how bitterly they had wanted to get away from one another, he and she. The emotion of parting gave a slight tug at her emotions, but only caused the iron that had gone into her soul to gore deeper.

So, they looked at their sleeping son, and the father's eyes were wet. But it is not the wetting of the eyes that counts, it is the deep iron rhythm of habit, the year-long, life-long habits; the deep-set stroke of power.

And in their two lives, the stroke of power was hostile,

his and hers. Like two engines running at variance, they shattered one another.

'All ashore! All ashore!'

'Maurice, you must go!'

And she thought to herself: For him it is All Ashore! For me it is Out to Sea!

Well, he waved his hanky on the midnight dreariness of the pier, as the boat inched away; one among a crowd. One among a crowd! C'est ça!

The ferry-boats, like great dishes piled with rows of lights, were still slanting across the Hudson. That black mouth must be the Lackawanna Station.

The ship ebbed on between the lights, the Hudson seemed interminable. But at last they were round the bend, and there was the poor harvest of lights at the Battery. Liberty flung up her torch in a tantrum. There was the wash of the sea.

And though the Atlantic was grey as lava, they did come at last into the sun. Even she had a house above the bluest of seas, with a vast garden, or vineyard, all vines and olives, dropping steeply, terrace after terrace, to the strip of coast plain; and the garden full of secret places, deep groves of lemon far down in the cleft of earth, and hidden, pure green reservoirs of water; then a spring issuing out of a little cavern, where the old Sicules had drunk before the Greeks came; and a grey goat bleating, stabled in an ancient tomb with the niches empty. There was the scent of mimosa, and beyond, the snow of the volcano.

She saw it all, and in a measure it was soothing. But it was all external. She didn't really care about it. She was herself just the same, with all her anger and frustration inside her, and her incapacity to feel anything real. The child irritated her, and preyed on her peace of mind. She felt so horribly, ghastly responsible for him: as if she must be responsible for every breath he drew. And that was torture to her, to the child, and to everybody else concerned.

'You know, Juliet, the doctor told you to lie in the sun, without your clothes. Why don't you?' said her mother.

'When I am fit to do so, I will. Do you want to kill me?' Juliet flew at her.

'To kill you, no! Only to do you good.'

'For God's sake, leave off wanting to do me good.'

The mother at last was so hurt and incensed, she departed.

The sea went white, and then invisible. Pouring rain fell. It was cold, in the house built for the sun.

Again a morning when the sun lifted himself molten and sparkling, naked over the sea's rim. The house faced southeast, Juliet lay in her bed and watched him rise. It was as if she had never seen the sun rise before. She had never seen the naked sun stand up pure upon the sea-line, shaking the night off himself, like wetness. And he was full and naked. And she wanted to come to him.

So the desire sprang secretly in her, to go naked to the sun. She cherished her desire like a secret. She wanted to come together with the sun.

But she wanted to go away from the house – away from people. And it is not easy, in a country where every olive tree has eyes, and every slope is seen from afar, to go hidden, and have intercourse with the sun.

But she found a place: a rocky bluff, shoved out to the sea and sun, and overgrown with the large cactus called prickly pear. Out of this thicket of cactus rose one cypress tree, with a pallid, thick trunk, and a tip that leaned over, flexible, in the blue. It stood like a guardian looking to sea; or a candle whose huge flame was darkness against light: the long tongue of darkness licking up at the sky.

Juliet sat down by the cypress tree, and took off her

clothes. The contorted cactus made a forest, hideous yet fascinating, about her. She sat and offered her bosom to the sun, sighing, even now, with a certain hard pain, against the cruelty of having to give herself: but exulting that at last it was no human lover.

But the sun marched in blue heaven and sent down his rays as he went. She felt the soft air of the sea on her breasts, that seemed as if they would never ripen. But she hardly felt the sun. Fruits that would wither and not mature, her breasts.

Soon, however, she felt the sun inside them, warmer than ever love had been, warmer than milk or the hands of her baby. At last, at last her breasts were like long white grapes in the hot sun.

She slid off all her clothes, and lay naked in the sun, and as she lay she looked up through her fingers at the central sun, his blue pulsing roundness, whose outer edges streamed brilliance. Pulsing with marvellous blue, and alive, and streaming white fire from his edges, the Sun! He faced down to her with blue body of fire, and enveloped her breasts and her face, her throat, her tired belly, her knees, her thighs and her feet.

She lay with shut eyes, the colour of rosy flame through her lids. It was too much. She reached and put leaves over her eyes. Then she lay again, like a long gourd in the sun, green that must ripen to gold.

She could feel the sun penetrating into her bones; nay, further, even into her emotions and her thoughts. The dark tensions of her emotion began to give way, the cold dark clots of her thoughts began to dissolve. She was beginning to be warm right through. Turning over, she let her shoulders lie in the sun, her loins, the backs of her thighs, even her heels. And she lay half stunned with the strangeness of the thing that was happening to her. Her weary, chilled heart was melting, and in melting, evaporating. Only her womb remained tense and resistant, the eternal resistance. It would resist even the sun.

When she was dressed again she lay once more and looked up at the cypress tree, whose crest, a filament, fell this way and that in the breeze. Meanwhile, she was conscious of the great sun roaming in heaven, and of her own resistance.

So, dazed, she went home, only half-seeing, sun-blinded and sun-dazed. And her blindness was like a richness to her, and her dim, warm, heavy half-consciousness was like wealth.

'Mummy! Mummy!' her child came running towards her, calling in that peculiar bird-like little anguish of want, always wanting her. She was surprised that her drowsed heart for once felt none of the anxious love-tension in return. She caught the child up in her arms, but she thought: He should not be such a lump! If he had any sun in him, he would spring up. And she felt again the unyielding resistance of her womb, against him and everything.

She resented, rather, his little hands clutching at her, especially her neck. She pulled her throat away. She did not want him getting hold of it. She put the child down.

'Run!' she said. 'Run in the sun!'

And there and then she took off his clothes and set him naked on the warm terrace.

'Play in the sun!' she said.

He was frightened and wanted to cry. But she, in the warm indolence of her body, and the complete indifference of her heart, and the resistance of her womb, rolled him an orange across the red tiles, and with his soft, unformed little body he toddled after it. Then, immediately he had it, he dropped it because it felt strange against his flesh. And he looked back at her, wrinkling his face to cry, frightened because he was stark.

'Bring me the orange,' she said, amazed at her own deep indifference to his trepidation. 'Bring Mummy the orange.'

'He shall not grow up like his father,' she said to herself. 'Like a worm that the sun has never seen.'

2

She had had the child so much on her mind, in a torment of responsibility, as if, having borne him, she had to answer for his whole existence. Even if his nose were running, it had been repulsive and a goad in her vitals, as if she must say to herself: Look at the thing you brought forth!

Now a change took place. She was no longer vitally consumed about the child, she took the strain of her anxiety and her will from off him. And he thrived all the more for it.

She was thinking inside herself, of the sun in his splendour, and his entering into her. Her life was now a secret ritual. She always lay awake, before dawn, watching for the grey to colour to pale gold, to know if clouds lay on the sea's edge. Her joy was when he rose all molten in his nakedness, and threw off blue-white fire, into the tender heaven.

But sometimes he came ruddy, like a big, shy creature. And sometimes slow and crimson red, with a look of anger, slowly pushing and shouldering. Sometimes again she could not see him, only the level cloud threw down gold and scarlet from above, as he moved behind the wall.

She was fortunate. Weeks went by, and though the dawn was sometimes clouded, and afternoon was sometimes grey, never a day passed sunless, and most days, winter though it was, streamed radiant. The thin little wild crocuses came up mauve and striped, the wild narcissi hung their winter stars.

Every day, she went down to the cypress tree, among the cactus grove on the knoll with yellowish cliffs at the foot. She was wiser and subtler now, wearing only a dove-grey wrapper, and sandals. So that in an instant, in any hidden niche, she was naked to the sun. And the moment she was covered again she was grey and invisible.

Every day, in the morning towards noon, she lay at the foot of the powerful, silver-pawed cypress tree, while the sun strode jovial in heaven. By now she knew the sun in every thread of her body. Her heart of anxiety, that anxious, straining heart, had disappeared altogether, like a flower that falls in the sun, and leaves only a little ripening fruit. And her tense womb, though still closed, was slowly unfolding, slowly, slowly, like a lily bud under water, as the sun mysteriously touched it. Like a lily bud under water it was slowly rising to the sun, to expand at last, to the sun, only to the sun.

She knew the sun in all her body, the blue-molten with his white fire edges, throwing off fire. And, though he shone on all the world, when she lay unclothed he focused on her. It was one of the wonders of the sun, he could shine on a million people and still be the radiant, splendid, unique sun, focused on her alone.

With her knowledge of the sun, and her conviction that the sun was gradually penetrating her to know her in the cosmic carnal sense of the word, came over her a feeling of detachment from people, and a certain contemptuous tolerance for human beings altogether. They were so un-elemental, so un-sunned. They were so like graveyard worms.

Even the peasants passing up the rocky, ancient little road with their donkeys, sun-blackened as they were, were not sunned right through. There was a little soft white core of fear, like a snail in a shell, where the soul of the man cowered in fear of the natural blaze of life. He dared not quite see the sun: always innerly cowed. All men were like that.

Why admit men!

With her indifference to people, to men, she was not now so cautious about being seen. She had told Marinina, who went shopping for her in the village, that the doctor had ordered sun-baths. Let that suffice.

Marinina was a woman of sixty or more, tall, thin, erect, with curling dark-grey hair, and dark-grey eyes that had the shrewdness of thousands of years in them, with the laugh, half mockery, that underlies all long experience. Tragedy is lack of experience.

'It must be beautiful to go naked in the sun,' said Marinina, with a shrewd laugh in her eyes, as she looked keenly at the other woman. Juliet's fair, bobbed hair curled in a little cloud at her temples. Marinina was a woman of Magna Graecia, and had far memories. She looked again at Juliet. 'But when a woman is beautiful, she can show herself to the sun? eh? isn't it true?' she added, with that queer, breathless little laugh of the women of the past.

'Who knows if I am beautiful!' said Juliet.

But beautiful or not, she felt that by the sun she was appreciated. Which is the same.

When, out of the sun at noon, sometimes she stole down over the rocks and past the cliff-edge, down to the deep gully where the lemons hung in cool eternal shadow, and in the silence slipped off her wrapper to wash herself quickly at one of the deep, clear green basins, she would notice, in the bare green twilight under the lemon leaves, that all her body was rosy, rosy and turning to gold. She was like another person. She was another person.

So she remembered that the Greeks had said a white, unsunned body was unhealthy, and fishy.

And she would rub a little olive oil into her skin, and wander a moment in the dark underworld of the lemons, balancing a lemon-flower in her navel, laughing to herself. There was just a chance some peasant might see her. But if he did he would be more afraid of her than she of him. She knew the white core of fear in the clothed bodies of men.

She knew it even in her little son. How he mistrusted her, now that she laughed at him, with the sun in her face! She insisted on his toddling naked in the sunshine, every day. And now his little body was pink, too, his blond hair was pushed thick from his brow, his cheeks had a pomegranate scarlet, in the delicate gold of the sunny skin. He was bonny and healthy, and the servants, loving his gold and red and blue, called him an angel from heaven.

But he mistrusted his mother: she laughed at him. And she saw, in his wide blue eyes, under the little frown, that centre of fear, misgiving, which she believed was at the centre of all male eyes, now. She called it fear of the sun. And her womb stayed shut against all men, sun-fearers.

'He fears the sun,' she would say to herself, looking down into the eyes of the child.

And as she watched him toddling, swaying, tumbling in the sunshine, making his little, bird-like noises, she saw that he held himself tight and hidden from the sun, inside himself, and his balance was clumsy, his movements a little gross. His spirit was like a snail in a shell, in a damp, cold crevice inside himself. It made her think of his father. She wished she could make him come forth, break out in a gesture of recklessness, a salutation, to the sun.

She determined to take him with her, down to the cypress tree among the cactus. She would have to watch him, because of the thorns. But surely in that place he would come forth from the little shell, deep inside him. That little civilized tension would disappear off his brow.

She spread a rug for him and sat down. Then she slid off her wrapper and lay down herself, watching a hawk high in the blue, and the tip of the cypress hanging over.

The boy played with stones on the rug. When he got up to toddle away, she got up too. He turned and looked at her. Almost, from his blue eyes, it was the challenging, warm look of the true male. And he was handsome, with the scarlet in the golden blond of his skin. He was not really white. His skin was gold-dusky.

'Mind the thorns, darling,' she said.

'Thorns!' re-echoed the child, in a birdy chirp, still looking at her over his shoulder, like some naked *putto* in a picture, doubtful.

'Nasty prickly thorns.'

'Ickly thorns!'

He staggered in his little sandals over the stones, pulling at the dry mint. She was quick as a serpent, leaping to him, when he was going to fall against the prickles. It surprised even herself. 'What a wild cat I am, really!' she said to herself.

She brought him every day, when the sun shone, to the cypress tree.

'Come!' she said. 'Let us go to the cypress tree.'

And if there was a cloudy day, with the tramontana blowing, so that she could not go down, the child would chirp incessantly: 'Cypress tree! Cypress tree!'

He missed it as much as she did.

It was not just taking sunbaths. It was much more than that. Something deep inside her unfolded and relaxed, and she was given to a cosmic influence. By some mysterious will inside her, deeper than her known consciousness and her known will, she was put into connection with the sun, and the stream flowed through her, round her womb. She herself, her conscious self, was secondary, a secondary person, almost an onlooker. The true Juliet lived in the dark flow of the sun within her deep body, like a river of dark rays circling, circling dark and violet round the sweet, shut bud of her womb.

She had always been mistress of herself, aware of what she was doing, and held tense in her own command. Now she felt inside her quite another sort of power, something greater than herself, darker and more savage, the element flowing upon her. Now she was vague, in the spell of a power beyond herself.

3

The end of February was suddenly very hot. Almond blossom was falling like pink snow, in the touch of the smallest breeze. The mauve, silky little anemones were out, the asphodels tall in bud, and the sea was corn-flower blue.

Juliet had ceased to care about anything. Now, most of the day, she and the child were naked in the sun, and it was all she wanted. Sometimes she went down to the sea to bathe: often she wandered in the gullies where the sun shone in, and she was out of sight. Sometimes she saw a peasant with an ass, and he saw her. But she went so simply and quietly with her child; and the fame of the sun's healing power, for the soul as well as for the body, had already spread among the people; so that there was no excitement.

The child and she were now both tanned with a rosy-golden tan, all over. 'I am another being,' she said to herself, as she looked at her red-gold breasts and thighs.

The child, too, was another creature, with a peculiar, quiet, sun-darkened absorption. Now he played by himself in silence, and she need hardly notice him. He seemed no longer to notice when he was alone.

There was not a breeze, and the sea was ultramarine. She sat by the great silver paw of the cypress tree, drowsed in the sun, but her breasts alert, full of sap. She was becoming aware of an activity rousing in her, an activity which would bring another self awake in her. Still she did not want to be aware. The new rousing would mean a new contact, and this she did not want. She knew well enough the vast cold apparatus of civilization, and what contact with it meant; and how difficult it was to evade.

The child had gone a few yards down the rocky path, round the great sprawling of a cactus. She had seen him, a real gold-brown infant of the winds, with burnt gold hair and red cheeks, collecting the speckled pitcher-flowers and laying them in rows. He could balance now, and was quick for his own emergencies, like an absorbed young animal playing.

Suddenly she heard him speaking: *Look, Mummy! Mummy, look!* A note in his bird-like voice made her lean forward sharply.

Her heart stood still. He was looking over his naked little shoulder at her, and pointing with a loose little hand at a snake which had reared itself up a yard away from him, and was opening its mouth so that its forked, soft tongue flickered black like a shadow, uttering a short hiss.

'Look, Mummy!'

'Yes, darling, it's a snake!' came the slow deep voice.

He looked at her, his wide blue eyes uncertain whether to be afraid or not. Some stillness of the sun in her re-assured him.

'Snake!' he chirped.

'Yes, darling! Don't touch it, it can bite.'

The snake had sunk down, and was reaching away from

the coils in which it had been basking asleep, and slowly was easing its long, gold-brown body into the rocks, with slow curves. The boy turned and watched it in silence. Then he said:

'Snake going!'

'Yes! Let it go. It likes to be alone.'

He still watched the slow, easing length as the creature drew itself apathetic out of sight.

'Snake gone back,' he said.

'Yes, it's gone back. Come to Mummy a moment.'

He came and sat with his plump, naked little body on her naked lap, and she smoothed his burnt, bright hair. She said nothing, feeling that everything was passed. The curious careless power of the sun filled her, filled the whole place like a charm, and the snake was part of the place, along with her and the child.

Another day, in the dry stone wall of one of the olive terraces, she saw a black snake horizontally creeping.

'Marinina,' she said, 'I saw a black snake. Are they harmful?'

'Ah, the black snakes, no! But the yellow ones, yes! If the yellow one bites you, you die. But they frighten me, they frighten me, even the black ones, when I see one.'

Juliet still went to the cypress tree with the child. But she always looked carefully round, before she sat down, examining everywhere where the child might go. Then she would lie and turn to the sun again, her tanned, pear-shaped breasts pointing up. She would take no thought for the morrow. She refused to think outside the garden, and she could not write letters. She would tell the nurse to write. So she lay in the sun, but not for long, for it was getting strong, fierce. And in spite of herself, the bud that had been tight and deep immersed in the innermost gloom of her, was rearing, rearing and straightening its curved stem, to open its dark tips and show a gleam of rose. Her womb was coming open wide with rosy ecstasy, like a lotus flower.

4

Spring was becoming summer, in the south of the sun, and the rays were very powerful. In the hot hours she would lie in the shade of trees, or she would even go down to the depths of the cool lemon grove. Or sometimes she went in the shadowy deeps of the gullies, at the bottom of the little ravine, towards home. The child fluttered around in silence, like a young animal absorbed in life.

Going slowly home in her nakedness down among the bushes of the dark ravine, one noon, she came round a rock suddenly upon the peasant of the next *podere*, who was stooping binding up a bundle of brushwood he had cut, his ass standing near. He was wearing summer cotton trousers, and stooping his buttocks towards her. It was utterly still and private down in the dark bed of the little ravine. A weakness came over her, for a moment she could not move. The man lifted the bundle of wood with powerful shoulders, and turned to the ass. He started and stood transfixed as he saw her, as if it were a vision. Then his eyes met hers, and she felt the blue fire running through her limbs to her womb, which was spreading in the helpless ecstasy. Still they looked into each other's eyes, and the fire flowed between them, like the blue, streaming fire from the heart of the sun. And she saw the phallus rise under his clothing, and knew he would come towards her.

'Mummy, a man! Mummy!' The child had put a hand against her thigh. 'Mummy, a man!'

She heard the note of fear and swung round.

'It's all right, boy!' she said, and taking him by the hand, she led him back round the rock again, while the peasant watched her naked, retreating buttocks lift and fall.

She put on her wrap, and taking the boy in her arms, began to stagger up a steep goat-track through the yellow-flowering tangle of shrubs, up the level of day, and the olive trees below the house. There she sat down to collect herself.

The sea was blue, very blue and soft and still-looking, and her womb inside her was wide open, wide open like a lotus flower, or a cactus flower, in a radiant sort of eagerness. She could feel it, and it dominated her consciousness. And a biting chagrin burned in her breast, against the child, against the complication of frustration.

She knew the peasant by sight: a man something over thirty, broad and very powerfully set. She had many times watched him from the terrace of her house: watched him come with his ass, watched him trimming the olive trees, working alone, always alone and physically powerful, with a broad red face and a quiet self-possession. She had spoken to him once or twice, and met his big blue eyes, dark and southern hot. And she knew his sudden gestures, a little violent and over-generous. But she had never thought of him. Save that she had noticed that he was always very clean and well-cared for: and then she had seen his wife one day, when the latter had brought the man's meal, and they sat in the shade of a carob tree, on either side the spread white cloth. And then Juliet had seen the man's wife was older than he, a dark, proud, gloomy woman. And then a young woman had come with a child, and the man had danced with the child, so young and passionate. But it was not his own child: he had no children. It was when he danced with the child, in such a sprightly way, as if full of suppressed passion, that Juliet had first really noticed him. But even then, she had never thought of him. Such a broad red face, such a great chest, and rather short legs. Too much a crude beast for her to think of, a peasant.

But now the strange challenge of his eyes had held her, blue and overwhelming like the blue sun's heart. And she had seen the fierce striving of the phallus under his thin trousers: for her. And with his red face, and with his broad body, he was like the sun to her, the sun in its broad heat.

She felt him so powerfully, that she would not go further from him. She continued to sit there under the tree. Then she heard nurse tinkling a bell at the house, and calling. And the child called back. She had to rise and go home.

In the afternoon she sat on the terrace of her house, that looked over the olive slopes to the sea. The man came and went, came and went to the little hut on his *podere*, on the edge of the cactus grove. And he glanced again at her house, at her sitting on the terrace. And her womb was open to him.

Yet she had not the courage to go down to him. She was paralysed. She had tea, and sat still there on the terrace. And the man came and went, and glanced, and glanced again. Till the evening bell had jangled from the capuchin church at the village gate, and the darkness came on. And still she sat on the terrace. Till at last in the moonlight she saw him load his ass and drive it sadly along the path to the little road. She heard him pass on the stones of the road behind her house. He was gone – gone home to the village, to sleep, to sleep with his wife, who would want to know why he was so late. He was gone in dejection.

Juliet sat late on into the night, watching the moon on the sea. The sun had opened her womb, and she was no longer free. The trouble of the open lotus blossom had come upon her, and now it was she who had not the courage to take the steps across the gully.

But at last she slept. And in the morning she felt better. Her womb seemed to have closed again: the lotus flower seemed back in bud again. She wanted so much that it should be so. Only the immersed bud, and the sun! She would never think of that man.

She bathed in one of the great tanks away down in the lemon-grove, down in the far ravine, far as possible from the other wild gully, and cool. Below, under the lemons, the child was wading among the yellow oxalis flowers of the shadow, gathering fallen lemons, passing with his tanned little body into flecks of light, moving all dappled.

She sat in the sun on the steep bank of the gully, feeling almost free again, the flower drooping in shadowy bud, safe inside her.

Suddenly, high over the land's edge, against the full-lit pale blue sky, Marinina appeared, a black cloth tied round her head, calling quietly: *Signora! Signora Giulietta!*

Juliet faced round, standing up. Marinina paused a moment, seeing the naked woman standing alert, her sun-faded fair hair in a little cloud. Then the swift old woman came down the slant of the steep sun-blazed track.

She stood a few steps, erect, in front of the sun-coloured woman, and eyed her shrewdly.

'But how beautiful you are, you!' she said coolly, almost cynically. 'Your husband has come.'

'What husband?' cried Juliet.

The old woman gave a shrewd bark of a little laugh, the mockery of the woman of the past.

'Haven't you got one, a husband, you?' she said, taunting.

'How? Where? In America,' said Juliet.

The old woman glanced over her shoulder, with another noiseless laugh.

'No America at all. He was following me here. He will

have missed the path.' And she threw back her head in the noiseless laugh of women.

The paths were all grown high with grass and flowers and nepitella, till they were like bird-tracks in an eternally wild place. Strange, the vivid wildness of the old classic places, that have known men so long.

Juliet looked at the Sicilian woman with meditating eyes.

'Oh, very well!' she said at last. 'Let him come.'

And a little flame leaped in her. It was the opening flower. At least he was a man.

'Bring him here? Now?' asked Marinina, her mocking smoke-grey eyes looking with laughter into Juliet's eyes. Then she gave a little jerk of her shoulders.

'All right! As you wish! But for him it is a rare one!'

She opened her mouth with a noiseless laugh of amusement, then she pointed down to the child, who was heaping lemons against his little chest. 'Look how beautiful the child is? An angel from heaven. That certainly will please him, poor thing. Then I shall bring him.'

'Bring him,' said Juliet.

The old woman scrambled rapidly up the track again and found Maurice at a loss among the vine terraces standing there in his grey felt hat and dark grey city suit. He looked pathetically out of place, in that resplendent sunshine and the grace of the old Greek world; like a blot of ink on the pale, sun-glowing slope.

'Come!' said Marinina to him. 'She is down here.'

And swiftly she led the way, striding with a long stride, making the way through the grasses. Suddenly she stopped on the brow of the slope. The tops of the lemon trees were dark, away below.

'You, you go down here,' she said to him, and he thanked her, glancing up at her swiftly.

He was a man of forty, clean-shaven, grey-faced, very

quiet and really shy. He managed his own business carefully, without startling success, but efficiently. And he confided in nobody. The old woman of Magna Graecia saw him at a glance: he is good, she said to herself, but not a man, poor thing.

'Down there is the Signora,' said Marinina, pointing like one of the Fates.

And again he said 'Thank you! Thank you!' without a twinkle, and stepped carefully into the track. Marinina lifted her chin with a joyful wickedness. Then she strode off towards the house.

Maurice was watching his step, through the tangle of Mediterranean herbage, so he did not catch sight of his wife till he came round a little bend, quite near her. She was standing erect and nude by the jutting rock, glistening with the sun and with warm life. Her breasts seemed to be lifting up, alert, to listen, her thighs looked brown and fleet. Inside her, the lotus of her womb was wide open, spread almost gaping in the violet rays of the sun, like a great lotus flower. And she thrilled helplessly: a man was coming. Her glance on him, as he came gingerly, like ink on blotting-paper, was swift and nervous.

Maurice, poor fellow, hesitated, and glanced away from her, turning his face aside.

'Hello, Julie!' he said, with a little nervous cough. 'Splendid! Splendid!'

He advanced with his face averted, shooting further glances at her furtively, as she stood with the peculiar satiny gleam of the sun on her tanned skin. Somehow she did not seem so terribly naked. It was the golden-rose of the sun that clothed her.

'Hello, Maurice!' she said, hanging back from him, and a cold shadow falling on the open flower of her womb. 'I wasn't expecting you so soon.'

'No,' he said, 'No! I managed to slip away a little earlier.'

And again he coughed unawares. Furtively, purposely he had taken her by surprise.

They stood several yards away from one another, and there was silence. But this was a new Julie to him, with the sun-tanned, wind-stroked thighs: not that nervous New York woman.

'Well!' he said, 'er – this is splendid, splendid! You are – er – splendid! Where is the boy?'

He felt, in his far-off depths, the desire stirring in him for the limbs and sun-wrapped flesh of the woman: the woman of flesh. It was a new desire in his life, and it hurt him. He wanted to side-track.

'There he is,' she said, pointing down to where a naked urchin in the deep shade was piling fallen lemons together.

The father gave an odd little laugh, almost neighing.

'Ah, yes! There he is! So there's the little man! Fine!' His nervous, suppressed soul was thrilling with violent thrills, he clung to the straw of his upper consciousness. 'Hello, Johnny!' he called, and it sounded rather feeble. 'Hello, Johnny!'

The child looked up, spilling lemons from his chubby arms, but did not respond.

'I guess we'll go down to him,' said Juliet, as she turned and went striding down the path. In spite of herself, the cold shadow was lifting off the open flower of her womb, and every petal was thrilling again. Her husband followed, watching the rosy, fleet-looking lifting and sinking of her quick hips, as she swayed a little in the socket of her waist. He was dazed with admiration, but also at a deadly loss. He was used to her as a person. And this was no longer a person, but a fleet sun-strong body, soulless and alluring as a nymph, twinkling its haunches. What would he do with himself? He was utterly out of the picture, in his dark grey suit and pale grey hat, and his grey, monastic face of a shy business man, and his grey mercantile mentality. Strange thrills shot through his loins and his legs. He was terrified, and he felt he might give a wild whoop of triumph, and jump towards that woman of tanned flesh.

'He looks all right, doesn't he,' said Juliet, as they came through the deep sea of yellow-flowering oxalis, under the lemon trees.

'Ah! – yes! yes! Splendid! Splendid! – Hello, Johnny! Do you know Daddy? Do you know Daddy, Johnny?'

He squatted down, forgetting his trouser-crease, and held out his hands.

'Lemons!' said the child, birdily chirping. 'Two lemons!'

'Two lemons!' replied the father. 'Lots of lemons!'

The infant came and put a lemon in each of his father's open hands. Then he stood back to look.

'Two lemons!' repeated the father. 'Come, Johnny! Come and say Hello! to Daddy.'

'Daddy going back?' said the child.

'Going back? Well – well – not today.'

And he gathered his son in his arms.

'Take a coat off! Daddy take a coat off!' said the boy, squirming debonair away from the cloth.

'All right, son! Daddy take a coat off.'

He took off his coat and laid it carefully aside, then looked at the creases in his trousers, hitched them a little and crouched down and took his son in his arms. The child's warm naked body against him made him feel faint. The naked woman looked down at the rosy infant in the arms of the man in his shirt sleeves. The boy had pulled off his father's hat, and Juliet looked at the sleek, black-and-grey hair of her husband, not a hair out of place. And utterly, utterly sunless! The cold shadow was over the flower of her womb again. She was silent for a long time, while the father talked to the child, who had been fond of his Daddy.

'What are you going to do about it, Maurice?' she said, suddenly.

He looked at her swiftly, sideways, hearing her abrupt American voice. He had forgotten her.

'Er – about what, Julie?'

'Oh, everything! About this! I can't go back into East Forty-Seventh.'

'Er –' he hesitated, 'no, I suppose not – Not just now, at least.'

'Never!' she said, and there was a silence.

'Well – er – I don't know,' he said.

'Do you think you can come out here?' she said savagely.

'Yes! – I can stay for a month. I think I can manage a month,' he hesitated. Then he ventured a complicated, shy peep at her, and turned away his face again.

She looked down at him, her alert breasts lifted with a sigh, as if she would impatiently shake the cold shadow of sunlessness off her.

'I can't go back,' she said slowly. 'I can't go back on this sun. If you can't come here –'

She ended on an open note. But the voice of the abrupt, personal American woman had died out, and he heard the voice of the woman of flesh, the sun-ripe body. He glanced at her again and again, with growing desire and lessening fear.

'No!' he said. 'This kind of thing suits you. You are splendid. No, I don't think you can go back.'

And at the caressive sound of his voice, in spite of her, her womb-flower began to open and thrill its petals.

He was thinking visionarily of her in the New York flat,

pale, silent, oppressing him terribly. He was the soul of gentle timidity in his human relations, and her silent, awful hostility after the baby was born had frightened him deeply. Because he had realized that she could not help it. Women were like that. Their feelings took a reverse direction, even against their own selves, and it was awful – devastating. Awful, awful to live in the house with a woman like that, whose feelings were reversed even against herself. He had felt himself borne down under the stream of her heavy hostility. She had ground even herself down to the quick, and the child as well. No, anything rather than that. Thank God, that menacing ghost-woman seemed to be sunned out of her now.

'But what about *you*?' she asked.

'I? Oh, I! – I can carry on the business, and – er – come over here for long holidays – so long as you like to stay here. You stay as long as you wish – ' He looked down a long time at the earth. He was so frightened of rousing that menacing, avenging spirit of womanhood in her, he did so hope she might stay as he had seen her now, like a naked, ripening strawberry, a female like a fruit. He glanced up at her with a touch of supplication in his uneasy eyes.

'Even for ever?' she said.

'Well – er – yes, if you like. For ever is a long time. One can't set a date.'

'And I can do anything I like?' She looked him straight in the eyes, challenging. And he was powerless against her rosy, wind-hardened nakedness, in his fear of arousing that other woman in her, the personal American woman, spectral and vengeful.

'Er – yes! – I suppose so! So long as you don't make yourself unhappy – or the boy.'

Again he looked up at her with a complicated, uneasy appeal – thinking of the child, but hoping for himself.

'I won't,' she said quickly.

'No!' he said. 'No! I don't think you will.'

There was a pause. The bells of the village were hastily clanging mid-day. That meant lunch.

She slipped into her grey crepe kimono, and fastened a broad green sash round her waist. Then she slipped a little blue shirt over the boy's head, and they went up to the house.

At table she watched her husband, his grey city face, his glued, black-grey hair, his very precise table manners, and his extreme moderation in eating and drinking. Sometimes he glanced at her furtively, from under his black lashes. He had the uneasy gold-grey eyes of a creature that has been caught young, and reared entirely in captivity, strange and cold, knowing no warm hopes. Only his black eye-brows and eye-lashes were nice. She did not take him in. She did not realize him. Being so sunned, she could not see him, his sunlessness was like nonentity.

They went on to the balcony for coffee, under the rosy mass of the bougainvillaea. Below, beyond, on the next *podere*, the peasant and his wife were sitting under the carob tree, near the tall green wheat, sitting facing one another across a little white cloth spread on the ground. There was still a huge piece of bread – but they had finished eating and sat with dark wine in their glasses. The peasant looked up at the terrace, as soon as the American emerged. Juliet put her husband with his back to the scene. Then she sat down, and looked back at the peasant. Until she saw his dark-visaged wife turn to look too.

5

The man was hopelessly in love with her. She saw his broad, rather short red face gazing up at her fixedly: till his wife turned too to look, then he picked up his glass and tossed the wine down his throat. The wife stared long at the figures on the balcony. She was handsome and rather gloomy, and surely older than he, with that great difference that lies between a rather overwhelming, superior woman over forty, and her more irresponsible husband of thirty-five or so. It seemed like the difference of a whole generation. 'He is my generation,' thought Juliet, 'and she is Maurice's generation.' Juliet was not yet thirty.

The peasant in his white cotton trousers and pale pink shirt, and battered old straw hat, was attractive, so clean, and full of the cleanliness of health. He was stout and broad, and seemed shortish, but his flesh was full of vitality, as if he were always about to spring into movement, to work, even, as she had seen him with the child, to play. He was the type of Italian peasant that wants to make an offering of himself, passionately wants to make an offering of himself, of his powerful flesh and thudding blood-stroke. But he was also completely a peasant, in that he would wait for the woman to make the move. He would hang round in a long, consuming passivity of desire, hoping, hoping for the woman to come for him. But he would never try to advance to her: never. She would have to make the advance. Only he would hang round, within reach.

Feeling her look at him, he flung off his old straw hat, showing his round, close-cropped, brown head, and reached out with a large brown-red hand for the great loaf, from which he broke a piece and started chewing with bulging cheek. He knew she was looking at him. And she had such power over him, the hot, inarticulate animal, with such a hot, massive blood-stream down his great veins! He was hot through with countless suns, and mindless as noon. And shy with a violent, farouche shyness, that would wait for her with consuming wanting, but would never, never move towards her.

With him, it would be like bathing in another kind of sunshine, heavy and big and perspiring: and afterwards one would forget. Personally, he would not exist. It would be just a bath of warm, powerful life – then separating and forgetting. Then again, the procreative bath, like sun.

But would that not be good! She was so tired of personal contacts, and having to talk with the man afterwards. With that healthy creature, one would just go satisfied away, afterwards. As she sat there, she felt the life stemming from him to her, and her to him. She knew by his movements he felt her even more than she felt him. It was almost a definite pain of consciousness in the body of each of them, and each sat as if distracted, watched by a keen-eyed spouse, possessor. And Juliet thought: Why shouldn't I go to him! Why shouldn't I bear his child? It would be like bearing a child to the unconscious sun and the unconscious earth, a child like a fruit. And the flower of her womb radiated. It did not care about sentiment or possession. It wanted man-dew only, utterly improvident.

But her heart was clouded with fear. She dare not! She dare not! If only the man would find some way! But he would not. He would only hover and wait, hover in endless desire, waiting for her to cross the gully. And she dare not. And he would hang round.

'You are not afraid of people seeing you when you take your sun-baths?' said her husband, turning round and looking across at the peasants. The saturnine wife over the gully, turned also to stare at the Villa. It was a kind of battle.

'No! One needn't be seen. Will you do it too? Will you take sun-baths?' said Juliet to him.

'Why – er – yes! I think I should like to, while I am here.'

There was a gleam in his eyes, a desperate kind of courage of desire to taste this new fruit, this woman with rosy, sun-ripening breasts tilting within her wrapper. And she thought of him with his blanched, etiolated little city figure, walking in the sun in the desperation of a husband's rights. And her mind swooned again. The strange, branded little fellow, the good citizen, branded like a criminal in the naked eye of the sun. How he would hate exposing himself!

And the flower of her womb went dizzy, dizzy. She knew she would take him. She knew she would bear his child. She knew it was for him, the branded little city man, that her womb was open radiating like a lotus, like the purple spread of a daisy anemone, dark at the core. She knew she would not go across to the peasant; she had not enough courage, she was not free enough.

And she knew the peasant would never come for her, he had the dogged passivity of the earth, and would wait, wait, only putting himself in her sight, again and again, lingering across her vision, with the persistency of animal yearning.

She had seen the flushed blood in the peasant's burnt face, and felt the jetting, sudden blue heat pouring over her from his kindled eyes, and the rousing of his big penis against his body – for her, surging for her. Yet she would never come to him – she daren't, so much was against her.

And the little etiolated body of her husband, city-branded, would possess her, and his little, frantic penis would beget another child in her. She could not help it. She was bound to the vast, fixed wheel of circumstance, and there was no Perseus in the universe to cut the bonds.

Mercury

It was Sunday, and very hot. The holiday-makers flocked to the hill of Mercury, to rise two thousand feet above the steamy haze of the valleys. For the summer had been very wet, and the sudden heat covered the land in hot steam.

Every time it made the ascent, the funicular was crowded. It hauled itself up the steep incline, that towards the top looked almost perpendicular, the steel thread of the rails in the gulf of pine-trees hanging like an iron rope against a wall. The women held their breath, and didn't look. Or they looked back towards the sinking levels of the river, steamed and dim, far-stretching over the frontier.

When you arrived at the top, there was nothing to do. The hill was a pine-covered cone; paths wound between the high tree-trunks, and you could walk round and see the glimpses of the world all round, all round: the dim, far river-plain, with a dull glint of the great stream, to westwards; southwards the black, forest-covered, agile-looking hills, with emerald-green clearings and a white house or two; east, the inner valley, with two villages, factory chimneys, pointed churches, and hills beyond; and north, the steep hills of forest, with reddish crags and reddish castle ruins. The hot sun burned overhead, and all was in steam.

Only on the very summit of the hill there was a tower, an outlook tower; a long restaurant with its beer-garden, all the little yellow tables standing their round disks under the horse-chestnut trees; then a bit of a rock-garden on the slope. But the great trees began again in wilderness a few yards off.

The Sunday crowd came up in waves from the funicular.

In waves they ebbed through the beer-garden. But not many sat down to drink. Nobody was spending any money. Some paid to go up the outlook tower, to look down on a world of vapours and black, agile-crouching hills, and half-cooked towns. Then everybody dispersed along the paths, to sit among the trees in the cool air.

There was not a breath of wind. Lying and looking upwards at the shaggy, barbaric middle-world of the pine trees, it was difficult to decide whether the pure high trunks supported the upper thicket of darkness, or whether they descended from it like great cords stretched downwards. Anyhow, in between the tree-top world and the earth-world went the wonderful clean cords of innumerable proud tree-trunks, clear as rain. And as you watched, you saw that the upper world was faintly moving, faintly, most faintly swaying, with a circular movement, though the lower trunks were utterly motionless and monolithic.

There was nothing to do. In all the world, there was nothing to do, and nothing to be done. Why have we all come to the top of the Merkur? There is nothing for us to do.

What matter? We have come a stride beyond the world. Let it steam and cook its half-baked reality below there. On the hill of Mercury we take no notice. Even we do not trouble to wander and pick the fat, blue, sourish bilberries. Just lie and see the rain-pure tree-trunks like chords of music between two worlds.

The hours pass by: people wander and disappear and reappear. All is hot and quiet. Humanity is rarely boisterous any more. You go for a drink: finches run among the few people at the tables: everybody glances at everybody, but with remoteness.

There is nothing to do but to return and lie down under the pine trees. Nothing to do. But why do anything, anyhow? The desire to do anything has gone. The tree-trunks, living like rain, they are quite active enough.

At the foot of the obsolete tower there is an old tablet-stone with a very much battered Mercury, in relief. There is also an altar, or votive stone, both from the Roman times. The Romans are supposed to have worshipped Mercury on the summit. The battered god, with his round sun-head, looks very hollow-eyed and unimpressive in the purplish-red sandstone of the district. And no one any more will throw grains of offering in the hollow of the votive stone: also common, purplish-red sandstone, very local and un-Roman.

The Sunday people do not even look. Why should they? They keep passing on into the pine trees. And many sit on the benches; many lie upon the long chairs. It is very hot, in the afternoon, and very still.

Till there seems a faint whistling in the tops of the pine trees, and out of the universal semi-consciousness of the afternoon arouses a bristling uneasiness. The crowd is astir, looking at the sky. And sure enough, there is a great flat blackness reared up in the western sky, curled with white wisps and loose breast-feathers. It looks very sinister, as only the elements still can look. Under the sudden weird whistling of the upper pine trees, there is a subdued babble and calling of frightened voices.

They want to get down; the crowd want to get down off the hill of Mercury, before the storm comes. At any price to get off the hill! They stream towards the funicular, while the sky blackens with incredible rapidity. And as the crowd presses down towards the little station, the first blaze of lightning opens out, followed immediately by a crash of thunder, and great darkness. In one strange movement, the crowd takes refuge in the deep veranda of the restaurant, pressing among the little tables in silence. There is no rain, and no definite wind, only a sudden coldness which makes the crowd press closer.

They press closer, in the darkness and the suspense. They have become curiously unified, the crowd, as if they had fused into one body. As the air sends a chill waft under the veranda the voices murmur plaintively, like birds under leaves, the bodies press closer together, seeking shelter in contact.

The gloom, dark as night, seems to continue a long time. Then suddenly the lightning dances white on the floor, dances and shakes upon the ground, up and down, and lights up the white striding of a man, lights him up only to the hips, white and naked and striding, with fire on his heels. He seems to be hurrying, this fiery man whose upper half is invisible, and at his naked heels white little flames seem to flutter. His flat, powerful thighs, his legs white as fire stride rapidly across the open, in front of the veranda, dragging little white flames at the ankles, with the movement. He is going somewhere, swiftly.

In the great bang of the thunder the apparition disappears. The earth moves, and the house jumps in complete darkness. A faint whimpering of terror comes from the crowd, as the cold air swirls in. But still, upon the darkness, there is no rain. There is no relief: a long wait.

Brilliant and blinding, the lightning falls again; a strange bruising thud comes from the forest, as all the little tables and the secret tree-trunks stand for one unnatural second exposed. Then the blow of the thunder, under which the house and the crowd reel as under an explosion. The storm is playing directly upon the Merkur. A belated sound of tearing branches comes out of the forest.

And again the white splash of the lightning on the ground: but nothing moves. And again the long, rattling, instantaneous volleying of the thunder, in the darkness.

The crowd is panting with fear, as the lightning again strikes white, and something again seems to burst, in the forest, as the thunder crashes.

At last, into the motionlessness of the storm, in rushes the wind, with the fiery flying of bits of ice, and the sudden sea-like roaring of the pine trees. The crowd winces and draws back, as the bits of ice hit in the face like fire. The roar of the trees is so great, it becomes like another silence. And through it is heard the crashing and splintering of timber, as the hurricane concentrates upon the hill.

Down comes the hail, in a roar that covers every other sound, threshing ponderously upon the ground and the roofs and the trees. And as the crowd surges irresistibly into the interior of the building, from the crushing of this ice-fall, still amid the sombre hoarseness sounds the tinkle and crackle of things breaking.

After an eternity of dread, it ends suddenly. Outside is a faint gleam of yellow light, over the snow and the endless debris of twigs and things broken. It is very cold, with the atmosphere of ice and deep winter. The forest looks wan, above the white earth, where the ice-balls lie in their myriads, six inches deep, littered with all the twigs and things they have broken.

'Yes! Yes!' say the men, taking sudden courage as the yellow light comes into the air. 'Now we can go!'

The first brave ones emerge, picking up the big hail-stones, pointing to the overthrown tables. Some, however, do not linger. They hurry to the funicular station, to see if the apparatus is still working.

The funicular station is on the north side of the hill. The men come back, saying there is no one there. The crowd begins to emerge upon the wet, crunching whiteness of the hail, spreading around in curiosity, waiting for the men who operate the funicular.

On the south side of the outlook tower two bodies lay in the cold but thawing hail. The dark-blue of the uniforms showed blackish. Both men were dead. But the lightning had completely removed the clothing from the legs of one man, so that he was naked from the hips down. There he lay, his face sideways on the snow, and two drops of blood running from his nose into his big, blond, military moustache. He lay there near the votive stone of the Mercury. His companion, a young man, lay face downwards, a few yards behind him.

The sun began to emerge. The crowd gazed in dread, afraid to touch the bodies of the men. Why had they, the dead funicular men, come round to this side of the hill, anyhow?

The funicular would not work. Something had happened to it in the storm. The crowd began to wind down the bare hill, on the sloppy ice. Everywhere the earth bristled with broken pine boughs and twigs. But the bushes and the leafy trees were stripped absolutely bare, to a miracle. The lower earth was leafless and naked as in winter.

'Absolute winter!' murmured the crowd, as they hurried, frightened, down the steep, winding descent, extricating themselves from the fallen pine-branches.

Meanwhile the sun began to steam in great heat.

The Man Who Was Through
with the World

THERE was a man not long ago, who felt he was through with the world, so he decided to be a hermit. He had a little money, and he knew that nowadays there are no hermitages going rent-free. So he bought a bit of wild land on a mountain-side, with a few chestnut trees growing on it. He waited till spring; then went up and started building himself a little cabin, with the stones from the hillside. By summer, he had got himself a nice little hut with a chimney and one little window, a table, a chair, a bed, and the smallest number of things a hermit may need. Then he considered himself set up as a hermit.

His hermitage stood in a sheltered nook in the rocks of the mountain, and through the open door he looked out on the big, staggering chestnut trees of the upper region. These trees, this bit of property was his legal own, but he wanted to dedicate it to somebody: to God, preferably.

He felt, however, a bit vague about God. In his youth he had been sent to Sunday School, but he had long been through with all that. He had, as a matter of fact, even forgotten the Lord's Prayer, like the old man in the Tolstoi parable. If he tried to remember it, he mixed it up with The Lord is my Shepherd, and felt annoyed. He might, of course, have fetched himself a Bible. But he was through with all that.

Because, before he was through with everything, he had read quite a lot about Brahma and Krishna and Shiva, and Buddha and Confucius and Mithras, not to mention Zeus and Aphrodite and that bunch, nor the Wotan family. So when he began to think: The Lord is my Shepherd, somehow Shiva would start dancing a Charleston in the back of his mind, and Mithras would take the bull by the horns, and Mohammed would start patting the buttery flanks of Ayesha, and Abraham would be sitting down to a good meal off a fat ram, till the grease ran down his beard. So that it was very difficult to concentrate on God with a large 'g', and the hermit had a natural reluctance to go into refinements of the great I Am, or of thatness. He wanted to get away from all that sort of thing. For what else had he become a hermit?

But alas, he found it wasn't so easy. If you're a hermit, you've got to concentrate. You've got to sit in the door of your hut in the sunshine, and concentrate on something holy. This hermit would sit in the door of his hut in the sunshine right enough, but he couldn't find anything holy enough really to keep him concentrated. If he tried some nice Eastern mode of meditation, and sat cross-legged with a faint lotus-like smile on his face, some dog-in-the-manger inside him growled: Oh, cut it out, Henry, Nirvana's a cold egg for the likes of you.

So gradually the hermit became desperate. There he was, all rigged up quite perfect as a holy man, a hermit, and an anchorite, and he felt like an acrobat trying to hang on to a tight wire with his eyebrows. He simply had nothing to hold on to. There wasn't a single holiness or high-and-mightiness that interested him enough to bring concentration. And a hermit with nothing to concentrate on is like a fly in the cream jug.

Spring changed into summer. The primroses by the little stream where the hermit dipped his water faded and were gone, only their large leaves spread to the hotter days. The violets flickered to a finish; at last not a purple spark was left. The chestnut burrs upon the ground finally had melted away, the leaves overhead had emerged and overlapped one another, to make the green roof of summer.

And the hermit was bored, and rather angry with himself and everything else. He saw nobody up there: an occasional goat-boy, an occasional hunter shooting little birds went by, looking askance. The hermit nodded a salutation, but no more.

Then at intervals he went down to the village for food. The village was four long miles away, down the steep side of the mountain. And when you got there, you found nothing but the silence, the dirt, the poverty and the suspicion of a mountain hamlet. And there was very little to buy.

The hermit always hurried back to his hermitage in disgust. Absence from his fellow-men did not make him love them any the more. On the contrary, they seemed more repulsive and smelly, when he came among them, after his isolation among the chestnut trees, and their weird sort of greed about money, tiny sums of money, made them seem like a plague of caterpillars to him. 'People badly need to have souls, to hatch out with wings after death,' he thought to himself, 'for they really are repulsive pale grubs in this life.'

So he went back to his hermitage glad to get away from his fellow-men, but no happier at having to hang on to his solitude by his eyebrows, in danger of slipping off any minute. For he still had nothing to concentrate on, and no sense of holiness came to soothe him.

He had brought no books with him, having renounced the world of which they are part. Sometimes he regretted this, sometimes he didn't. But he did nothing about it. He lived stubbornly on from day to day, letting his brown beard grow bushy round his nose, and his black hair long on his neck. When it was warm enough, he went nude, with just a loincloth. For long hours he sat near his hut in the sun, not meditating, not even musing, just being stubborn, and getting browned to a beautiful gold-brown colour. He did not mind so much, while the sun shone, and he could stroll nude through the trees, or sit out in the glow or in the shade. Then he didn't mind not being able to meditate nor to concentrate, and not having any holiness to bless himself with. The sun on his body seemed to do all the meditating and concentrating he needed. His limbs were thin, and golden brown, and his thin body was as brown as his face. He was, like the savage in the story, 'face all over'.

'I am face all over,' he thought to himself, with a smile.

The strings of the chestnut flowers had fallen, the fruits set and grew big, of a clear green colour, and fuzzy. The hermit had to decide whether he would stay on after the chestnuts had come down, when the snow would fall and the mountains lapse into isolation. He was still hanging on to solitude by his eye-brows, and nothing holy had turned up for him to concentrate on.

But he was getting used to the condition. And the very fact that he was alone, that no people came near him, was a source of positive satisfaction. He decided he would stay on all winter.

This, however, meant getting in certain supplies for the cold months, and especially boots and clothing and bedding, for he had no mind to mortify the flesh by shivering with cold. The snow would lie round his cabin, and the icy wind would whistle through his chestnut trees in huge blasts. Prepare for the wrath to come.

So he put on his decent suit of clothes, clipped his beard a little, descended, took the post-omnibus and then the train, and found himself in the city. His chief feeling was that everything smelled unpleasantly, that the noise was hellish, and that people had terrible and repulsive faces;

and that everywhere was a rancid odour of money, a terrible over-smell that reeked from everything animate and inanimate.

He bought his necessities with disgust, hurrying to get it over. Everybody stared at him as if he were a cameleopard, and he knew the police wanted to arrest him at sight. He had to spend the night in town, so he stayed at the big hotel near the station. And he fixed the clerk with a cold and haughty eye, and spoke in his coldest, calmly arrogant voice, knowing that if he were for one moment modest or uncertain, the worm behind the desk would deny him a room.

As it was, he had to put up with an inner bedroom, beside the lift. But at dawn, he left the place, having settled his bill the night before, and getting all his bundles into a carriage, drove across to the station. The porter who helped him eyed him with the usual insolent stare, and took his tip and dodged away with the air of a contemptuous human being who has just about had enough of attending to animals in a menagerie.

The hermit, for his part, hired a donkey at the village, piled his goods upon it, and shook the stink of his fellowmen out of his clothing. Never had he been so glad to climb through the trees. Never had anything looked so nice as his stone hut with its barrel roof, the first yellow leaves of the chestnuts dropping around it, and the rosy little cyclamens in the moss just near the door.

It was a warm afternoon. He hastily took off his clothing and put it in the sun, to remove the taint of the city and the train. He went down to his pool to wash himself, and stayed naked in the sun till sunset, to clear himself from the pollution of people.

There followed a busy period. He gathered the chestnuts scrupulously as they fell, piling them in a heap near the door, then carefully getting them from their burrs, and spreading the bright nuts on his small roof. He built a lean-to against his little house, and stacked his wood there, that he cut in the forest. Also he began to collect the big pine-cones that have pine-kernels inside them: though for these it was as yet full early.

Already the mornings and evenings were touched with ice. He emerged in the morning in warm woollen clothing, which he peeled off as the sun rose, and at last went about in his own brown skin. But many days were cold, and many were rainy, and he had to remain covered up.

Then he was never happy. He found, the more clothing he had to wear, the more he was restless and needed to think, needed some sort of salvation; and on the other hand, the more he could go naked in the sun, the less he went in need of any salvation. So while he could, he went about stark, and gradually he grew tougher. But as winter and the snow-winds swept the mountains, he could less and less afford to lose his bodily heat, by exposing himself.

In the days of cold rain, he did his chores in his hut, and made himself bread, and cooked pies, and mended his clothes.

(Unfinished)

A Dream of Life

NOTHING depresses me more than to come home to the place where I was born, and where I lived my first twenty years, here, at Newthorpe, this coal-mining village on the Nottingham-Derby border. The place has grown, but not very much, the pits are poor. Only it has changed. There is a tram-line from Nottingham through the one street, and buses to Nottingham and Derby. The shops are bigger, more plate-glassy: there are two picture-palaces, and one Palais de Danse.

But nothing can save the place from the poor, grimy, mean effect of the Midlands, the little grimy brick houses with slate roofs, the general effect of paltriness, smallness, meanness, fathomless ugliness, combined with a sort of chapel-going respectability. It is the same as when I was a boy, only more so.

Now, it is all tame. It was bad enough, thirty years ago, when it was still on the upward grade, economically. But then the old race of miners were not immensely respectable. They filled the pubs with smoke and bad language, and they went with dogs at their heels. There was a sense of latent wildness and unbrokenness, a weird sense of thrill and adventure in the pitch-dark Midland nights, and roaring footballing Saturday afternoons. The country in between the colliery regions had a lonely sort of fierceness and beauty, half-abandoned, and threaded with poaching colliers and whippet dogs. Only thirty years ago!

Now it seems so different. The colliers of today are the men of my generation, lads I went to school with. I find it hard to believe. They were rough, wild lads. They are not rough, wild men. The board-school, the Sunday-school, the Band of Hope, and, above all, their mothers got them under. Got them under, made them tame. Made them sober, conscientious, and decent. Made them good husbands. When I was a boy, a collier who was a good husband was an exception to the rule, and while the women with bad husbands pointed him out as a shining example, they also despised him a little, as a petticoat man.

But nearly all the men of my generation are good husbands. There they stand, at the street corners, pale, shrunken, well-dressed, decent, and *under*. The drunken colliers of my father's generation were not got under. The decent colliers of my generation are got under entirely. They are so patient, so forbearing, so willing to listen to reason, so ready to put themselves aside. And there they stand, at the street corners and the entry-ends, the rough lads I went to school with, men now, with smart daughters and bossy wives and cigarette-smoking lads of their own. There they stand, then, and white as cheap wax candles, spectral, as if they had no selves any more: decent, patient, self-effacing sort of men, who have seen the war and the high-watermark wages, and now are down again, under, completely under, with not a tuppence to rattle in their pockets. There they are, poor as their fathers before them, but poor with a hopeless outlook and a new and expensive world around them.

When I was a boy, the men still used to sing: 'There's a good time coming, boys, there's a good time coming!' Well, it has come and gone. If anybody sang now, they'd sing: 'It's a bad time now, and a worse time coming.' But the men of my generation are dumb: they have been got under and made good.

As for the next generation, that is something different. As soon as mothers become self-conscious, sons become what their mothers make them. My mother's generation was the first generation of working-class mothers to become really self-conscious. Our grandmothers were still too much under our grandfathers' thumb, and there was still too much masculine kick against petticoat rule. But with the next generation, the woman freed herself at least mentally and spiritually from the husband's domination, and then she became that great institution, that character-forming power, the mother of my generation. I am sure the character of nine-tenths of the men of my generation was formed by the mother: the character of the daughters too.

And what sort of characters? Well, the woman of my mother's generation was in reaction against the ordinary high-handed, obstinate husband who went off to the pub to enjoy himself and to waste the bit of money that was so precious to the family. The woman felt herself the higher moral being: and justly, as far as economic morality goes. She therefore assumed the major responsibility for the family, and the husband let her. So she proceeded to mould a generation.

Mould it to the shape of her own unfulfilled desire, of course. What had she wanted, all her life? – a 'good' husband, gentle and understanding and moral, one who did not go to pubs and drink and waste the bit of wages, but who lived for his wife and his children.

Millions of mothers in Great Britain, in the latter half of Victoria's reign, unconsciously proceeded to produce sons to pattern. And they produced them, by the million: good sons, who would make good, steady husbands who would live for their wives and families. And there they are! we've got 'em now! the men of my generation, men between forty and fifty, men who almost all had Mothers with a big *m*.

And then the daughters! Because the mothers who produced so many 'good sons' and future 'good husbands' were at the same time producing daughters, perhaps without taking so much thought or exercising so much will-power over it, but producing them just as inevitably.

What sort of daughters came from these morally responsible mothers? As we should expect, daughters morally confident. The mothers had known some little hesitancy in their moral supremacy. But the daughters were quite assured. The daughters were always right. They were born with a sense of self-rightness that sometimes was hoity-toity, and sometimes was seemingly wistful: but there it was, the inevitable sense that I-am-right. This the women of my generation drew in with their mothers' milk, this feeling that they were 'right' and must be 'right' and nobody must gainsay them. It is like being born with one eye: you can't help it.

We are such stuff as our grandmothers' dreams are made on. This terrible truth should never be forgotten. Our grandmothers dreamed of wonderful 'free' womanhood in a 'pure' world, surrounded by 'adoring, humble, high-minded' men. Our mothers started to put the dream into practice. And we are the fulfilment. We are such stuff as our grandmothers' dreams were made on.

For I think it cannot be denied that ours is the generation of 'free' womanhood, and a helplessly 'pure' world, and of pathetic 'adoring, humble, high-minded' men.

We are, more or less, such stuff as our grandmothers' dreams are made on. But the dream changes with every new generation of grandmothers. Already my mother, while having a definite ideal for her sons, of 'humble, adoring, high-minded' men, began to have secret dreams of her own: dreams of some Don Juan sort of person whose influence would make the vine of Dionysus grow and coil over the pulpit of our Congregational Chapel. I myself, her son, could see the dream peeping out, thrusting little tendrils through her paved intention of having 'good sons'. It was my turn to be the 'good son'. It would be my son's turn to fulfil the other dream, or dreams: the secret ones.

Thank God I have no son to undertake the onerous burden. Oh, if only every father could say to his boy: Look here, my son! These are your grandmother's dreams of a man. Now you look out! – My dear old grandmother, my mother's mother, I'm sure she dreamed me almost to a *t*, except for a few details.

But the daughter starts, husbandly speaking, where the mother leaves off. The daughters of my mother, and of the mothers of my generation, start, as a rule, with 'good husbands', husbands who never fundamentally contradict them, whose lifelong attitude is: All right, dear! I know I'm wrong, as usual. This is the attitude of the husband of my generation.

It alters the position of the wife entirely. It is a fight for the woman to get the reins into her own hands, but once she's got them, there she is! the reins have got her. She's got to drive somewhere, to steer the matrimonial cart in some direction. 'All right, dear! I'll let you decide it, since you know better than I do!' says the husband, in every family matter. So she must keep on deciding. Or, if the husband balks her occasionally, she must keep up the pressure till he gives in.

Now driving the matrimonial cart is quite an adventure for a time, while the children are little, and all that. But later, the woman begins to think to herself: 'Oh, damn the cart! Where do *I* come in?' She begins to feel she's getting nothing out of it. It's not good enough. Whether you're the horse or whether you're the driver doesn't make any odds. So long as you're both harnessed to the cart.

Then the woman of my generation begins to have ideas

about her sons. They'd better not be so all-forsaken 'good' as their father has been. They'd better be more sporting, and give a woman a bit more 'life'. After all, what's a family? It swallows a woman up until she's fifty, and then puts the remains of her aside. Not good enough! No! My sons must be more manly, make plenty of money for a woman and give her a 'life', and not be such a muff about 'goodness' and being 'right'. What is being 'right', after all? Better enjoy yourself while you've got the chance.

So the sons of the younger generation emerge into the world – my sons, if I'd got any – with the intrinsic maternal charge ringing in their ears: 'Make some money and give yourself a good time – and all of us. Enjoy yourself!'

The young men of the younger generation begin to fulfil the hidden dreams of my mother. They are jazzy – but not coarse. They are a bit Don-Juanish, but, let us hope, entirely without brutality or vulgarity. They are more elegant, and not much more moral. But they are still humble before a woman, especially *the* woman!

It is the secret dream of my mother, coming true.

And if you want to know what the next generation will be like, you must fathom the secret dreams of your wife: the woman of forty or so. There you will find the clue. And if you want to be more precise, then find out what is the young woman of twenty's ideal of a man.

The poor young woman of twenty, she is rather stumped for an ideal of a man. So perhaps the next generation but one won't be anything at all.

We are such stuff as our grandmothers' dreams are made on. Even colliers are such stuff as their grandmothers' dreams are made on. And if Queen Victoria's dream was King George, then Queen Alexandra's was the Prince of Wales, and Queen Mary's will be – what?

But all this doesn't take away from the fact that my home

place is more depressing to me than death, and I wish my grandmother and all her generation had been better dreamers. 'Those maids, thank God, are 'neath the sod,' but their dreams we still have with us. It is a terrible thing to dream dreams that shall become flesh.

And when I see the young colliers dressed up like the Prince of Wales, dropping in to the Miners' Welfare for another drink, or into the 'Pally' for a dance – in evening suit to beat the band – or scooting down the black roads on a motor-bike, a leggy damsel behind – then I wish the mothers of my own generation, my own mother included, had been a little less *frivolous* as a dreamer. In life, so deadly earnest! And oh, what frivolous dreams our mothers must have had, as they sat in the pews of the Congregational Chapel with faces like saints! They must unconsciously have been dreaming jazz and short skirts, the Palais de Danse, the Film, and the motor-bike. It is enough to embitter one's most sacred memories. 'Lead Kindly Light' – unto the 'Pally'. The eleventh commandment: 'Enjoy yourselves!'

Well, well! Even grandmothers' dreams don't always come true, that is, they aren't allowed to. They'd come true right enough otherwise. But sometimes fate, and that long dragon the concatenation of circumstance, intervene. I am sure my mother never dreamed a dream that wasn't well-off. My poor old grandmother might still dream noble poverty – myself, to wit! But my mother? Impossible! In her secret dreams, the sleeve-links were solid gold, and the socks were silk.

And now fate, the monster, frustrates. The pits don't work. There's reduced wages and short pay. The young colliers will have a hard time buying another pair of silk socks for the 'Pally' when these are worn out. They'll have to go in wool. As for the young lady's fur coat – well, well!

let's hope it is seal, or some other hard-wearing skin, and not that evanescent chinchilla or squirrel that moults in a season.

For the young lady won't get another fur coat in a hurry, if she has to wait for her collier father to buy it. Not that he would refuse it her. What is a man for, except to provide for his wife and daughters? But you can't get blood out of a stone, nor cash out of a collier, not any more.

It is a soft, hazy October day, with the dark green Midlands fields looking somewhat sunken, and the oak trees brownish, the mean houses shabby and scaly, and the whole countryside somewhat dead, expunged, faintly blackened under the haze. It is a queer thing that countries die along with their inhabitants. This countryside is dead: or so inert, it is as good as dead. The old sheep-bridge where I used to swing as a boy is now an iron affair. The brook where we caught minnows now runs on a concrete bed. The old sheep-dip, the dipping-hole, as we called it, where we bathed, has somehow disappeared, so has the mill-dam and the little water-fall. It's all a concrete arrangement now, like a sewer. And the people's lives are the same, all running in concrete channels like a vast cloaca.

At Engine Lane Crossing, where I used to sit as a tiny child and watch the trucks shunting with a huge grey horse and a man with a pole, there are now no trucks. It is October, and there should be hundreds. But there are no orders. The pits are turning half-time. Today they are not turning at all. The men are all at home: no orders, no work.

And the pit is fuming silently, there is no rattle of screens, and the head-stock wheels are still. That was always an ominous sign, except on Sundays: even when I was a small child. The head-stock wheels twinkling against the sky, that meant work and life, men 'earning a living', if living can be earned.

But the pit is foreign to me anyhow, so many new big buildings round it, electric plant and all the rest. It's a wonder even the shafts are the same. But they must be: the shafts where we used to watch the cage-loads of colliers coming up suddenly, with a start: then the men streaming out to turn in their lamps, then trailing off, all grey, along the lane home; while the screens still rattled, and the pony on the sky-line still pulled along the tub of 'dirt', to tip over the edge of the pit-bank.

It is different now: all is much more impersonal and mechanical and abstract. I don't suppose the children of today drop 'nuts' of coal down the shaft, on Sunday afternoons, to hear them hit, hit with an awful resonance against the sides far down, before there comes the last final plump into the endlessly far-off sump. My father was always so angry if he knew we dropped coals down the shaft: If there was a man at t'bottom, it'd kill 'im straight off. How should you like that? – We didn't quite know how we should have liked it.

But anyhow Moorgreen is no more what it was: or it is too much more. Even the rose-bay willow-herb, which seems to love collieries, no longer showed its hairy autumn thickets and its last few spikes of rose around the pit-pond and on the banks. Only the yellow snapdragon, toad-flax, still was there.

Up from Moorgreen goes a footpath past the quarry and up the fields, out to Renshaw's farm. This was always a favourite walk of mine. Beside the path lies the old quarry, part of it very old and deep and filled in with oak trees and guelder-rose and tangle of briars, the other part open, with square wall neatly built up with dry-stone on the side under the plough-fields, and the bed still fairly level and open. This open part of the quarry was blue with dog-violets in spring, and, on the smallish brambles, the first handsome blackberries came in autumn. Thank heaven, it is late October, and too late for blackberries, or there would still be here some wretched men with baskets, ignominiously combing the brambles for the last berry. When I was a boy, how a man, a full-grown miner, would have been despised for going with a little basket lousing the hedges for a blackberry or two. But the men of my generation put their pride in their pocket, and now their pockets are empty.

The quarry was a haunt of mine, as a boy. I loved it because, in the open part, it seemed so sunny and dry and warm, the pale stone, the pale, slightly sandy bed, the dogviolets and the early daisies. And then the old part, the deep part, was such a fearsome place. It was always dark – you had to crawl under bushes. And you came upon honeysuckle and nightshade, that no one ever looked upon. And at the dark sides were little, awful rocky caves, in which I imagined the adders lived.

There was a legend that these little caves or niches in the rocks were 'everlasting wells', like the everlasting wells at Matlock. At Matlock the water drips in caves, and if you put an apple in there, or a bunch of grapes, or even if you cut your hand off and put it in, it won't decay, it will turn everlasting. Even if you put a bunch of violets in, they won't die, they'll turn everlasting.

Later, when I grew up and went to Matlock – only sixteen miles away – and saw the infamous everlasting wells, that the water only made a hoary nasty crust of stone on everything, and the stone hand was only a glove stuffed with sand, being 'petrified', I was disgusted. But still, when I see the stone fruits that people have in bowls for decoration, purple, semi-translucent stone grapes, and lemons, I think: *these* are the real fruits from the everlasting wells.

In the soft, still afternoon I found the quarry not very

much changed. The red berries shone quietly on the briars. And in this still, warm, secret place of the earth I felt my old childish longing to pass through a gate, into a deeper, sunnier, more silent world.

The sun shone in, but the shadows already were deep. Yet I had to creep away into the darkness of bushes, into the lower hollow of the tree-filled quarry. I felt, as I had always felt, there was something there. And as I wound my way, stooping, through the unpleasant tangle, I started, hearing a sudden rush and clatter of falling earth. Some part of the quarry must be giving way.

I found the place, away at the depth under the trees and bushes, a new place where yellow earth and whitish earth and pale rock had slid down new in a heap. And at the top of the heap was a crack, a little slantingly upright slit or orifice in the rock.

I looked at the new place curiously, the pallid new earth and rock among the jungle of vegetation, the little opening above, into the earth. A touch of sunlight came through the oak-leaves and fell on the new place and the aperture, and the place flashed and twinkled. I had to climb up to look at it.

It was a little crystalline cavity in the rock, all crystal, a little pocket or womb of quartz, among the common stone. It was pale and colourless, the stuff we call spar, from which they make little bowls and mementoes, in Matlock. But through the flat-edged, colourless crystal of the spar ran a broad vein of purplish crystal, wavering inwards as if it were arterial. And that was a vein of the Blue John spar that is rather precious.

The place fascinated me, especially the vein of purple, and I had to clamber into the tiny cave, which would just hold me. It seemed warm in there, as if the shiny rock were warm and alive, and it seemed to me there was a strange perfume, of rock, of living rock like hard, bright flesh, faintly perfumed with phlox. It was a subtle yet most fascinating secret perfume, an inward perfume. I crept right into the little cavity, into the narrow inner end where the vein of purple ran, and I curled up there, like an animal in its hole. 'Now,' I thought, 'for a little while I am safe and sound, and the vulgar world doesn't exist for me.' I curled together with soft, curious voluptuousness. The scent of inwardness and of life, a queer scent like phlox, with a faint narcotic inner quality like opium or like truffles, became very vivid to me, then faded. I suppose I must have gone to sleep.

Later, I don't know how much later, it may have been a minute, or an eternity, I was wakened by feeling something lifting me, lifting me with a queer, half-sickening motion, curiously exciting, in a slow little rhythmic heave that was at once soft and powerful, gentle and violent, grateful and violating. I could do nothing, not even wake up: yet I was not really terrified, only utterly wonderstruck.

Then the lifting and heaving ceased, and I was cold. Something harsh passed over me: I realized it was my face: I realized I had a face. Then immediately a sharpness and bitingness flew into me, flew right into me, through what must have been my nostrils, into my body, what must have been my breast. Roused by a terrific shock of amazement, suddenly a new thing rushed into me, right into me, with a sweep that swept me away, and at the same time I felt that first thing moving somewhere in me, there was a movement that came aloud.

There were some dizzy moments when my I, my consciousness, wheeled and swooped like an eagle that is going to wheel away into the sky and be gone. Yet I felt her, my I, my life, wheeling closer, closer, my consciousness. And suddenly she closed with me, and I knew, I came awake.

I knew. I knew I was alive. I even heard a voice say: 'He's alive!' Those were the first words I heard.

And I opened my eyes again and blinked with terror, knowing the light of day. I shut them again, and felt sensations out in space, somewhere, and yet upon *me*. Again my eyes were opened, and I even saw objects, great things that were here and were there and then were not there. And the sensations out in space drew nearer, as it were, to me, the middle me.

So consciousness swooped and swerved, returning in great swoops. I realized that I was I, and that this I was also a body that ended abruptly in feet and hands. Feet! yes, feet! I remembered even the word. Feet!

I roused a little, and saw a greyish pale nearness that I recognized was my body, and something terrible moving upon it and making sensations in it. Why was it grey, my own nearness? Then I felt that other sensation, that I call aloudness, and I knew it. It was 'Dust of ages!' That was the aloudness: 'Dust of ages!'

In another instant I knew that violent movingness that was making sensations away out upon me. It was somebody. In terror and wonder the realization came to me: it was somebody, another one, a man. A man, making sensations on me! A man, who made the aloudness: 'Dust of ages.' A man! Still I could not grasp it. The conception would not return whole to me.

Yet once it had lodged within me, my consciousness established itself. I moved. I even moved my legs, my far-off feet. Yes! And an aloudness came out of me, even of me. I knew. I even knew now that I had a throat. And in another moment I should know something else.

It came all of a sudden. I saw the man's face. I saw it, a ruddy sort of face with a nose and a trimmed beard. I even knew more. I said: 'Why –?'

And the face quickly looked at me, with blue eyes into my eyes, and I struggled as if to get up.

'Art awake?' it said.

And somewhere, I knew there was the word Yes! But it had not yet come to me.

But I knew, I knew! Dimly I came to know that I was lying in sun on new earth that was spilled before my little, opened cave. I remembered my cave. But why I should be lying grey and stark-naked on earth in the sun outside I did not know; nor what the face was, nor whose.

Then there was more aloudness, and there was another one. I realized there could be more than one other one. More than one! More than one! I felt a new sudden something that made all of me move at once, in many directions, it seemed, and I became once more aware of the extent of me, and an aloudness came from my throat. And I remembered even that new something that was upon me. Many sensations galloping in all directions! But it was one dominant, drowning. It was water. Water! I even remembered water, or I knew I knew it. They were washing me. I even looked down and saw the whiteness: me, myself, white, a body.

And I remembered, that when all of me had moved to the touch of water, and I had made an aloudness in my throat, the men had laughed. Laughed! I remembered laughter.

So as they washed me, I came to myself. I even sat up. And I saw earth and rock, and a sky that I knew was afternoon. And I was stark-naked, and there were two men washing me, and they too were stark-naked. But I was white, pure white, and thin, and they were ruddy, and not thin.

They lifted me, and I leaned on one, standing, while the

other washed me. The one I leaned on was warm, and his life softly warmed me. The other one rubbed me gently. I was alive. I saw my white feet like two curious flowers, and I lifted them one after another, remembering walking.

The one held me, and the other put a woollen shirt or smock over me. It was pale grey and red. Then they fastened shoes on my feet. Then the free one went to the cave, peering, and he came back with things in his hands: buttons, some discoloured yet unwasted coins, a dull but not rusted pocket-knife, a waistcoat buckle, and a discoloured watch, whose very face was dark. Yet I knew these things were mine.

'Where are my clothes?' I said.

I felt eyes looking at me, two blue eyes, two brown eyes, full of strange life.

'My clothes!' I said.

They looked at one another, and made strange speech. Then the blue-eyed one said to me:

'Gone! Dust of ages!'

They were strange men to me, with their formal, peaceful faces and trimmed beards, like old Egyptians. The one on whom I was unconsciously leaning stood quite still, and he was warmer than the afternoon sunshine. He seemed to give off life to me, I felt a warmth suffusing into me, an inflooding of strength. My heart began to lift with strange, exultant strength. I turned to look at the man I was resting on, and met the blue, quiet shimmer of his eyes. He said something to me, in the quiet, full voice, and I nearly understood, because it was like the dialect. He said it again, softly and calmly, speaking to the inside of me, so that I understood as a dog understands, from the voice, not from the words.

'Can ta goo, o shollt be carried?'

It sounded to me like that, like the dialect.

'I think I can walk,' said I, in a voice that sounded harsh after the soft, deep modulation of the other.

He went slowly down the heap of loose earth and stones, which I remembered had fallen. But it was different. There were no trees in an old quarry hollow. This place was bare, like a new working. And when we came out, it was another place altogether. Below was a hollow of trees, and a bare, grassy hillside swept away, with clumps of trees, like parkland. There was no colliery, no railway, no hedges, no square, shut-in fields. And yet the land looked tended.

We stood on a little path of paved stone, only about a yard wide. Then the other man came up from the quarry, carrying tools and wearing a grey shirt or smock with a red cord. He spoke with that curious soft inwardness, and we turned down the path, myself still leaning on the shoulder of the first man. I felt myself quivering with a new strength, and yet ghostlike. I had a curious sensation of lightness, not touching the ground as I walked, as if my hand that rested on the man's shoulder buoyed me up. I wanted to know whether I was really buoyant, as in a dream.

I took my hand suddenly from the man's shoulder, and stood still. He turned and looked at me.

'I can walk alone,' I said, and as in a dream I took a few paces forward. It was true. I was filled with a curious rushing strength that made me almost buoyant, scarcely needing to touch the ground. I was curiously, quiveringly strong, and at the same time buoyant.

'I can go alone!' I said to the man.

They seemed to understand, and to smile, the blue-eyed one showing his teeth when he smiled. I had a sudden idea: How beautiful they are, like plants in flower! But still, it was something I felt, rather than saw.

The blue-eyed one went in front, and I walked on the

narrow path with my rushing buoyancy, terribly elated and proud, forgetting everything, the other man following silently behind. Then I was aware that the path had turned and ran beside a road in a hollow where a stream was, and a cart was clanking slowly ahead, drawn by two oxen and led by a man who was entirely naked.

I stood still, on the raised, paved path, trying to think, trying, as it were, to come awake. I was aware that the sun was sinking behind me, golden in the October afternoon. I was aware that the man in front of me also had no clothes on whatsoever, and he would soon be cold.

Then I made an effort, and looked round. On the slopes to the left were big, rectangular patches of dark plough-land. And men were ploughing still. On the right were hollow meadows, beyond the stream, with tufts of trees and many speckled cattle being slowly driven forwards. And in front the road swerved on, past a mill-pond and a mill, and a few little houses, and then swerved up a rather steep hill. And at the top of the hill was a town, all yellow in the late afternoon light, with yellow, curved walls rising massive from the yellow-leaved orchards, and above, buildings swerving in a long, oval curve, and round, faintly conical towers rearing up. It had something at once soft and majestical about it, with its soft yet powerful curves, and no sharp angles or edges, the whole substance seeming soft and golden like the golden flesh of a city.

And I knew, even while I looked at it, that it was the place where I was born, the ugly colliery townlet of dirty red brick. Even as a child, coming home from Moorgreen, I had looked up and seen the squares of miners' dwellings, built by the Company, rising from the hill-top in the afternoon light like the walls of Jerusalem, and I had wished it were a golden city, as in the hymns we sang in the Congregational Chapel.

Now it had come true. But the very realization, and the very intensity of my *looking*, had made me lose my strength and my buoyancy. I turned forlorn to the men who were with me. The blue-eyed one came and took my arm, and laid it across his shoulder, laying his left hand round my waist, on my hip.

And almost immediately the soft, warm rhythm of his life pervaded me again, and the memory in me which was my old self went to sleep. I was like a wound, and the touch of these men healed me at once. We went on again, along the raised pavement.

Three horsemen came cantering up, from behind. All the world was turning home towards the town, at sunset. The horsemen slackened pace as they came abreast. They were men in soft, yellow sleeveless tunics, with the same still, formal Egyptian faces and trimmed beards as my companions. Their arms and legs were bare, and they rode without stirrups. But they had curious hats of beech-leaves on their heads. They glanced at us sharply and my companions saluted respectfully. Then the riders cantered ahead again, the golden tunics softly fluttering. No one spoke at all. There was a great stillness in all the world, and yet a magic of close-interwoven life.

The road now began to be full of people, slowly passing up the hill towards the town. Most were bare-headed, wearing the sleeveless woollen shirt of grey and red, with a red girdle, but some were clean-shaven, and dressed in grey shirts, and some carried tools, some fodder. There were women too, in blue or lilac smocks, and some men in scarlet smocks. But among the rest, here and there were men like my guide, quite naked, and some young women, laughing together as they went, had their blue smocks folded to a pad on their heads, as they carried their bundles, and their slender, rosy-tanned bodies were quite naked, save for a little girdle of white and green and purple cord fringe that hung round their hips and swung as they walked. Only they had soft shoes on their feet.

They all glanced at me, and some spoke a word of salute to my companions, but no one asked questions. The naked girls went very stately, with bundles on their heads, yet they laughed more than the men. And they were comely as berries on a bush. That was what they reminded me of: rose-berries on a bush. That was the quality of all the people: an inner stillness and ease, like plants that come to flower and fruit. The individual was like a whole fruit, body and mind and spirit, without split. It made me feel a curious, sad sort of envy, because I was not so whole, and at the same time, I was wildly elated, my rushing sort of energy seemed to come upon me again. I felt as if I were just going to plunge into the deeps of life, for the first time: belated, and yet a pioneer of pioneers.

I saw ahead the great rampart walls of the town – then the road suddenly curved to gateway, all the people flowing in, in two slow streams, through the narrow side entrances.

It was a big gateway of yellow stone, and inside was a clear space, paved mostly with whitish stones, and around it stood buildings in the yellow stone, golden-looking, with pavement arcades supported on yellow pillars. My guides turned into a chamber where men in green stood on guard, and several peasants were waiting. They made way, and I was taken before a man who reclined on a dark-yellow couch, himself wearing a yellow tunic. He was blond, with the trimmed beard and hair worn long, cut round like the hair of a Florentine page. Though he was not handsome, he had a curious quality of beauty, that came from within. But this time, it was the beauty of a flower rather than of a berry.

My guides saluted him and explained briefly and quietly, in words I could only catch a drift of. Then the man looked at me, quietly, gently, yet I should have been afraid, if I had been his enemy. He spoke to me, and I thought he asked if I wanted to stay in their town.

'Did you ask me if I want to stay here?' I replied. 'You see, I don't even know where I am.'

'You are in this town of Nethrupp,' he said, in slow English, like a foreigner. 'Will you stay some time with us?'

'Why, thank you, if I may,' I said, too helplessly bewildered to know what I was saying.

We were dismissed, with one of the guards in green. The people were all streaming down the side street, between the yellow-coloured houses, some going under the pillared porticoes, some in the open road. Somewhere ahead a wild music began to ring out, like three bagpipes squealing and droning. The people pressed forward, and we came to a great oval space on the ramparts, facing due west. The sun, a red ball, was near the horizon.

We turned into a wide entrance and went up a flight of stairs. The man in green opened a door and ushered me in.

'All is thine!' he said.

My naked guide followed me into the room, which opened on to the oval and the west. He took a linen shirt and a woollen tunic from a small cupboard, and smilingly offered them to me. I realized he wanted his own shirt back, and quickly gave it him, and his shoes. He put my hand quickly between his two hands, then slipped into his shirt and shoes, and was gone.

I dressed myself in the clothes he had laid out, a blue-and-white striped tunic, and white stockings, and blue cloth shoes, and went to the window. The red sun was almost touching the tips of the tree-covered hills away in the west, Sherwood Forest grown dense again. It was the landscape I knew best on earth, and still I knew it, from the shapes.

There was a curious stillness in the square. I stepped out of my window on to the terrace, and looked down. The crowd had gathered in order, a cluster of men on the left, in grey, grey-and-scarlet, and pure scarlet, and a cluster of women on the right, in tunics of all shades of blue and crocus lilac. In the vaulted porticoes were more people. And the red sun shone on all, till the square glowed again.

When the ball of fire touched the tree-tops, there was a queer squeal of bagpipes, and the square suddenly started into life. The men were stamping softly, like bulls, the women were softly swaying, and softly clapping their hands, with a strange noise, like leaves. And from under the vaulted porticoes, at opposite ends of the egg-shaped oval, came the soft booming and trilling of women and men singing against one another in the strangest pattern of sound.

It was all kept very soft, soft-breathing. Yet the dance swept into swifter and swifter rhythm, with the most extraordinary incalculable unison. I do not believe there was any outside control of the dance. The thing happened by instinct, like the wheeling and flashing of a shoal of fish or of a flock of birds dipping and spreading in the sky. Suddenly, in one amazing wing-movement, the arms of all the men would flash up into the air, naked and glowing, and with the soft, rushing sound of pigeons alighting the men ebbed in a spiral, grey and sparkled with scarlet, bright arms slowly leaning, upon the women, who rustled all crocus-blue, rustled like an aspen, then in one movement scattered like sparks, in every direction, from under the enclosing, sinking arms of the men, and suddenly formed slender rays of lilac branching out from red and grey knot of the men.

All the time the sun was slowly sinking, shadow was falling, and the dance was moving slower, the women wheeling blue around the obliterated sun. They were dancing the sun down, and dancing as birds wheel and dance, and fishes in shoals, controlled by some strange unanimous instinct. It was at once terrifying and magnificent, I wanted to die, so as not to see it, and I wanted to rush down, to be one of them. To be a drop in that wave of life.

The sun had gone, the dance unfolded and faced inwards to the town, the men softly stamping, the women rustling and softly clapping, the voices of the singers drifting on like a twining wind. And slowly, in one slow wing-movement, the arms of the men rose up unanimous, in a sort of salute, and as the arms of the men were sinking, the arms of the women softly rose. It gave the most marvellous impression of soft, slow flight of two many-pinioned wings, lifting and sinking like the slow drift of an owl. Then suddenly everything ceased. The people scattered silently.

And two men came into the oval, the one with glowing lamps hung on a pole he carried across his shoulder, while the other quickly hung up the lamps within the porticoes, to light the town. It was night.

Someone brought us a lighted lamp, and was gone. It was evening, and I was alone in a smallish room with a small bed, a lamp on the floor, and an unlighted fire of wood on the small hearth. It was very simple and natural. There was a small outfit of clothing in the cupboard, with a thick blue cloak. And there were a few plates and dishes. But in the room there were no chairs, but a long, folded piece of dark felt, on which one could recline. The light shone upwards from below, lighting the walls of creamy smoothness, like a chalk enamel. And I was alone, utterly alone, within a couple of hundred yards of the very spot where I was born.

I was afraid: afraid for myself. These people, it seemed to me, were not people, not human beings in my sense of the word. They had the stillness and the completeness of plants. And see how they could melt into one amazing instinctive thing, a human flock of motion.

I sat on the ground on the dark-blue felt, wrapped in the blue mantle, because I was cold and had no means of lighting the fire. Someone tapped at the door, and a man of the green guard entered. He had the same quiet, fruit-like glow of the men who had found me, a quality of beauty that came from inside, in some queer physical way. It was a quality I loved, yet it made me angry. It made me feel like a green apple, as if they had had all the real sun.

He took me out, and showed me lavatories and baths, with two lusty men standing under the douches. Then he took me down to a big circular room with a raised hearth in the centre, and a blazing wood fire whose flame and smoke rose to a beautiful funnel-shaped canopy or chimney of stone. The hearth spread out beyond the canopy, and here some men reclined on the folded felts, with little white cloths before them, eating an evening meal of stiff porridge and milk, with liquid butter, fresh lettuce, and apples. They had taken off their clothes, and lay with the firelight flickering on their healthy, fruit-like bodies, the skin glistening faintly with oil. Around the circular wall ran a broad dais where other men reclined, either eating or resting. And from time to time a man came in with his food, or departed with his dishes.

My guide took me out, to peep in a steaming room where each man washed his plate and spoon and hung them in his own little rack. Then my guide gave me a cloth and tray and dishes, and we went to a simple kitchen, where the porridge stood in great bowls over a slow fire, the melted butter was in a deep silver pan, the milk and the lettuce and fruit stood near the door. Three cooks guarded the kitchen, but the men from outside came quietly and took what they needed or what they wanted, helping themselves, then returning to the great round room, or going away to their own little rooms. There was an instinctive cleanliness and decency everywhere, in every movement, in every act. It was as if the deepest instinct had been cultivated in the people, to be comely. The soft, quiet comeliness was like a dream, a dream of life at last come true.

I took a little porridge, though I had little desire to eat. I felt a curious surge of force in me: yet I was like a ghost, among these people. My guide asked me, would I eat in the round hall, or go up to my room? I understood, and chose the round hall. So I hung my cloak in the curving lobby, and entered the men's hall. There I lay on a felt against the wall, and watched the men, and listened.

They seemed to slip out of their clothing as soon as they were warm, as if clothes were a burden or a slight humiliation. And they lay and talked softly, intermittently, with low laughter, and some played games with draughtsmen and chessmen, but mostly they were still.

The room was lit by hanging lamps, and it had no furniture at all. I was alone, and I was ashamed to take off my white sleeveless shirt. I felt, somehow, these men had no right to be so unashamed and self-possessed.

The green guard came again, and asked me, would I go to see somebody whose name I did not make out. So I took my mantle, and we went into the softly-lighted street, under the porticoes. People were passing, some in cloaks, some only in tunics, and women were tripping along.

We climbed up towards the top of the town, and I felt I must be passing the very place where I was born, near where the Wesleyan Chapel stood. But now it was all softly lighted, golden-coloured porticoes, with people passing in green or blue or grey-and-scarlet cloaks.

We came out on top into a circular space, it must have been where our Congregational Chapel stood, and in the centre of the circle rose a tower shaped tapering rather like a lighthouse, and rosy-coloured in the lamplight. Away in the sky, at the club-shaped tip of the tower, glowed one big ball of light.

We crossed, and mounted the steps of another building, through the great hall where people were passing, on to a door at the end of a corridor, where a green guard was seated. The guard rose and entered to announce us, then I followed through an antechamber to an inner room with a central hearth and a fire of clear-burning wood.

A man came forward to meet me, wearing a thin, carmine-coloured tunic. He had brown hair and a stiff, reddish-brown beard, and an extraordinary glimmering kind of beauty. Instead of the Egyptian calmness and fruit-like impassivity of the ordinary people, or the steady, flower-like radiance of the chieftain in yellow, at the city gates, this man had a quavering glimmer like light coming through water. He took my cloak from me; and I felt at once he understood.

'It is perhaps cruel to awaken,' he said, in slow, conscious English, 'even at a good moment.'

'Tell me where I am!' I said.

'We call it Nethrupp – but was it not Newthorpe? – Tell me, when did you go to sleep?'

'This afternoon, it seems – in October, 1927.'

'October, nineteen-twenty-seven!' He repeated the words curiously, smiling.

'Did I really sleep? Am I really awake?'

'Are you not awake?' he said smiling. 'Will you recline upon the cushons? Or would you rather sit? See!' – He showed me a solid oak armchair, of the modern furniture-revival sort, standing alone in the room. But it was black with age, and shrunken-seeming. I shivered.

'How old is that chair?' I said.

'It is just about a thousand years! a case of special pre-servation,' he said.

I could not help it. I just sat on the rugs and burst into tears, weeping my soul away.

The man sat perfectly still for a long time. Then he came and put my hand between his two.

'Don't cry!' he said. 'Don't cry! Man was a perfect child so long. Now we try to be men, not fretful children. Don't cry! Is not this better?'

'When is it? What year is this?' I asked.

'What year? We call it the year of the acorn. But you mean its arithmetic? You would call it the year two thousand nine hundred and twenty-seven.'

'It cannot be,' I said.

'Yet still it is.'

'Then I am a thousand and forty-two years old!'

'And why not?'

'But how can I be?'

'How? You went to sleep, like a chrysalis: in one of the earth's little chrysalis wombs: and your clothes turned to dust, yet they left the buttons: and you woke up like a butterfly. But why not? Why are you afraid to be a butterfly that wakes up out of the dark for a little while, beautiful? Be beautiful, then, like a white butterfly. Take off your clothes and let the firelight fall on you. What is given, accept then –'

'How long shall I live now, do you think?' I asked him.

'Why will you always measure? Life is not a clock.'
It is true. I am like a butterfly, and I shall only live a little while. That is why I don't want to eat.

(Unfinished)

The Undying Man

LONG ago in Spain there were two very learned men, so clever and knowing so much that they were famous all over the world. One was called Rabbi Moses Maimonides, a Jew – blessed be his memory! – and the other was called Aristotle, a Christian who belonged to the Greeks.

These two were great friends, because they had always studied together and found out many things together. At last after many years, they found out a thing they had been specially trying for. They discovered that if you took a tiny little vein out of a man's body, and put it in a glass jar with certain leaves and plants, it would gradually begin to grow, and would grow and grow until it became a man. When it had grown as big as a boy, you could take it out of the jar, and then it would live and keep on growing till it became a man, a fine man who would never die. He would be undying. Because he had never been born, he would never die, but live for ever and ever. Because the wisest men on earth had made him, and he didn't have to be born.

When they were quite sure it was so, then the Rabbi Moses Maimonides and the Christian Aristotle decided they would really make a man. Up till then, they had only experimented. But now they would make the real undying man.

The question was, from whom should they take the little vein? Because the man they took it from would die. So at first they decided to take it from a slave. But then they thought, a slave wasn't good enough to make the beginnings of the undying man. So they decided to ask one of their devoted students to sacrifice himself. But that did not seem right either, because they might get a man they didn't really like, and whom they wouldn't want to be the beginning of the man who would never die. So at last, they decided to leave it to fate; they gathered together their best and most learned disciples, and they all agreed to draw lots. The lot fell to Aristotle, to have the little vein cut from his body.

So Aristotle had to agree. But before he would have the little vein cut out of his body, Aristotle asked Maimonides to take him by the hand and swear by their clasped hands that he would never interfere with the growth of the little vein, never at any time or in any way. Maimonides took him by the hand and swore. And then Aristotle had the little vein cut out of his body by Maimonides himself.

So now Maimonides alone took the little vein and placed it among the leaves and herbs, as they had discovered, in the great glass jar, and he sealed the jar. Then he set the jar on a shelf in his own room where nobody entered but himself, and he waited. The days passed by, and he recited his prayers, pacing back and forth in his room among his books, and praying loudly as he paced, as the Jews do. Then he returned to his books and his chemistry. But every day he looked at the jar, to see if the little vein had changed. For a long time it did not change. So he thought it was in vain.

Then at last it seemed to change, to have grown a little. Rabbi Moses Maimonides gazed at the jar transfixed, and forgot everything else in all the wide world; lost to all and everything, he gazed into the jar. And at last he saw the tiniest, tiniest tremor in the little vein, and he knew it was a tremor of growth. He sank on the floor and lay unconscious, because he had seen the first tremor of growth of the undying man.

When he came to himself, the room was dusk, it was almost night. And Rabbi Moses Maimonides was afraid. He did not know what he was afraid of. He rose to his feet, and glanced towards the jar. And it seemed to him, in the darkness on the shelf there was a tiny red glow, like the smallest ember of fire. But it did not go out, as the last ember of fire goes out while you watch. It stayed on, and glowed a tiny dying glow that did not die. Then he knew he saw the glow of the life of the undying man, and he was afraid.

He locked his room, where no one ever entered but himself, and went out into the town. People greeted him with bows and reverences, for he was the most learned of all rabbis. But tonight they all seemed very far from him. They looked small and they grimaced like monkeys in his eyes. And he thought to himself: they will all die! They grimace in this fashion, like monkeys, because they will all die. Only I shall not die!

But as he thought this, his heart stood still, because he knew that he too would die. He stood still in the street, though rain was falling, and people crept past him humbly, thinking he was praying some great prayer. But he was only locked in this one thought: I shall die and pass away, but that little red spark which came from Aristotle the Christian, it will never die. It will live for ever and ever, like God. God alone lives for ever and ever. But this man in the jar will also live for ever and ever, even that red spark. He will be a man, and live for ever and ever, as good as God. Nay, better than God! For surely, to be as good as God, and to be also a man and alive, that would be better even than being God!

Rabbi Moses Maimonides started at this thought as if he had been stung. And immediately he began to walk down the street towards home, to see if the red glow were really glowing. When he got to his door, he stood still, afraid to open. He could not open.

So suddenly he cried a great fierce cry to God, to help him and His people. A great fierce cry for help. For they were God's people, God's chosen people. Though they grimaced in the sight of Rabbi Moses Maimonides like monkeys, they were beautiful in the sight of God, and the best Jews among them would sit in high, high places in the eternal glory of God, in the after-life.

This thought so emboldened Maimonides that he opened his door and entered his room. But he stood again as if pierced through the body by that strange red light, like no light of God, which glowed so tiny and yet was so fierce and strong. 'Fierce and strong! fierce and strong!' he kept muttering to himself as he paced back and forth in his room. 'Fierce and strong!' His servant thought he was praying, and she dared not bring his food to the door. 'Fierce and strong!' – he paced back and forth. And he himself thought he was praying. He was so used to praying the ritual prayers as he paced in his room, that now he thought he was praying to the one and only God. But in fact, all he was saying was 'Fierce and strong! Fierce and strong!'

At last he sank down in exhaustion, and then his woman tapped at his door and set down the tray. But he told her to take the tray away, he would not eat in his room, but would come downstairs. For he could not eat in the presence of that little red glow.

So he made his ablutions and went downstairs and ate. And he slept in the guest-room, for he could not sleep in the presence of the little red glow. Indeed he could not sleep at all, but lay and groaned in spirit, thinking of that little red light which alone of all light was not the light of God. And he knew it would grow and grow, and be a man, most splendid, a man who would never die. And all the people would think: What is the most wonderful of all things, seen or unseen? – And there would come the

(Unfinished)

The Blue Moccasins

THE fashion in women changes nowadays even faster than women's fashions. At twenty, Lina McLeod was almost painfully modern. At sixty, almost obsolete!

She started off in life to be really independent. In that remote day, forty years ago, when a woman said she was going to be independent, it meant she was having no nonsense with men. She was kicking over the masculine traces, and living her own life, manless.

Today, when a girl says she is going to be independent, it means she is going to devote her attentions almost exclusively to men; though not necessarily to 'a man'.

Miss McLeod had an income from her mother. Therefore, at the age of twenty, she turned her back on that image of tyranny, her father, and went to Paris to study art. Art having been studied, she turned her attention to the globe of earth. Being terribly independent, she soon made Africa look small: she dallied energetically with vast hinterlands of China: and she knew the Rocky Mountains and the deserts of Arizona as if she had been married to them. All this, to escape mere man.

It was in New Mexico she purchased the blue moccasins, blue bead moccasins, from an Indian who was her guide and her subordinate. In her independence she made use of men, of course, but merely as servants, subordinates.

When the war broke out she came home. She was then forty-five, and already going grey. Her brother, two years older than herself, but a bachelor, went off to the war; she stayed at home in the small family mansion in the country, and did what she could. She was small and erect and brief in her speech, her face was like pale ivory, her skin like a very delicate parchment, and her eyes were very blue. There was no nonsense about her, though she did paint pictures. She never even touched her delicately parchment face with pigment. She was good enough as she was, honest-to-God, and the country town had a tremendous respect for her.

In her various activities she came pretty often into contact with Percy Barlow, the clerk at the bank. He was only twenty-two when she first set eyes on him, in 1914, and she immediately liked him. He was a stranger in the town, his father being a poor country vicar in Yorkshire. But he was of the confiding sort. He soon confided in Miss McLeod, for whom he had a towering respect how he disliked his step-mother, how he feared his father, was but as wax in the hands of that downright woman, and how, in consequence, he was homeless. Wrath shone in his pleasant features, but somehow it was an amusing wrath; at least to Miss McLeod.

He was distinctly a good-looking boy, with stiff dark hair and odd, twinkling grey eyes under thick dark brows, and a rather full mouth and a queer, deep voice that had a caressing touch of hoarseness. It was his voice that somehow got behind Miss McLeod's reserve. Not that he had the faintest intention of so doing. He looked up to her immensely: 'She's miles above me.'

When she watched him playing tennis, letting himself go a bit too much, hitting too hard, running too fast, being too nice to his partner, her heart yearned over him. The orphan in him! Why should he go and be shot? She kept him at home as long as possible, working with her at all kinds of war-work. He was so absolutely willing to do everything she wanted: devoted to her.

But at last the time came when he must go. He was now twenty-four and she forty-seven. He came to say good-bye, in his awkward fashion. She suddenly turned away, leaned her forehead against the wall, and burst into bitter tears. He was frightened out of his wits. Before he knew what was happening he had his arm in front of his face and was sobbing too.

She came to comfort him. 'Don't cry, dear, don't! It will all be all right.'

At last he wiped his face on his sleeve and looked at her sheepishly. 'It was you crying as did me in,' he said. Her blue eyes were brilliant with tears. She suddenly kissed him.

'You are such a dear!' she said wistfully. Then she added, flushing suddenly vivid pink under her transparent parchment skin: 'It wouldn't be right for you to marry an old thing like me, would it?'

He looked at her dumbfounded.

'No, I'm too old,' she added hastily.

'Don't talk about old! You're not old!' he said hotly.

'At least I'm too old for *that*,' she said sadly.

'Not as far as I'm concerned,' he said. 'You're younger than me, in most ways, I'm hanged if you're not!'

'Are you hanged if I'm not?' she teased wistfully.

'I am,' he said. 'And if I thought you wanted me, I'd be jolly proud if you married me. I would, I assure you.'

'Would you?' she said, still teasing him.

Nevertheless, the next time he was home on leave she married him, very quietly, but very definitely. He was a young lieutenant. They stayed in her family home, Twybit Hall, for the honeymoon. It was her house now, her brother being dead. And they had a strangely happy month. She had made a strange discovery: a man.

He went off to Gallipoli, and became a captain. He came home in 1919, still green with malaria, but otherwise sound. She was in her fiftieth year. And she was almost white-haired; long, thick, white hair, done perfectly, and perfectly creamy, colourless face, with very blue eyes.

He had been true to her, not being very forward with women. But he was a bit startled by her white hair. However, he shut his eyes to it, and loved her. And she, though frightened and somewhat bewildered, was happy. But she was bewildered. It always seemed awkward to her, that he should come wandering into her room in his pyjamas when she was half dressed, and brushing her hair. And he would sit there silent, watching her brush the long swinging river of silver, of her white hair, the bare, ivory-white, slender arm working with a strange mechanical motion, sharp and forcible, brushing down the long silvery stream of hair. He would sit as if mesmerized, just gazing. And she would at last glance round sharply, and he would rise, saying some little casual thing to her and smiling to her oddly with his eyes. Then he would go out, his thin cotton pyjamas hitching up over his hips, for he was a rather big-built fellow. And she would feel dazed, as if she did not quite know her own self any more. And the queer, ducking motion of his silently going out of her door impressed her ominously, his curious cat head, his big hips and limbs.

They were alone in the house, save for the servants. He had no work. They lived modestly, for a good deal of her money had been lost during the war. But she still painted pictures. Marriage had only stimulated her to this. She painted canvases of flowers, beautiful flowers that thrilled her soul. And he would sit, pipe in fist, silent, and watch her. He had nothing to do. He just sat and watched her small, neat figure and her concentrated movements as she painted. Then he knocked out his pipe, and filled it again.

She said that at last she was perfectly happy. And he said that he was perfectly happy. They were always together. He hardly went out, save riding in the lanes. And practically nobody came to the house.

But still, they were very silent with one another. The old chatter had died out. And he did not read much. He just sat still, and smoked, and was silent. It got on her nerves sometimes, and she would think as she had thought in the past, that the highest bliss a human being can experience is perhaps the bliss of being quite alone, quite, quite alone.

His bank firm offered to make him manager of the local branch, and, at her advice, he accepted. Now he went out of the house every morning and came home every evening, which was much more agreeable. The rector begged him to sing again in the church choir: and again she advised him to accept. These were the old grooves in which his bachelor life had run. He felt more like himself.

He was popular: a nice, harmless fellow, everyone said of him. Some of the men secretly pitied him. They made rather much of him, took him home to luncheon, and let him loose with their daughters. He was popular among the daughters too: naturally, for if a girl expressed a wish, he would instinctively say: 'What! Would you like it? I'll get it for you.' And if he were not in a position to satisfy the desire, he would say: 'I only wish I could do it for you. I'd do it like a shot.' All of which he meant.

At the same time, though he got on so well with the maidens of the town, there was no coming forward about him. He was, in some way, not wakened up. Good-looking, and big, and serviceable, he was inwardly remote, without self-confidence, almost without a self at all.

The rector's daughter took upon herself to wake him up. She was exactly as old as he was, a smallish, rather sharp-faced young woman who had lost her husband in the war, and it had been a grief to her. But she took the stoic attitude of the young: You've got to live, so you may as well do it!

She was a kindly soul, in spite of her sharpness. And she had a very perky little red-brown pomeranian dog that she had bought in Florence in the street, but which had turned out a handsome little fellow. Miss McLeod looked down a bit on Alice Howells and her pom, so Mrs Howells felt no special love for Miss McLeod – 'Mrs Barlow, that is!' she would add sharply. 'For it's quite impossible to think of her as anything but Miss McLeod!'

Percy was really more at ease at the rectory, where the pom yapped and Mrs Howells changed her dress three or four times a day and looked it, than in the semi-cloisteral atmosphere of Twybit Hall, where Miss McLeod wore tweeds and a natural knitted jumper, her skirts rather long, her hair done up pure silver, and painted her wonderful flower pictures in the deepening silence of the daytime. At evening she would go up to change, after he came home. And though it thrilled her to have a man coming into her room as he dressed, snapping his collar-stud, to tell her something trivial as she stood bare-armed in her silk slip, rapidly coiling up the rope of silver hair behind her head, still, it worried her. When he was there, he couldn't keep away from her. And he would watch her, watch her, watch her as if she was the ultimate revelation. Sometimes it made her irritable. She was so absolutely used to her own privacy. What was he looking at? She never watched *him*. Rather she looked the other way. His watching tried her nerves. She was turned fifty. And his great silent body loomed almost dreadful.

He was quite happy playing tennis or croquet with Alice Howells and the rest. Alice was choir-mistress, a bossy little person outwardly, inwardly rather forlorn and affectionate, and not very sure that life hadn't let her down for good. She was now over thirty – and had no one but the pom and her father and the parish – nothing in her really intimate life. But she was very cheerful, busy, even gay, with her choir and school work, her dancing and flirting and dressmaking.

She was intrigued by Percy Barlow. 'How *can* a man be so nice to *everybody*?' she asked him, a little exasperated. 'Well, why not?' he replied, with the odd smile of his eyes. 'It's not why he shouldn't, but how he manages to do it! How can you have so much good-nature? I *have* to be catty to some people, but you're nice to *everybody*.'

'Oh, am I!' he said ominously.

He was like a man in a dream, or in a cloud. He was quite a good bank-manager, in fact very intelligent. Even in appearance, his great charm was his beautifully-shaped head. He had plenty of brains, really. But in his will, in his body, he was asleep. And sometimes this lethargy, or coma, made him look haggard. And sometimes it made his body seem inert and despicable, meaningless.

Alice Howells longed to ask him about his wife. '*Do* you love her? *Can* you really care for her?' But she daren't. She daren't ask him one word about his wife. Another thing she couldn't do, she couldn't persuade him to dance. Never, not once. But in everything else he was pliable as wax.

Mrs Barlow – Miss McLeod – stayed out at Twybit all the time. She did not even come in to church on Sunday. She had shaken off church, among other things. And she watched Percy depart, and felt just a little humiliated. He was going to sing in the choir! Yes, marriage was also a humiliation to her. She had distinctly married beneath her.

The years had gone by: she was now fifty-seven, Percy was thirty-four. He was still, in many ways, a boy. But in his curious silence, he was ageless. She managed him with perfect ease. If she expressed a wish, he acquiesced at once. So now it was agreed he should not come to her room any more. And he never did. But sometimes she went to him in his room, and was winsome in a pathetic, heart-breaking way.

She twisted him round her little finger, as the saying goes. And yet secretly she was afraid of him. In the early years he had displayed a clumsy but violent sort of passion, from which she had shrunk away. She felt it had nothing to do with her. It was just his indiscriminating desire for Woman, and for his own satisfaction. Whereas she was not just unidentified Woman, to give him his general satisfaction. So she had recoiled, and withdrawn herself. She had put him off. She had regained the absolute privacy of her room.

He was perfectly sweet about it. Yet she was uneasy with him now. She was afraid of him; or rather, not of him, but of a mysterious something in him. She was not a bit afraid of *him*, oh no! And when she went to him now, to be nice to him, in her pathetic winsomeness of an unused woman of fifty-seven, she found him sweet-natured as ever, but really indifferent. He saw her pathos and her winsomeness. In some way, the mystery of her, her thick white hair, her vivid blue eyes, her ladylike refinement still fascinated him. But his bodily desire for her had gone, utterly gone. And secretly, she was rather glad. But as he looked at her, looked at her, as he lay there so silent, she was afraid, as if some finger were pointed at her. Yet she knew, the moment she spoke to him, he would twist his eyes to that good-natured and 'kindly' smile of his.

It was in the late, dark months of this year that she missed the blue moccasins. She had hung them on a nail in his room. Not that he ever wore them: they were too small. Nor did she: they were too big. Moccasins are male foot-wear, among the Indians, not female. But they were of a lovely turquoise-blue colour, made all of little turquoise beads, with little forked flames of dead-white and dark-green. When, at the beginning of their marriage, he had exclaimed over them, she had said: 'Yes! Aren't they a lovely colour! So blue!' And he had replied: 'Not as blue as your eyes, even then.'

So, naturally, she had hung them up on the wall in his room, and there they had stayed. Till, one November day, when there were no flowers, and she was pining to paint a still-life with something blue in it – oh, so blue, like delphiniums! – she had gone to his room for the moccasins. And they were not there. And though she hunted, she could not find them. Nor did the maids know anything of them.

So she asked him: 'Percy, do you know where those blue moccasins are, which hung in your room?' There was a moment's dead silence. Then he looked at her with his good-naturedly twinkling eyes, and said: 'No, I know nothing of them.' There was another dead pause. She did not believe him. But being a perfect lady, she only said, as she turned away: 'Well then, how curious it is!' And there was another dead pause. Out of which he asked her what she wanted them for, and she told him. Whereon the matter lapsed.

It was November, and Percy was out in the evening fairly often now. He was rehearsing for a 'play' which was to be given in the church schoolroom at Christmas. He had asked her about it. 'Do you think it's a bit *infra dig*, if I play one of the characters?' She had looked at him mildly, disguising her real feeling. 'If you don't feel *personally* humiliated,' she said, 'then there's nothing else to consider.' And he had answered: 'Oh, it doesn't upset *me* at all.' So she mildly said: 'Then do it, by all means.' Adding at the back of her mind: If it amuses you, child! – but she thought, a change had indeed come over the world, when the master of Twybit Hall, or even, for that matter, the manager of the dignified Stubbs' Bank, should perform in public on a schoolroom stage in amateur theatricals. And she kept calmly aloof, preferring not to know any details. She had a world of her own.

When he had said to Alice Howells: 'You don't think other folk'll mind – clients of the bank and so forth – think it beneath my dignity?' she had cried, looking up into his twinkling eyes: 'Oh, you don't have to keep *your* dignity on ice, Percy – any more than I do mine.'

The play was to be performed for the first time on Christmas Eve: and after the play, there was the midnight service in church. Percy therefore told his wife not to expect him home till the small hours, at least. So he drove himself off in the car.

As night fell, and rain, Miss McLeod felt a little forlorn. She was left out of everything. Life was slipping past her. It was Christmas Eve, and she was more alone than she had ever been. Percy only seemed to intensify her aloneness, leaving her in this fashion.

She decided not to be left out. She would go to the play too. It was past six o'clock, and she had worked herself into a highly nervous state. Outside was darkness and rain: inside was silence, forlornness. She went to the telephone and rang up the garage in Shewbury. It was with great difficulty she got them to promise to send a car for her: Mr Slater would have to fetch her himself in the two-seater runabout: everything else was out.

She dressed nervously, in a dark-green dress with a few modest jewels. Looking at herself in the mirror, she still thought herself slim, young-looking and distinguished. She did not see how old-fashioned she was, with her uncompromising erectness, her glistening knob of silver hair sticking out behind, and her long dress.

It was a three-miles drive in the rain, to the small country town. She sat next to old Slater, who was used to driving horses and was nervous and clumsy with a car, without saying a word. He thankfully deposited her at the gate of St Barnabas' School.

It was almost half-past seven. The schoolroom was packed and buzzing with excitement. 'I'm afraid we haven't a seat left, Mrs Barlow!' said Jackson, one of the church sidesmen, who was standing guard in the school porch, where people were still fighting to get in. He faced her in consternation. She faced him in consternation. 'Well, I shall have to stay somewhere, till Mr Barlow can drive me home,' she said. 'Couldn't you put me a chair somewhere?'

Worried and flustered, he went worrying and flustering the other people in charge. The schoolroom was simply packed solid. But Mr Simmons, the leading grocer, gave up his chair in the front row to Mrs Barlow, whilst he sat in a chair right under the stage, where he couldn't see a thing. But he could see Mrs Barlow seated between his wife and daughter, speaking a word or two to them occasionally, and that was enough.

The lights went down: *The Shoes of Shagput* was about to begin. The amateur curtains were drawn back, disclosing the little amateur stage with a white amateur back-cloth daubed to represent a Moorish courtyard. In stalked Percy, dressed as a Moor, his face darkened. He looked quite handsome, his pale grey eyes queer and startling in his dark face. But he was afraid of the audience – he spoke away from them, stalking around clumsily. After a certain amount of would-be funny dialogue, in tripped the heroine, Alice Howells, of course. She was an eastern Houri, in white gauze Turkish trousers, silver veil, and – the blue moccasins. The whole stage was white, save for her blue moccasins, Percy's dark-green sash, and a negro boy's red fez.

When Mrs Barlow saw the blue moccasins, a little bomb of rage exploded in her. This, of all places! The blue moccasins that she had bought in the western deserts! The blue moccasins that were not so blue as her own eyes! *Her* blue moccasins! On the feet of that creature, Mrs Howells.

Alice Howells was not afraid of the audience. She looked full at them, lifting her silver veil. And of course she saw Mrs Barlow, sitting there like the Ancient of Days in judgement, in the front row. And a bomb of rage exploded in *her* breast too.

In the play, Alice was the wife of the grey-bearded old Caliph, but she captured the love of the young Ali, otherwise Percy, and the whole business was the attempt of these two to evade Caliph and negro-eunuchs and ancient crones, and get into each other's arms. The blue shoes were very important: for while the sweet Leila wore them, the gallant Ali was to know there was danger. But when she took them off, he might approach her.

It was all quite childish, and everybody loved it, and Miss McLeod might have been quite complacent about it all, had not Alice Howells got her monkey up, so to speak. Alice, with a lot of make-up, looked boldly handsome. And suddenly bold she was, bold as the devil. All these years the poor young widow had been 'good', slaving in the parish, and only even flirting just to cheer things up, never going very far and knowing she could never get anything out of it, but determined never to mope.

Now the sight of Miss McLeod sitting there so erect, so coolly 'higher plane', and calmly superior, suddenly let loose a devil in Alice Howells. All her limbs went suave and molten, as her young sex, long pent up, flooded even to her finger-tips. Her voice was strange, even to herself, with its long, plaintive notes. She felt all her movements soft and fluid, she felt herself like living liquid. And it was lovely. Underneath it all was the sting of malice against Miss McLeod, sitting there so erect, with her great knob of white hair.

Alice's business, as the lovely Leila, was to be seductive to the rather heavy Percy. And seductive she was. In two minutes, she had him spell-bound. He saw nothing of the audience. A faint, fascinated grin came on to his face, as he acted up to the young woman in the Turkish trousers. His rather full, hoarse voice changed and became clear, with a new, naked clang in it. When the two sang together, in the simple banal duets of the play, it was with a most fascinating intimacy. And when, at the end of Act One, the lovely Leila kicked off the blue moccasins, saying: 'Away, shoes of bondage, shoes of sorrow!' and danced a little dance all alone, barefoot, in her Turkish trousers, in front of her fascinated hero, his smile was so spell-bound that everybody else was spell-bound too.

Miss McLeod's indignation knew no bounds. When the blue moccasins were kicked across the stage by the brazen Alice, with the words: 'Away, shoes of bondage, shoes of sorrow!' the elder woman grew pink with fury, and it was all she could do not to rise and snatch the moccasins from the stage, and bear them away. She sat in speechless indignation during the brief curtain between Act one and Act two. Her moccasins! Her blue moccasins! Of the sacred blue colour, the turquoise of heaven.

But there they were, in Act two, on the feet of the bold Alice. It was becoming too much. And the love-scenes between Percy and the young woman were becoming nakedly shameful. Alice grew worse and worse. She was worked up now, caught in her own spell, and unconscious of everything save of him, and the sting of that other woman, who presumed to own him. Own him? Ha-ha!

For he was fascinated. The queer smile on his face, the concentrated gleam of his eyes, the queer way he leaned forward from his loins towards her, the new, reckless, throaty twang in his voice – the audience had before their eyes a man spell-bound and lost in passion.

Miss McLeod sat in shame and torment, as if her chair was red-hot. She too was fast losing her normal consciousness, in the spell of rage. She was outraged. The second Act was working to its climax. The climax came. The lovely Leila kicked off the blue shoes: 'Away, shoes of bondage, away!' and flew barefoot to the enraptured Ali, flinging herself into his arms. And if ever a man was gone in sheer desire, it was Percy, as he pressed the woman's lithe form against his body, and seemed unconsciously to envelop her, unaware of everything else. While she, blissful in his spell, but still aware of the audience and of the superior Miss McLeod, let herself be wrapped closer and closer.

Miss McLeod rose to her feet and looked towards the door. But the way out was packed with people standing holding their breath as the two on the stage remained wrapped in each other's arms, and the three fiddles and the flute softly woke up. Miss McLeod could not bear it. She was on her feet, and beside herself. She could not get out. She could not sit down again.

'Percy!' she said, in a low clear voice. 'Will you hand me my moccasins?'

He lifted his face like a man startled in a dream, lifted his face from the shoulder of his Leila. His gold-grey eyes were like softly-startled flames. He looked in sheer horrified wonder at the little white-haired woman standing below.

'Eh?' he said, purely dazed.

'Will you please hand me my moccasins!' – and she pointed to where they lay on the stage.

Alice had stepped away from him, and was gazing at the

risen viper of the little elderly woman on the tip of the audience. Then she watched him move across the stage, bending forward from the loins in his queer mesmerized way, pick up the blue moccasins, and stoop down to hand them over the edge of the stage to his wife, who reached up for them.

'Thank you!' said Miss McLeod, seating herself, with the blue moccasins in her lap.

Alice recovered her composure, gave a sign to the little orchestra, and began to sing at once, strong and assured, to sing her part in the duet that closed the Act. She knew she could command public opinion in her favour.

He too recovered at once, the little smile came back on his face, he calmly forgot his wife again as he sang his share in the duet. It was finished. The curtains were pulled to. There was immense cheering. The curtains opened, and Alice and Percy bowed to the audience, smiling both of them their peculiar secret smile, while Miss McLeod sat with the blue moccasins in her lap.

The curtains were closed, it was the long interval. After a few moments of hesitation, Mrs Barlow rose with dignity, gathered her wrap over her arm, and with the blue moccasins in her hand, moved towards the door. Way was respectfully made for her.

'I should like to speak to Mr Barlow,' she said to Jackson, who had anxiously ushered her in, and now would anxiously usher her out.

'Yes, Mrs Barlow.'

He led her round to the smaller class-room at the back, that acted as dressing-room. The amateur actors were drinking lemonade, and chattering freely. Mrs Howells came forward, and Jackson whispered the news to her. She turned to Percy.

'Percy, Mrs Barlow wants to speak to you. Shall I come with you?'

'Speak to me? Aye, come on with me.'

The two followed the anxious Jackson into the other half-lighted class-room, where Mrs Barlow stood in her wrap, holding the moccasins. She was very pale, and she watched the two butter-muslin Turkish figures enter, as if they could not possibly be real. She ignored Mrs Howells entirely.

'Percy,' she said, 'I want you to drive me home.'

'Drive you home?' he echoed.

'Yes, please!'

'Why – when?' he said, with vague bluntness.

'Now, – if you don't mind –'

'What – in this get-up?' He looked at himself.

'I could wait while you changed.'

There was a pause. He turned and looked at Alice Howells, and Alice Howells looked at him. The two women saw each other out of the corners of their eyes: but it was beneath notice. He turned to his wife, his black face ludicrously blank, his eyebrows cocked.

'Well, you see,' he said, 'it's rather awkward. I can hardly hold up the third Act while I've taken you home and got back here again, can I?'

'So you intend to play in the third Act?' she asked with cold ferocity.

'Why, I must, mustn't I?' he said blankly.

'Do you *wish* to?' she said, in all her intensity.

'I do, naturally. I want to finish the thing up properly,' he replied, in the utter innocence of his head; about his heart he knew nothing.

She turned sharply away.

'Very well!' she said. And she called to Jackson, who was standing dejectedly by the door: 'Mr Jackson, will you please find some car or conveyance to take me home?'

'Aye! I say, Mr Jackson,' called Percy in his strong, democratic voice, going forward to the man. 'Ask Tom Lomas if he'll do me a good turn and get my car out of the rectory garage, to drive Mrs Barlow home. Aye, ask Tom Lomas! And if not him, ask Mr Pilkington – Leonard. The key's there. You don't mind, do you? I'm ever so much obliged –'

The three were left awkwardly alone again.

'I expect you've had enough with two acts,' said Percy soothingly to his wife. 'These things aren't up to your mark. I know it. They're only child's play. But, you see, they please the people. We've got a packed house, haven't we?'

His wife had nothing to answer. He looked so ludicrous, with his dark-brown face and butter-muslin bloomers. And his mind was so ludicrously innocent. His body, however, was not so ridiculously innocent as his mind, as she knew when he turned to the other woman.

'You and I, we're more on the nonsense level, aren't we?' he said, with the new, throaty clang of naked intimacy in his voice. His wife shivered.

'Absolutely on the nonsense level,' said Alice, with easy assurance.

She looked into his eyes, then she looked at the blue moccasins in the hand of the other woman. He gave a little start, as if realizing something for himself.

At that moment Tom Lomas looked in, saying heartily: 'Right you are, Percy! I'll have my car here in half a tick. I'm more handy with it than yours.'

'Thanks, old man! You're a Christian.'

'Try to be! – especially when you turn Turk! Well –' He disappeared.

'I say, Lina,' said Percy in his most amiable democratic

way, 'would you mind leaving the moccasins for the next act? We s'll be in a bit of a hole without them.'

Miss McLeod faced him and stared at him with the full blast of her forget-me-not blue eyes, from her white face.

'Will you pardon me if I don't?' she said.

'What!' he exclaimed. 'Why? Why not? It's nothing but play, to amuse the people. I can't see how it can hurt the *moccasins*. I understand you don't quite like seeing me make a fool of myself. But anyhow, I'm a bit of a born fool. What?' – and his blackened face laughed with a Turkish laugh. 'Oh yes, you have to realize I rather enjoy playing the fool,' he resumed. 'And, after all, it doesn't really hurt *you*, now does it? Shan't you leave us those moccasins for the last act?'

She looked at him, then at the moccasins in her hand. No, it was useless to yield to so ludicrous a person. The vulgarity of his wheedling, the commonness of the whole performance! It was useless to yield even the moccasins. It would be treachery to herself.

'I'm sorry,' she said. 'But I'd so much rather they weren't used for this kind of thing. I never intended them to be.' She stood with her face averted from the ridiculous couple.

He changed as if she had slapped his face. He sat down on top of the low pupils' desk, and gazed with glazed interest round the class-room. Alice sat beside him, in her white gauze and her bedizened face. They were like two rebuked sparrows on one twig, he with his great, easy, intimate limbs, she so light and alert. And as she sat he sank into an unconscious physical sympathy with her. Miss McLeod walked towards the door.

'You'll have to think of something as'll do instead,' he muttered to Alice in a low voice, meaning the blue moccasins. And leaning down, he drew off one of the grey shoes she had on, caressing her foot with the slip of his hand over its slim, bare shape. She hastily put the bare foot behind her other, shod foot.

Tom Lomas poked in his head, his overcoat collar turned up to his ears.

'Car's there,' he said.

'Right-o! Tom! I'll chalk it up to thee, lad!' said Percy with heavy breeziness. Then, making a great effort with himself, he rose heavily and went across to the door, to his wife, saying to her, in the same stiff voice of false heartiness:

'You'll be as right as rain with Tom. You won't mind if I don't come out? No! I'd better not show myself to the audience. Well – I'm glad you came, if only for a while. Good-bye then! I'll be home after the service – but I shan't disturb you. Good-bye! Don't get wet now –' And his voice, falsely cheerful, stiff with anger, ended in a clang of indignation.

Alice Howells sat on the infants' bench in silence. She was ignored. And she was unhappy, uneasy, because of the scene.

Percy closed the door after his wife. Then he turned with a looming slowness to Alice, and said in a hoarse whisper: 'Think o' that, now!'

She looked up at him anxiously. His face, in its dark pigment, was transfigured with indignant anger. His yellow-grey eyes blazed, and a great rush of anger seemed to be surging up volcanic in him. For a second his eyes rested on her upturned, troubled, dark-blue eyes, then glanced away, as if he didn't want to look at her in his anger. Even so, she felt a touch of tenderness in his glance.

'And that's all she's ever cared about – her own things and her own way,' he said, in the same hoarse whisper, hoarse with suddenly-released rage. Alice Howells hung her head in silence.

'Not another damned thing, but what's her own, her own – and her own holy way – damned holy-holy-holy, all to herself.' His voice shook with hoarse, whispering rage, burst out at last.

Alice Howells looked up at him in distress.

'Oh, don't say it!' she said. 'I'm sure she's fond of you.'

'*Fond* of me! Fond of *me*!' he blazed, with a grin of transcendent irony. 'It makes her sick to look at me. I am a hairy brute, I own it. Why, she's never once touched me to be fond of me – never once – though she pretends sometimes. But a man knows –' and he made a grimace of contempt. 'He knows when a woman's just stroking him, good doggie! – and when she's really a bit woman-fond of him. That woman's never been real fond of anybody or anything, all her life – she couldn't, for all her show of kindness. She's limited to herself, that woman is; and I've looked up to her as if she was God. More fool me! If God's not good-natured and good-hearted, then what is He –?'

Alice sat with her head dropped, realizing once more that men aren't really fooled. She was upset, shaken by his rage, and frightened, as if she too were guilty. He had sat down blankly beside her. She glanced up at him.

'Never mind!' she said soothingly. 'You'll like her again tomorrow.'

He looked down at her with a grin, a grey sort of grin. 'Are you going to stroke me good doggie! as well?' he said.

'Why?' she asked, blank.

But he did not answer. Then after a while he resumed: 'Wouldn't even leave the moccasins! And she'd hung them up in my room, left them there for years – any man'd consider they were his. And I did want this show tonight to be a success! What are you going to do about it?'

'I've sent over for a pair of pale-blue satin bed-slippers of mine – they'll do just as well,' she replied.

'Aye! For all that, it's done me in.'

'You'll get over it.'

'Happen so! She's curdled my inside, for all that. I don't know how I'm going to be civil to her.'

'Perhaps you'd better stay at the rectory tonight,' she said softly.

He looked into her eyes. And in that look, he transferred his allegiance.

'*You* don't want to be drawn in, do you?' he asked, with troubled tenderness.

But she only gazed with wide, darkened eyes into his eyes, so she was like an open, dark doorway to him. His heart beat thick, and the faint, breathless smile of passion came into his eyes again.

'You'll have to go on, Mrs Howells. We can't keep them waiting any longer.'

It was Jim Stokes, who was directing the show. They heard the clapping and stamping of the impatient audience.

'Goodness!' cried Alice Howells, darting to the door.

Things

THEY were true idealists, from New England. But that is some time ago: before the war. Several years before the war, they met and married; he a tall, keen-eyed young man from Connecticut, she a smallish, demure, Puritan-looking young woman from Massachusetts. They both had a little money. Not much, however. Even added together, it didn't make three thousand dollars a year. Still – they were free. Free!

Ah! Freedom! To be free to live one's own life! To be twenty-five and twenty-seven, a pair of true idealists with a mutual love of beauty, and an inclination towards 'Indian thought' – meaning, alas, Mrs Besant – and an income a little under three thousand dollars a year! But what is money? All one wishes to do is to live a full and beautiful life. In Europe, of course, right at the fountain-head of tradition. It might possibly be done in America: in New England, for example. But at a forfeiture of a certain amount of 'beauty'. True beauty takes a long time to mature. The baroque is only half-beautiful, half-matured. No, the real silver bloom, the real golden-sweet bouquet of beauty had its roots in the Renaissance, not in any later or shallower period.

Therefore the two idealists, who were married in New Haven, sailed at once to Paris: Paris of the old days. They had a studio apartment on the Boulevard Montparnasse, and they became real Parisians, in the old, delightful sense, not in the modern, vulgar. It was the shimmer of the pure impressionists, Monet and his followers, the world seen in terms of pure light, light broken and unbroken. How lovely! How lovely the nights, the river, the mornings in the old streets and by the flower-stalls and the book-stalls, the afternoons up on Montmartre or in the Tuileries, the evenings on the boulevards!

They both painted, but not desperately. Art had not taken them by the throat, and they did not take Art by the throat. They painted: that's all. They knew people – nice people, if possible, though one had to take them mixed. And they were happy.

Yet it seems as if human beings must set their claws in *something*. To be 'free', to be 'living a full and beautiful life', you must, alas, be attached to something. A 'full and beautiful life' means a tight attachment to *something* – at least, it is so for all idealists – or else a certain boredom supervenes; there is a certain waving of loose ends upon the air, like the waving, yearning tendrils of the vine that spread and rotate, seeking something to clutch, something up which to climb towards the necessary sun. Finding nothing, the vine can only trail, half-fulfilled, upon the ground. Such is freedom! – a clutching of the right pole. And human beings are all vines. But especially the idealist. He is a vine, and he needs to clutch and climb. And he despises the man who is a mere *potato*, or turnip, or lump of wood.

Our idealists were frightfully happy, but they were all the time reaching out for something to cotton on to. At first, Paris was enough. They explored Paris *thoroughly*. And they learned French till they almost felt like French people, they could speak it so glibly.

Still, you know, you never talk French with your *soul*. It can't be done. And though it's very thrilling, at first, talking in French to clever Frenchmen – they seem *so* much cleverer than oneself – still, in the long run, it is not satisfying. The endlessly clever *materialism* of the French leaves you cold, in the end, gives a sense of barrenness and incompatibility with true New England depth. So our two idealists felt.

They turned away from France – but ever so gently. France had disappointed them. 'We've loved it, and we've got a great deal out of it. But after a while, after a considerable while, several years, in fact, Paris leaves one feeling disappointed. It hasn't quite got what one wants.'

'But Paris isn't France.'

'No, perhaps not. France is quite different from Paris. And France is lovely – quite lovely. But *to us*, though we love it, it doesn't say a great deal.'

So, when the war came, the idealists moved to Italy. And they loved Italy. They found it beautiful, and more poignant than France. It seemed much nearer to the New England conception of beauty: something pure, and full of sympathy, without the *materialism* and the *cynicism* of the French. The two idealists seemed to breathe their own true air in Italy.

And in Italy, much more than in Paris, they felt they could thrill to the teachings of the Buddha. They entered the swelling stream of modern Buddhistic emotion, and they read the books, and they practised meditation, and they deliberately set themselves to eliminate from their own souls greed, pain, and sorrow. They did not realize – yet – that Buddha's very eagerness to free himself from pain and sorrow is in itself a sort of greed. No, they dreamed of a perfect world, from which all greed, and nearly all pain, and a great deal of sorrow, were eliminated.

But America entered the war, so the two idealists had to help. They did hospital work. And though their experience made them realize more than ever that greed, pain, and sorrow *should* be eliminated from the world, nevertheless the Buddhism, or the theosophy, didn't emerge very triumphant from the long crisis. Somehow, somewhere, in some part of themselves, they felt that greed, pain, and sorrow would never be eliminated, because most people don't care about eliminating them, and never will care. Our idealists were far too western to think of abandoning all the world to damnation, while they saved their two selves. They were far too unselfish to sit tight under a bho-tree and reach Nirvana in a mere couple.

It was more than that, though. They simply hadn't enough *Sitz fleisch* to squat under a bho-tree and get to Nirvana by contemplating anything, least of all their own navel. If the whole wide world was not going to be saved, they, personally, were not so very keen on being saved just by themselves. No, it would be so lonesome. They were New Englanders, so it must be all or nothing. Greed, pain, and sorrow must either be eliminated from *all the world*, or else, what was the use of eliminating them from oneself? No use at all! One was just a victim.

And so, although they still *loved* 'Indian thought', and felt very tender about it: well, to go back to our metaphor, the pole up which the green and anxious vines had clambered so far now proved dry-rotten. It snapped, and the vines came slowly subsiding to earth again. There was no crack and crash. The vines held themselves up by their own foliage, for a while. But they subsided. The beanstalk of 'Indian thought' had given way before Jack and Jill had climbed off the tip of it to a further world.

They subsided with a slow rustle back to earth again. But they made no outcry. They were again 'disappointed'. But they never admitted it. 'Indian thought' had let them down. But they never complained. Even to one another, they never said a word. They were disappointed, faintly but deeply disillusioned, and they both knew it. But the knowledge was tacit.

And they still had so much in their lives. They still had

Italy – dear Italy. And they still had freedom, the priceless treasure. And they still had so much 'beauty'. About the fullness of their lives they were not quite so sure. They had one little boy, whom they loved as parents should love their children, but whom they wisely refrained from fastening upon, to build their lives on him. No, no, they must live their own lives! They still had strength of mind to know that.

But they were now no longer very young. Twenty-five and twenty-seven had become thirty-five and thirty-seven. And though they had had a very wonderful time in Europe, and though they still loved Italy – dear Italy! – yet: they were disappointed. They had got a lot out of it: oh, a very great deal indeed! Still, it hadn't given them quite, not *quite*, what they had expected. Europe was lovely, but it was dead. Living in Europe, you were living on the past. And Europeans, with all their superficial charm, were not *really* charming. They were materialistic, they had no *real* soul. They just did not understand the inner urge of the spirit, because the inner urge was dead in them, they were all survivals. There, that was the truth about Europeans: they were survivals, with no more getting ahead in them.

It was another bean-pole, another vine-support crumbled under the green life of the vine. And very bitter it was, this time. For up the old tree-trunk of Europe the green vine had been clambering silently for more than ten years, ten hugely important years, the years of real living. The two idealists had *lived* in Europe, lived on Europe and on European life and European things as vines in an everlasting vineyard.

They had made their home here: a home such as you could never make in America. Their watchword had been 'beauty'. They had rented, the last four years, the second floor of an old palazzo on the Arno, and here they had all their 'things'. And they derived a profound, profound satisfaction from their apartment: the lofty, silent, ancient rooms with windows on the river, with glistening, dark-red floors, and the beautiful furniture that the idealists had 'picked up'.

Yes, unknown to themselves, the lives of the idealists had been running with a fierce swiftness horizontally, all the time. They had become tense, fierce hunters of 'things' for their home. While their souls were climbing up to the sun of old European culture or old Indian thought, their passions were running horizontally, clutching at 'things'. Of course they did not buy the things for the things' sakes, but for the sake of 'beauty'. They looked upon their home as a place entirely furnished by loveliness, not by 'things' at all. Valerie had some very lovely curtains at the windows of the long *salotto*, looking on the river: curtains of queer ancient material that looked like finely-knitted silk, most beautifully faded down from vermilion and orange and gold and black, down to a sheer soft glow. Valerie hardly ever came into the *salotto* without mentally falling on her knees before the curtains. 'Chartres!' she said. 'To me they are Chartres!' And Melville never turned and looked at his sixteenth-century Venetian bookcase, with its two or three dozen of choice books, without feeling his marrow stir in his bones. The holy of holies!

The child silently, almost sinisterly, avoided any rude contact with these ancient monuments of furniture, as if they had been nests of sleeping cobras, or that 'thing' most perilous to the touch, the Ark of the Covenant. His childish awe was silent and cold, but final.

Still, a couple of New England idealists cannot live merely on the bygone glory of their furniture. At least, one couple could not. They got used to the marvellous Bologna cupboard, they got used to the wonderful Venetian bookcase, and the books, and the Siena curtains and bronzes, and the lovely sofas and side-tables and chairs they had 'picked up' in Paris. Oh, they had been picking things up since the first day they landed in Europe. And they were still at it. It is the last interest Europe can offer to an outsider: or to an insider either.

When people came, and were thrilled by the Melville interior, then Valerie and Erasmus felt they had not lived in vain: that they still were living. But in the long mornings, when Erasmus was desultorily working at Renaissance Florentine literature, and Valerie was attending to the apartment: and in the long hours after lunch; and in the long, usually very cold and oppressive evenings in the ancient palazzo: then the halo died from around the furniture, and the things became things, lumps of matter that just stood there or hung there, *ad infinitum*, and said nothing; and Valerie and Erasmus almost hated them. The glow of beauty, like every other glow, dies down unless it is fed. The idealists still dearly loved their things. But they had got them. And the sad fact is, things that glow vividly while you're getting them, go almost quite cold after a year or two. Unless, of course, people envy them very much, and the museums are pining for them. And the Melvilles' 'things', though very good, were not quite so good as that.

So, the glow gradually went out of everything, out of Europe, out of Italy – 'the Italians are *dears*' – even out of that marvellous apartment on the Arno. 'Why, if I had this apartment, I'd never, never even want to go out of doors! It's too lovely and perfect.' That was something, of course – to hear that.

And yet Valerie and Erasmus went out of doors: they even went out to get away from its ancient, cold-floored, stone-heavy silence and dead dignity. 'We're living on the past, you know, Dick,' said Valerie to her husband. She called him Dick.

They were grimly hanging on. They did not like to give in. They did not like to own up that they were through. For twelve years, now, they had been 'free' people living a 'full and beautiful life'. And America for twelve years had been their anathema, the Sodom and Gomorrah of industrial materialism.

It wasn't easy to own that you were 'through'. They hated to admit that they wanted to go back. But at last, reluctantly, they decided to go, 'for the boy's sake' – 'We can't *bear* to leave Europe. But Peter is an American, so he had better look at America while he's young.' The Melvilles had an entirely English accent and manner; almost; a little Italian and French here and there.

They left Europe behind, but they took as much of it along with them as possible. Several van-loads, as a matter of fact. All those adorable and irreplaceable 'things'. And all arrived in New York, idealists, child, and the huge bulk of Europe they had lugged along.

Valerie had dreamed of a pleasant apartment, perhaps on Riverside Drive, where it was not so expensive as east of Fifth Avenue, and where all their wonderful things would look marvellous. She and Erasmus house-hunted. But alas! their income was quite under three thousand dollars a year. They found – well, everybody knows what they found. Two small rooms and a kitchenette, and don't let us unpack a *thing*!

The chunk of Europe which they had bitten off went into a warehouse, at fifty dollars a month. And they sat in two small rooms and a kitchenette, and wondered why they'd done it.

Erasmus, of course, ought to get a job. This was what was written on the wall, and what they both pretended not to see. But it had been the strange, vague threat that the Statue of Liberty had always held over them: 'Thou shalt get a job!' Erasmus had the tickets, as they say. A scholastic career was still possible for him. He had taken his exams brilliantly at Yale, and had kept up his 'researches' all the time he had been in Europe.

But both he and Valerie shuddered. A scholastic career! The scholastic world! The *American* scholastic world! Shudder upon shudder! Give up their freedom, their full and beautiful life? Never! Never! Erasmus would be forty next birthday.

The 'things' remained in warehouse. Valerie went to look at them. It cost her a dollar an hour, and horrid pangs. The 'things', poor things, looked a bit shabby and wretched, in that warehouse.

However, New York was not all America. There was the great clean West. So the Melvilles went West, with Peter, but without the things. They tried living the simple life, in the mountains. But doing their own chores became almost a nightmare. 'Things' are all very well to look at, but it's awful handling them, even when they're beautiful. To be the slave of hideous things, to keep a stove going, cook meals, wash dishes, carry water and clean floors: pure horror of sordid anti-life!

In the cabin on the mountains, Valerie dreamed of Florence, the lost apartment; and her Bologna cupboard and Louis Quinze chairs, above all, her 'Chartres' curtains, stood in New York and costing fifty dollars a month.

A millionaire friend came to the rescue, offering them a cottage on the Californian coast – California! Where the new soul is to be born in man. With joy the idealists moved a little farther west, catching at new vine-props of hope.

And finding them straws! The millionaire cottage was

perfectly equipped. It was perhaps as labour-savingly perfect as is possible: electric heating and cooking, a white-and-pearl-enamelled kitchen, nothing to make dirt except the human being himself. In an hour or so the idealists had got through their chores. They were 'free' – free to hear the great Pacific pounding the coast, and to feel a new soul filling their bodies.

Alas! the Pacific pounded the coast with hideous brutality, brute force itself! And the new soul, instead of sweetly stealing into their bodies, seemed only meanly to gnaw the old soul out of their bodies. To feel you are under the fist of the most blind and crunching brute force: to feel that your cherished idealist's soul is being gnawed out of you, and only irritation left in place of it: well, it isn't good enough.

After about nine months, the idealists departed from the Californian west. It had been a great experience, they were glad to have had it. But, in the long run, the West was not the place for them, and they knew it. No, the people who wanted new souls had better get them. They, Valerie and Erasmus Melville, would like to develop the old soul a little further. Anyway, they had not felt any influx of new soul on the Californian coast. On the contrary.

So, with a slight hole in their material capital, they returned to Massachusetts and paid a visit to Valerie's parents, taking the boy along. The grandparents welcomed the child – poor expatriated boy – and were rather cold to Valerie, but really cold to Erasmus. Valerie's mother definitely said to Valerie, one day, that Erasmus ought to take a job, so that Valerie could live decently. Valerie haughtily reminded her mother of the beautiful apartment on the Arno, and the 'wonderful' things in store in New York, and of the 'marvellous and satisfying life' she and Erasmus had led. Valerie's mother said that she didn't think her daughter's life looked so very marvellous at present: homeless, with a husband idle at the age of forty, a child to educate, and a dwindling capital: looked the reverse of marvellous to *her*. Let Erasmus take some post in one of the universities.

'What post? What university?' interrupted Valerie.

'That could be found, considering your father's connections and Erasmus's qualifications,' replied Valerie's mother. 'And you could get all your valuable things out of store, and have a really lovely home, which everybody in America would be proud to visit. As it is, your furniture is eating up your income, and you are living like rats in a hole, with nowhere to go to.'

This was very true. Valerie was beginning to pine for a home, with her 'things'. Of course she could have sold her furniture for a substantial sum. But nothing would have induced her to. Whatever else passed away, religions, cultures, continents, and hopes, Valerie would *never* part from the 'things' which she and Erasmus had collected with such passion. To these she was nailed.

But she and Erasmus still would not give up that freedom, that full and beautiful life they had so believed in. Erasmus cursed America. He did not *want* to earn a living. He panted for Europe.

Leaving the boy in charge of Valerie's parents, the two idealists once more set off for Europe. In New York they paid two dollars and looked for a brief, bitter hour at their 'things'. They sailed 'student class' – that is, third. Their income now was less than two thousand dollars, instead of three. And they made straight for Paris – cheap Paris.

They found Europe, this time, a complete failure. 'We have returned like dogs to our vomit,' said Erasmus; 'but the vomit has staled in the meantime.' He found he couldn't stand Europe. It irritated every nerve in his body. He hated America too. But America at least was a darn sight better than this miserable, dirt-eating continent; which was by no means cheap any more, either.

Valerie, with her heart on her things – she had really burned to get them out of that warehouse, where they had stood now for three years, eating up two thousand dollars – wrote to her mother she thought Erasmus would come back if he could get some suitable work in America. Erasmus, in a state of frustration bordering on rage and insanity, just went round Italy in a poverty-stricken fashion, his coat-cuffs frayed, hating everything with intensity. And when a post was found for him in Cleveland University, to teach French, Italian and Spanish literature, his eyes grew more beady, and his long, queer face grew sharper and more rat-like, with utter baffled fury. He was forty, and the job was upon him.

'I think you'd better accept, dear. You don't care for Europe any longer. As you say, it's dead and finished. They offer us a house on the college lot, and mother says there's room in it for all our things. I think we'd better cable "Accept".'

He glowered at her like a cornered rat. One almost expected to see rat's whiskers twitching at the sides of the sharp nose.

'Shall I send the cablegram?' she asked.

'Send it!' he blurted.

And she went out and sent it.

He was a changed man, quieter, much less irritable. A load was off him. He was inside the cage.

But when he looked at the furnaces of Cleveland, vast and like the greatest of black forests, with red and white-hot cascades of gushing metal, and tiny gnomes of men, and terrific noises, gigantic, he said to Valerie:

'Say what you like, Valerie, this is the biggest thing the modern world has to show.'

And when they were in their up-to-date little house on the college lot of Cleveland University, and that woebegone débris of Europe; Bologna cupboard, Venice bookshelves, Ravenna bishop's chair, Louis Quinze side-tables, 'Chartres' curtains, Siena bronze lamps, all were arrayed, and all looked perfectly out of keeping, and therefore very impressive; and when the idealists had had a bunch of gaping people in, and Erasmus had showed off in his best European manner, but still quite cordial and American; and Valerie had been most ladylike, but for all that, 'we prefer America'; then Erasmus said, looking at her with queer, sharp eyes of a rat:

'Europe's the mayonnaise all right, but America supplies the good old lobster – what?'

'Every time!' she said, with satisfaction.

And he peered at her. He was in the cage: but it was safe inside. And she, evidently, was her real self at last. She had got the goods. Yet round his nose was a queer, evil scholastic look, of pure scepticism. But he liked lobster.

Mother and Daughter

VIRGINIA BODOIN had a good job: she was head of a
department in a certain government office, held a responsible position, and earned, to imitate Balzac and be precise
about it, seven hundred and fifty pounds a year. That is
already something. Rachel Bodoin, her mother, had an
income of about six hundred a year, on which she had
lived in the capitals of Europe since the effacement of a
never very important husband.

Now, after some years of virtual separation and 'freedom', mother and daughter once more thought of settling
down. They had become, in course of time, more like a
married couple than mother and daughter. They knew one
another very well indeed, and each was a little 'nervous' of
the other. They had lived together and parted several
times. Virginia was now thirty, and she didn't look like
marrying. For four years she had been as good as married
to Henry Lubbock, a rather spoilt young man who was
musical. Then Henry let her down: for two reasons. He
couldn't stand her mother. Her mother couldn't stand him.
And anybody whom Mrs Bodoin could not stand she
managed to sit on, disastrously. So Henry had writhed
horribly, feeling his mother-in-law sitting on him tight,
and Virginia after all, in a helpless sort of family loyalty,
sitting alongside her mother. Virginia didn't really want to
sit on Henry. But when her mother egged her on, she
couldn't help it. For ultimately her mother had power over
her; a strange *female* power, nothing to do with parental
authority. Virginia had long thrown parental authority to
the winds. But her mother had another, much subtler form
of domination, female and thrilling, so that when Rachel

said: 'Let's squash him!' Virginia had to rush wickedly and gleefully to the sport. And Henry knew quite well when he was being squashed. So that was one of his reasons for going back on Vinny. He called her Vinny, to the superlative disgust of Mrs Bodoin, who always corrected him: 'My daughter *Virginia* –'

The second reason was, again to be Balzacian, that Virginia hadn't a sou of her own. Henry had a sorry two hundred and fifty. Virginia, at the age of twenty-four, was already earning four hundred and fifty. But she was earning them. Whereas Henry managed to earn about twelve pounds per annum, by his precious music. He had realized that he would find it hard to earn more. So that marrying, except with a wife who could keep him, was rather out of the question. Vinny would inherit her mother's money. But then Mrs Bodoin had the health and muscular equipment of the Sphinx. She would live for ever, seeking whom she might devour, and devouring him. Henry lived with Vinny for two years, in the married sense of the words: and Vinny felt they *were* married, minus a mere ceremony. But Vinny had her mother always in the background; often as far back as Paris or Biarritz, but still, within letter reach. And she never realized the funny little grin that came on her own elvish face when her mother, even in a letter, spread her skirts and calmly sat on Henry. She never realized that in spirit she promptly and mischievously sat on him too: she could no more have helped it than the tide can help turning to the moon. And she did not dream that he felt it, and was utterly mortified in his masculine vanity. Women, very often, hypnotize one another, and then, hypnotized, they proceed gently to wring the neck of the man they think they are loving with all their hearts. Then they call it utter perversity on his part, that he doesn't like having his neck wrung. They think he is repudiating a heart-felt love. For hey are hypnotized. Women hypnotize one another, without knowing it.

In the end, Henry backed out. He saw himself being simply reduced to nothingness by two women, an old witch with muscles like the Sphinx, and a young, spell-bound witch, lavish, elvish and weak, who utterly spoilt him but who ate his marrow.

Rachel would write from Paris: 'My Dear Virginia, as I had a windfall in the way of an investment, I am sharing it with you. You will find enclosed my cheque for twenty pounds. No doubt you will be needing it to buy Henry a suit of clothes, since the spring is apparently come, and the sunlight may be tempted to show him up for what he is worth. I don't want my daughter going around with what is presumably a street-corner musician, but please pay the tailor's bill yourself, or you may have to do it over again later.' Henry got a suit of clothes, but it was as good as a shirt of Nessus, eating him away with subtle poison.

So he backed out. He didn't jump out, or bolt, or carve his way out at the sword's point. He sort of faded out, distributing his departure over a year or more. He was fond of Vinny, and he could hardly do without her, and he was sorry for her. But at length he couldn't see her apart from her mother. She was a young, weak, spendthrift witch, accomplice of her tough-clawed witch of a mother.

Henry made other alliances, got a good hold on else-where, and gradually extricated himself. He saved his life, but he had lost, he felt, a good deal of his youth and mar-row. He tended now to go fat, a little puffy, somewhat insignificant. And he had been handsome and striking-looking.

The two witches howled when he was lost to them. Poor Virginia was really half crazy, she didn't know what to do with herself. She had a violent recoil from her mother. Mrs

Bodoin was filled with furious contempt for her daughter
that she should let such a hooked fish slip out of her hands.
That she should allow such a person to turn her down! 'I
don't quite see my daughter seduced and thrown over by
a sponging individual such as Henry Lubbock,' she wrote.
'But if it has happened, I suppose it is somebody's fault –

There was a mutual recoil, which lasted nearly five years.
But the spell was not broken. Mrs Bodoin's mind never
left her daughter, and Virginia was ceaselessly aware of her
mother, somewhere in the universe. They wrote, and met
at intervals, but they kept apart in recoil.

The spell, however, was between them, and gradually it
worked. They felt more friendly. Mrs Bodoin came to
London. She stayed in the same quiet hotel with her
daughter: Virginia had had two rooms in an hotel for the
past three years. And, at last, they thought of taking an
apartment together.

Virginia was now over thirty. She was still thin and odd
and elvish, with a very slight and piquant cast in one of her
brown eyes, and she still had her odd, twisted smile, and her
slow, rather deep-toned voice, that caressed a man like the
stroking of subtle fingertips. Her hair was still a natural
tangle of curls, a bit dishevelled. She still dressed with a
natural elegance which tended to go wrong and a tiny bit
sluttish. She still might have a hole in her expensive and
perfectly new stockings, and still she might have to take off
her shoes in the drawing-room, if she came to tea, and sit
there in her stockinged-feet. True, she had elegant feet:
she was altogether elegantly shaped. But it wasn't that. It
was neither coquetry nor vanity. It was simply that, after
having gone to a good shoemaker and paid five guineas for
a pair of perfectly simple and natural shoes, made to her
feet, the said shoes would hurt her excruciatingly, when
she had walked half a mile in them, and she would simply

have to take them off, even if she sat on the kerb to do it. It was a fatality. There was a touch of the *gamin* in her very feet, a certain sluttishness that wouldn't let them stay properly in nice proper shoes. She practically always wore her mother's old shoes. 'Of course, I go through life in mother's old shoes. If she died and left me without a supply, I suppose I should have to go in a bath-chair,' she would say, with her odd twisted little grin. She was so elegant, and yet a slut. It was her charm, really.

Just the opposite of her mother. They could wear each other's shoes and each other's clothes, which seemed remarkable, for Mrs Bodoin seemed so much the bigger of the two. But Virginia's shoulders were broad; if she was thin, she had a strong frame, even when she looked a frail rag.

Mrs Bodoin was one of those women of sixty or so, with a terrible inward energy and a violent sort of vitality. But she managed to hide it. She sat with a perfect repose, and folded hands. One thought: What a calm woman! Just as one may look at the snowy summit of a quiescent volcano, in the evening light, and think: What peace!

It was a strange *muscular* energy which possessed Mrs Bodoin, as it possesses, curiously enough, many women over fifty, and is usually distasteful in its manifestations. Perhaps it accounts for the lassitude of the young.

But Mrs Bodoin recognized the bad taste in her energetic coevals, so she cultivated repose. Her very way of pronouncing the word, in two syllables: re-pòse, making the second syllable run on into the twilight, showed how much suppressed energy she had. Faced with the problem of iron-grey hair and black eyebrows, she was too clever to try dyeing herself back into youth. She studied her face, her whole figure, and decided that it was *positive*. There was no denying it. There was no wispiness, no hollowness, no limp frail blossom-on-a-bending-stalk about her. Her figure though not stout, was full, strong, and *cambré*. Her face had an aristocratic arched nose, aristocratic, who-the-devil-are-you grey eyes, and cheeks rather long but also rather full. Nothing appealing or youthfully skittish here.

Like an independent woman, she used her wits, and decided most emphatically not to be either youthful or skittish or appealing. She would keep her dignity, for she was fond of it. She was positive. She liked to be positive. She was used to her positivity. So she would just *be* positive.

She turned to the positive period; to the eighteenth century, to Voltaire, to Ninon de l'Enclos and the Pompadour, to Madame la Duchesse and Monsieur le Marquis. She decided that she was not much in the line of la Pompadour or la Duchesse, but almost exactly in the line of Monsieur le Marquis. And she was right. With hair silvering to white, brushed back clean from her positive brow and temples, cut short, but sticking out a little behind, with her rather full, pink face and thin black eyebrows plucked to two fine, superficial crescents, her arching nose and her rather full insolent eyes she was perfectly eighteenth century, the early half. That she was Monsieur le Marquis rather than Madame la Marquise made her really modern.

Her appearance was perfect. She wore delicate combinations of grey and pink, maybe with a darkening iron-grey touch, and her jewels were of soft old coloured paste. Her bearing was a sort of alert repose, very calm, but very assured. There was, to use a vulgarism, no getting past her.

She had a couple of thousand pounds she could lay hands on. Virginia, of course, was always in debt. But, after all, Virginia was not to be sniffed at. She made seven hundred and fifty a year.

Virginia was oddly clever, and not clever. She didn't *really* know anything, because anything and everything was interesting to her for the moment, and she picked it up at once. She picked up languages with extraordinary ease, she was fluent in a fortnight. This helped her enormously with her job. She could prattle away with heads of industry, let them come from where they liked. But she didn't *know* any language, nor even her own. She picked things up in her sleep, so to speak, without knowing anything about them.

And this made her popular with men. With all her curious facility, they didn't feel small in front of her, because she was like an instrument. She had to be prompted. Some man had to set her in motion, and then she worked, really cleverly. She could collect the most valuable information. She was very useful. She worked with men, spent most of her time with men, her friends were practically all men. She didn't feel easy with women.

Yet she had no lover, nobody seemed eager to marry her, nobody seemed eager to come close to her at all. Mrs Bodoin said: 'I'm afraid Virginia is a one-man woman. I am a one-man woman. So was my mother, and so was my grandmother. Virginia's father was the only man in my life, the only one. And I'm afraid Virginia is the same, tenacious. Unfortunately, the man was what he was, and her life is just left there.'

Henry had said, in the past, that Mrs Bodoin wasn't a one-man woman, she was a no-man woman, and that if she could have had her way, everything male would have been wiped off the face of the earth, and only the female element left.

However, Mrs Bodoin thought that it was now time to make a move. So she and Virginia took a quite handsome apartment in one of the old Bloomsbury squares, fitted it up and furnished it with extreme care, and with some quite lovely things, got in a very good man, an Austrian, to cook, and they set up married life together, mother and daughter.

At first it was rather thrilling. The two reception-rooms looking down on the dirty old trees of the Square gardens were of splendid proportions, and each with three great windows coming down low, almost to the level of the knees. The chimney-piece was late eighteenth-century. Mrs Bodoin furnished the rooms with a gentle suggestion of Louis Seize merged with Empire, without keeping to any particular style. But she had, saved from her own home, a really remarkable Aubusson carpet. It looked almost new, as if it had been woven two years ago, and was startling, yet somehow rather splendid, as it spread its rose-red borders and wonderful florid array of silver-grey and gold, grey roses, lilies and gorgeous swans and trumpeting volutes away over the floor. Very aesthetic people found it rather loud, they preferred the worn, dim yellowish Aubusson in the big bedroom. But Mrs Bodoin loved her drawing-room carpet. It was positive, but it was not vulgar. It had a certain grand air in its floridity. She felt it gave her a proper footing. And it behaved very well with her painted cabinets and grey-and-gold brocade chairs and big Chinese vases, which she liked to fill with big flowers, single Chinese peonies, big roses, great tulips, orange lilies. The dim room of London, with all its atmospheric colour, would stand the big, free, fisticuffing flowers.

Virginia, for the first time in her life, had the pleasure of making a home. She was again entirely under her mother's spell, and swept away, thrilled to her marrow. She had had no idea that her mother had got such treasures as the carpet and painted cabinets and brocade chairs up her sleeve; many of them the débris of the Fitzpatrick home in Ireland, Mrs Bodoin being a Fitzpatrick. Almost like a child, like a bride, Virginia threw herself into the business of fixing up the rooms. 'Of course, Virginia, I consider this is *your* apartment,' said Mrs Bodoin. 'I am nothing but your *dame de compagnie*, and shall carry out your wishes entirely, if you will only express them.'

Of course Virginia expressed a few, but not many. She introduced some wild pictures bought from impecunious artists whom she patronized. Mrs Bodoin thought the pictures positive about the wrong things, but as far as possible, she let them stay: looking on them as the necessary element of modern ugliness. But by that element of modern ugliness, wilfully so, it was easy to see the things that Virginia had introduced into the apartment.

Perhaps nothing goes to the head like setting up house. You can get drunk on it. You feel you are creating something. Nowadays it is no longer the 'home', the domestic nest. It is 'my rooms', or 'my house', the great garment which reveals and clothes 'my personality'. Mrs Bodoin, deliberately scheming for Virginia, kept moderately cool over it, but even she was thrilled to the marrow, and of an intensity and ferocity with the décorators and furnishers, astonishing. But Virginia was just all the time tipsy with it, as if she had touched some magic button on the grey wall of life, and with an Open Sesame! her lovely and coloured rooms had begun to assemble out of fairyland. It was far more vivid and wonderful to her than if she had inherited a duchy.

The mother and daughter, the mother in a sort of faded russet crimson and the daughter in silver, began to entertain. They had, of course, mostly men. It filled Mrs Bodoin with a sort of savage impatience to entertain women. Besides, most of Virginia's acquaintances were men. So there were dinners and well-arranged evenings.

It went well, but something was missing. Mrs Bodoin wanted to be gracious, so she held herself rather back. She stayed a little distant, was calm, reposed, eighteenth-century, and determined to be a foil to the clever and slightly-elvish Virginia. It was a pose, and alas, it stopped something. She was very nice with the men, no matter what her contempt of them. But the men were uneasy with her: afraid.

What they all felt, all the men guests, was that *for them*, nothing really happened. Everything that happened was between mother and daughter. All the flow was between mother and daughter. A subtle, hypnotic spell encompassed the two women, and, try as they might, the men were shut out. More than one young man, a little dazzled, *began* to fall in love with Virginia. But it was impossible. Not only was he shut out, he was, in some way, annihilated. The spontaneity was killed in his bosom. While the two women sat, brilliant and rather wonderful, in magnetic connection at opposite ends of the table, like two witches, a double Circe turning the men not into swine – the men would have liked that well enough – but into lumps.

It was tragic. Because Mrs Bodoin wanted Virginia to fall in love and marry. She really wanted it, and she attributed Virginia's lack of forthcoming to the delinquent Henry. She never realized the hypnotic spell, which of course encompassed her as well as Virginia, and made men just an impossibility to both women, mother and daughter alike.

At this time, Mrs Bodoin hid her humour. She had a really marvellous faculty of humorous imitation. She could imitate the Irish servants from her old home, or the American women who called on her, or the modern lady-like young men, the asphodels, as she called them: 'Of course, you know the asphodel is a kind of onion! Oh yes, just an over-bred onion': who wanted, with their murmuring voices and peeping under their brows, to make her feel very small and very bourgeois. She could imitate them all with a humour that was really touched with genius. But it was devastating. It demolished the objects of her humour so absolutely, smashed them to bits with a ruthless hammer, pounded them to nothing so terribly, that it frightened people, particularly men. It frightened men off.

So she hid it. She hid it. But there it was, up her sleeve, her merciless, hammer-like humour, which just smashed its object on the head and left him brained. She tried to disown it. She tried to pretend, even to Virginia, that she had the gift no more. But in vain; the hammer hidden up her sleeve hovered over the head of every guest, and every guest felt his scalp creep, and Virginia felt her inside creep with a little, mischievous, slightly idiotic grin, as still another fool male was mystically knocked on the head. It was a sort of uncanny sport.

No, the plan was not going to work: the plan of having Virginia fall in love and marry. Of course the men *were* such lumps, such *œufs farcis*. There was one, at least, that Mrs Bodoin had real hopes of. He was a healthy and normal and very good-looking boy of good family, with no money, alas, but clerking to the House of Lords and very hopeful, and not very clever, but simply in love with Virginia's cleverness. He was just the one Mrs Bodoin would have married for herself. True, he was only twenty-six, to Virginia's thirty-one. But he had rowed in the Oxford eight, and adored horses, talked horses adorably, and was simply infatuated by Virginia's cleverness. To him Virginia had the finest mind on earth. She was as wonderful as Plato, but infinitely more attractive, because she was a woman, and winsome with it. Imagine a winsome Plato with untidy curls and the tiniest little brown-eyed squint and just a hint of woman's pathetic need for a protector, and you may imagine Adrian's feeling for Virginia. He adored her on his knees, but he felt he could protect her.

'Of course, he's just a very nice *boy*!' said Mrs Bodoin. 'He's a boy, and that's all you can say. And he always will be a boy. But that's the very nicest kind of man, the only kind you can live with: the eternal boy. Virginia, aren't you attracted to him?'

'Yes, mother! I think he's an awfully nice *boy*, as you say,' replied Virginia, in her rather low, musical, whimsical voice. But the mocking little curl in the intonation put the lid on Adrian. Virginia was not marrying a nice *boy*! She could be malicious too, against her mother's taste. And Mrs Bodoin let escape her a faint gesture of impatience.

For she had been planning her own retreat, planning to give Virginia the apartment outright, and half of her own income, if she would marry Adrian. Yes, the mother was already scheming how best she could live with dignity on three hundred a year, once Virginia was happily married to that most attractive if slightly brainless *boy*.

A year later, when Virginia was thirty-two, Adrian, who had married a wealthy American girl and been transferred to a job in the legation at Washington in the meantime, faithfully came to see Virginia as soon as he was in London, faithfully kneeled at her feet, faithfully thought her the most wonderful spiritual being, and faithfully felt that she, Virginia, could have done wonders with him, which wonders would now never be done, for he had married in the meantime.

Virginia was looking haggard and worn. The scheme of a *ménage à deux* with her mother had not succeeded. And now, work was telling on the younger woman. It is true, she was amazingly facile. But facility wouldn't get her all the way. She had to earn her money, and earn it hard. She had to slog, and she had to concentrate. While she could work by quick intuition and without much responsibility, work thrilled her. But as soon as she had to get down to it, as they say, grip and slog and concentrate, in a really responsible position, it wore her out terribly. She had to do it all off her nerves. She hadn't the same sort of fighting power as a man. Where a man can summon his old Adam in him to fight through his work, a woman has to draw on her nerves, and on her nerves alone. For the old Eve in her will have nothing to do with such work. So that mental responsibility, mental concentration, mental slogging wear out a woman terribly, especially if she is head of a department, and not working *for* somebody.

So poor Virginia was worn out. She was thin as a rail. Her nerves were frayed to bits. And she could never forget her beastly work. She would come home at tea-time speechless and done for. Her mother, tortured by the sight of her, longed to say: 'Has anything gone wrong, Virginia? Have you had anything particularly trying at the office today?' But she learned to hold her tongue, and say nothing. The question would be the last straw to Virginia's poor overwrought nerves, and there would be a little scene which, despite Mrs Bodoin's calm and forbearance, offended the elder woman to the quick. She had learned, by bitter experience, to leave her child alone, as one would leave a frail tube of vitriol alone. But, of course, she could not keep her *mind* off Virginia. That was impossible. And poor Virginia, under the strain of work and the strain of her mother's awful ceaseless mind, was at the very end of her strength and resources.

Mrs Bodoin had always disliked the fact of Virginia's doing a job. But now she hated it. She hated the whole government office with violent and virulent hate. Not only was it undignified for Virginia to be tied up there, but it was turning her, Mrs Bodoin's daughter, into a thin, nagging, fearsome old maid. Could anything be more utterly English and humiliating to a well-born Irishwoman?

After a long day attending to the apartment, skilfully darning one of the brocade chairs, polishing the Venetian mirrors to her satisfaction, selecting flowers, doing certain shopping and housekeeping, attending perfectly to everything, then receiving callers in the afternoon, with never-ending energy, Mrs Bodoin would go up from the drawing-room after tea and write a few letters, take her bath, dress with great care – she enjoyed attending to her person – and come down to dinner as fresh as a daisy, but far more energetic than that quiet flower. She was ready now for a full evening.

She was conscious, with gnawing anxiety, of Virginia's presence in the house, but she did not see her daughter till dinner was announced. Virginia slipped in, and away to her room unseen, never going into the drawing-room to tea. If Mrs Bodoin heard her daughter's key in the latch, she quickly retired into one of the rooms till Virginia was safely through. It was too much for poor Virginia's nerves even to catch sight of anybody in the house, when she came in from the office. Bad enough to hear the murmur of visitors' voices behind the drawing-room door.

And Mrs Bodoin would wonder: How is she? How is she tonight? I wonder what sort of a day she's had? And this thought would roam prowling through the house, to where Virginia was lying on her back in her room. But the mother would have to consume her anxiety till dinner-time. And then Virginia would appear, with black lines under her eyes, thin, tense, a young woman out of an office, the stigma upon her: badly dressed, a little acid in humour, with an impaired digestion, not interested in anything, blighted by her work. And Mrs Bodoin, humiliated at the very sight of her, would control herself perfectly, say nothing but the mere smooth nothings of casual speech, and sit in perfect form presiding at a carefully-

cooked dinner thought out entirely to please Virginia.
Then Virginia hardly noticed what she ate.

Mrs Bodoin was pining for an evening with life in it.
But Virginia would lie on the couch and put on the loud-
speaker. Or she would put a humorous record on the
gramophone, and be amused, and hear it again, and be
amused, and hear it again, six times, and six times be amused
by a mildly funny record that Mrs Bodoin now knew off by
heart. 'Why, Virginia, I could repeat that record over to
you, if you wished it, without your troubling to wind up
that gramophone.' And Virginia, after a pause in which she
seemed not to have heard what her mother said, would
reply: 'I'm sure you could, mother.' And that simple
speech would convey such volumes of contempt for all
that Rachel Bodoin was or ever could be or ever had been,
contempt for her energy, her vitality, her mind, her body,
her very existence, that the elder woman would curl. It
seemed as if the ghost of Robert Bodoin spoke out of the
mouth of the daughter, in deadly venom. Then Virginia
would put on the record for the seventh time.

During the second ghastly year, Mrs Bodoin realized
that the game was up. She was a beaten woman, a woman
without object or meaning any more. The hammer of her
awful female humour, which had knocked so many people
on the head, all the people, in fact, that she had come into
contact with, had at last flown backwards and hit herself
on the head. For her daughter was her other self, her *alter
ego*. The secret and the meaning and the power of Mrs
Bodoin's whole life lay in the hammer, that hammer of her
living humour which knocked everything on the head.
That had been her lust and her passion, knocking everybody and everything humorously on the head. She had felt
inspired in it: it was a sort of mission. And she had hoped
to hand on the hammer to Virginia, her clever, unsolid but

still actual daughter, Virginia. Virginia was the continuation of Rachel's own self. Virginia was Rachel's *alter ego*, her other self.

But, alas, it was a half-truth. Virginia had had a father. This fact, which had been utterly ignored by the mother, was gradually brought home to her by the curious recoil of the hammer. Virginia was her father's daughter. Could anything be more unseemly, horrid, more perverse in the natural scheme of things? For Robert Bodoin had been fully and deservedly knocked on the head by Rachel's hammer. Could anything, then, be more disgusting than that he should resurrect again in the person of Mrs Bodoin's own daughter, her own *alter ego* Virginia, and start hitting back with a little spiteful hammer that was David's pebble against Goliath's battle-axe!

But the little pebble was mortal. Mrs Bodoin felt it sink into her brow, her temple, and she was finished. The hammer fell nerveless from her hand.

The two women were now mostly alone. Virginia was too tired to have company in the evening. So there was the gramophone or loud-speaker, or else silence. Both women had come to loathe the apartment. Virginia felt it was the last grand act of bullying on her mother's part, she felt bullied by the assertive Aubusson carpet, by the beastly Venetian mirrors, by the big over cultured flowers. She even felt bullied by the excellent food, and longed again for a Soho restaurant and her two poky shabby rooms in the hotel. She loathed the apartment: she loathed everything. But she had not the energy to move. She had not the energy to do anything. She crawled to her work, and for the rest, she lay flat, gone.

It was Virginia's worn-out inertia that really finished Mrs Bodoin. That was the pebble that broke the bone of her temple: 'To have to attend my daughter's funeral, and accept the sympathy of all her fellow-clerks in her office, no, that is a final humiliation which I must spare myself. No! If Virginia must be a lady-clerk, she must be it henceforth on her own responsibility. I will retire from her existence.'

Mrs Bodoin had tried hard to persuade Virginia to give up her work and come and live with her. She had offered her half her income. In vain. Virginia stuck to her office.

Very well! So be it! The apartment was a fiasco, Mrs Bodoin was longing, longing to tear it to pieces again. One last and final blow of the hammer! 'Virginia, don't you think we'd better get rid of this apartment, and live around as we used to do? Don't you think we'll do that?' – 'But all the money you've put into it? and the lease for ten years!' cried Virginia, in a kind of inertia. 'Never mind! We had the pleasure of making it. And we've had as much pleasure out of living in it as we shall ever have. Now we'd better get rid of it – quickly – don't you think?'

Mrs Bodoin's arms were twitching to snatch the pictures off the walls, roll up the Aubusson carpet, take the china out of the ivory-inlaid cabinet there and then, at that very moment.

'Let us wait till Sunday before we decide,' said Virginia.

'Till Sunday! Four days! As long as that? Haven't we already decided in our own minds?' said Mrs Bodoin.

'We'll wait till Sunday, anyhow,' said Virginia.

The next evening, the Armenian came to dinner. Virginia called him Arnold, with the French pronunciation, Arnault. Mrs Bodoin, who barely tolerated him, and could never get his name which seemed to have a lot of bouyoums in it, called him either the Armenian or the Rahat Lakoum, after the name of the sweetmeat, or simply The Turkish Delight.

'Arnault is coming to dinner to-night, mother.'

'Really! The Turkish Delight is coming here to dinner? Shall I provide anything special?' Her voice sounded as if she would suggest snails in aspic.

'I don't think so.'

Virginia had seen a good deal of the Armenian at the office, when she had to negotiate with him on behalf of the Board of Trade. He was a man of about sixty, a merchant, had been a millionaire, was ruined during the war, but was now coming on again, and represented trade in Bulgaria. He wanted to negotiate with the British Government, and the British Government sensibly negotiated with him: at first through the medium of Virginia. Now things were going satisfactorily between Monsieur Arnault, as Virginia called him, and the Board of Trade, so that a sort of friendship had followed the official relations.

The Turkish Delight was sixty, grey-haired and fat. He had numerous grandchildren growing up in Bulgaria, but he was a widower. He had a grey moustache cut like a brush, and glazed brown eyes over which hung heavy lids with white lashes. His manner was humble, but in his bearing there was a certain dogged conceit. One notices the combination sometimes in Jews. He had been very wealthy and kow-towed to, he had been ruined and humiliated, terribly humiliated, and now, doggedly, he was rising up again, his sons backing him, away in Bulgaria. One felt he was not alone. He had his sons, his family, his tribe behind him, away in the Near East.

He spoke bad English, but fairly fluent guttural French. He did not speak much, but he sat. He sat, with his short, fat thighs, as if for eternity, *there*. There was a strange potency in his fat immobile sitting, as if his posterior were connected with the very centre of the earth. And his brain, spinning away at the one point in question, business, was very agile. Business absorbed him. But not in a nervous, personal way. Somehow the family, the tribe was always felt behind him. It was business for the family, the tribe.

With the English he was humble, for the English like such aliens to be humble, and he had had a long schooling from the Turks. And he was always an outsider. Nobody would ever take any notice of him in society. He would just be an outsider, *sitting*.

'I hope, Virginia, you won't ask that Turkish-carpet gentleman when we have other people. I can bear it,' said Mrs Bodoin. 'Some people might mind.'

'Isn't it hard when you can't choose your own company in your own house,' mocked Virginia.

'No! *I* don't care. I can meet anything; and I'm sure, in the way of selling Turkish carpets, your acquaintance is very good. But I don't suppose you look on him as a personal friend –?'

'I do. I like him quite a lot.'

'Well –! As you will. But consider your *other* friends.'

Mrs Bodoin was really mortified this time. She looked on the Armenian as one looks on the fat Levantine in a fez who tries to sell one hideous tapestries at Port Said, or on the sea-front at Nice, as being outside the class of human beings, and in the class of insects. That he had been a millionaire, and might be a millionaire again, only added venom to her feeling of disgust at being forced into contact with such scum. She could not even squash him, or annihilate him. In scum, there is nothing to squash, for scum is only the unpleasant residue of that which was never anything but squashed.

However, she was not quite just. True, he was fat, and he sat, with short thighs, like a toad, as if seated for a toad's eternity. His colour was of a dirty sort of paste, his black eyes were glazed under heavy lids. And he never spoke until spoken to, waiting in his toad's silence, like a slave.

But his thick, fine white hair, which stood up on his head like a soft brush, was curiously virile. And his curious small hands, of the same soft dull paste, had a peculiar, fat, soft masculine breeding of their own. And his dull brown eye could glint with the subtlety of serpents, under the white brush of eyelash. He was tired, but he was not defeated. He had fought, and won, and lost, and was fighting again, always at a disadvantage. He belonged to a defeated race which accepts defeat, but which gets its own back by cunning. He was the father of sons, the head of a family, one of the heads of a defeated but indestructible tribe. He was not alone, and so you could not lay your finger on him. His whole consciousness was patriarchal and tribal. And somehow, he was humble, but he was indestructible.

At dinner he sat half-effaced, humble, yet with the conceit of the humble. His manners were perfectly good, rather French. Virginia chattered to him in French, and he replied with that peculiar nonchalance of the boulevards, which was the only manner he could command when speaking French. Mrs Bodoin understood, but she was what one would call a heavy-footed linguist, so when she said anything, it was intensely in English. And the Turkish Delight replied in his clumsy English, hastily. It was not his fault that French was being spoken. It was Virginia's.

He was very humble, conciliatory, with Mrs Bodoin. But he cast at her sometimes that rapid glint of a reptilian glance as if to say: 'Yes! I see you! You are a handsome figure. As an *objet de vertu* you are almost perfect.' Thus his connoisseur's, antique-dealer's eye would appraise her. But then his thick white eyebrows would seem to add: 'But what, under holy Heaven, are you as a woman? You are neither wife nor mother nor mistress, you have no perfume of sex, you are more dreadful than a Turkish soldier or an English official. No man on earth could embrace you. You

are a ghoul, you are a strange genie from the underworld!'
And he would secretly invoke the holy names, to shield him.

Yet he was in love with Virginia. He saw, first and fore-
most, the child in her, as if she were a lost child in the
gutter, a waif with a faint, fascinating cast in her brown
eyes, waiting till someone would pick her up. A fatherless
waif! And he was tribal father, father through all the ages.

Then, on the other hand, he knew her peculiar dis-
interested cleverness in affairs. That, too, fascinated him:
that odd, almost second-sight cleverness about business,
and entirely impersonal, entirely in the air. It seemed to
him very strange. But it would be an immense help to him
in his schemes. He did not really understand the English.
He was at sea with them. But with her, he would have a
clue to everything. For she was, finally, quite a somebody
among these English, these English officials.

He was about sixty. His family was established in the
East, his grandsons were growing up. It was necessary for
him to live in London, for some years. This girl would be
useful. She had no money, save what she would inherit
from her mother. But he would risk that: she would be an
investment in his business. And then the apartment. He
liked the apartment extremely. He recognized the *cachet*,
and the lilies and swans of the Aubusson carpet really did
something to him. Virginia said to him: 'Mother gave me
the apartment.' So he looked on that as safe. And finally,
Virginia was almost a virgin, probably quite a virgin, and,
as far as the paternal oriental male like himself was concerned, entirely virgin. He had a very small idea of the silly
puppy-sexuality of the English, so different from the pro-
longed male voluptuousness of his own pleasures. And
last of all, he was physically lonely, getting old, and tired.

Virginia of course did not know why she liked being
with Arnault. Her cleverness was amazingly stupid when

it came to life, to living. She said he was 'quaint'. She said
his nonchalant French of the boulevards was 'amusing'.
She found his business cunning 'intriguing', and the glint
in his dark glazed eyes, under the white, thick lashes,
'sheiky'. She saw him quite often, had tea with him in his
hotel, and motored with him one day down to the sea.

When he took her hand in his own soft still hands, there
was something so caressing, so possessive in his touch, so
strange and positive in his leaning towards her, that though
she trembled with fear, she was helpless. 'But you are so
thin, dear little thin thing, you need repose, repose, for the
blossom to open, poor little blossom, to become a little
fat!' he said in his French.

She quivered, and was helpless. It certainly was quaint!
He was so strange and positive, he seemed to have all the
power. The moment he realized that she would succumb
into his power, he took full charge of the situation, he lost
all his hesitation and his humility. He did not want just to
make love to her: he wanted to marry her, for all his multi-
farious reasons. And he must make himself master of her.

He put her hand to his lips, and seemed to draw her life
to his in kissing her thin hand. 'The poor child is tired, she
needs repose, she needs to be caressed and cared for,' he
said in his French. And he drew nearer to her.

She looked up in dread at his glinting, tired dark eyes
under the white lashes. But he used all his will, looking
back at her heavily and calculating that she must submit.
And he brought his body quite near to her, and put his hand
softly on her face, and made her lay her face against his
breast, as he soothingly stroked her arm with his other
hand. 'Dear little thing! Dear little thing! Arnault loves
her so dearly! Arnault loves her! Perhaps she will marry her
Arnault. Dear little girl, Arnault will put flowers in her life,
and make her life perfumed with sweetness and content.'

She leaned against his breast and let him caress her. She gave a fleeting, half poignant, half vindictive thought to her mother. Then she felt in the air the sense of destiny, destiny. Oh, so nice, not to have to struggle. To give way to destiny.

'Will she marry her old Arnault? Eh? Will she marry him?' he asked in a soothing, caressing voice, at the same time compulsive.

She lifted her head and looked at him: the thick white brows, the glinting, tired dark eyes. How queer and comic! How comic to be in his power! And he was looking a little baffled.

'Shall I?' she said, with her mischievous twist of a grin.

'Mais oui!' he said, with all the sang-froid of his old eyes. 'Mais oui! Je te contenterai, tu le verras.'

'Tu me contenteras!' she said, with a flickering smile of real amusement at his assurance. 'Will you really content me?'

'But surely! I assure it you. And you will marry me?'

'You must tell mother,' she said, and hid wickedly against his waistcoat again, while the male pride triumphed in him.

Mrs Bodoin had no idea that Virginia was intimate with the Turkish Delight: she did not inquire into her daughter's movements. During the famous dinner, she was calm and a little aloof, but entirely self-possessed. When, after coffee, Virginia left her alone with the Turkish Delight, she made no effort at conversation, only glanced at the rather short, stout man in correct dinner-jacket, and thought how his sort of fatness called for a fez and the full muslin breeches of a bazaar merchant in *The Thief of Baghdad*.

'Do you really prefer to smoke a hookah?' she asked him, with a slow drawl.

'What is a hookah, please?'

'One of those water-pipes. Don't you all smoke them, i
the East?'

He only looked mystified and humble, and silence re
sumed. She little knew what was simmering inside his still
ness.

'Madame,' he said, 'I want to ask you something.'

'You do? Then why not ask it?' came her slightl
melancholy drawl.

'Yes! It is this. I wish I may have the honour to marr
your daughter. She is willing.'

There was a moment's blank pause. Then Mrs Bodoi
leaned towards him from her distance, with curious por
tentousness.

'What was that you said?' she asked. 'Repeat it!'

'I wish I may have the honour to marry your daughter
She is willing to take me.'

His dark, glazed eyes looked at her, then glanced awa
again. Still leaning forward, she gazed fixedly on him, as i
spellbound, turned to stone. She was wearing pink topa
ornaments, but he judged they were paste, moderatel
good.

'Did I hear you say she is willing to take you?' came th
slow, melancholy, remote voice.

'Madame, I think so,' he said, with a bow.

'I think we'll wait till she comes,' she said, leaning back

There was silence. She stared at the ceiling. He looke
closely round the room, at the furniture, at the china in th
ivory-inlaid cabinet.

'I can settle five thousand pounds on Mademoisell
Virginia, Madame,' came his voice. 'Am I correct to assum
that she will bring this apartment and its appointments int
the marriage settlement?'

Absolute silence. He might as well have been on th

noon. But he was a good sitter. He just sat until Virginia came in.

Mrs Bodoin was still staring at the ceiling. The iron had entered her soul finally and fully. Virginia glanced at her, but said:

'Have a whisky-and-soda, Arnault?'

He rose and came towards the decanters, and stood beside her: a rather squat, stout man with white head, silent with misgiving. There was the fizz of the syphon: then they came to their chairs.

'Arnault has spoken to you, mother?' said Virginia.

Mrs Bodoin sat up straight, and gazed at Virginia with big, owlish eyes, haggard. Virginia was terrified, yet a little thrilled. Her mother was beaten.

'Is it true, Virginia, that you are *willing* to marry this – oriental gentleman?' asked Mrs Bodoin slowly.

'Yes, mother, quite true,' said Virginia, in her teasing soft voice.

Mrs Bodoin looked owlish and dazed.

'May I be excused from having any part in it, or from having anything to do with your future *husband* – I mean having any business to transact with him?' she asked dazedly, in her slow, distinct voice.

'Why, of course!' said Virginia, frightened, smiling oddly.

There was a pause. Then Mrs Bodoin, feeling old and haggard, pulled herself together again.

'Am I to understand that your future husband would like to possess this apartment?' came her voice.

Virginia smiled quickly and crookedly. Arnault just sat, planted on his posterior, and heard. She reposed on him.

'Well – perhaps!' said Virginia. 'Perhaps he would like to know that I possessed it.' She looked at him.

Arnault nodded gravely.

'And do you *wish* to possess it?' came Mrs Bodoin'
slow voice. 'Is it your intention to *inhabit* it, with you
husband?' She put eternities into her long, stressed words

'Yes, I think it is,' said Virginia. 'You know you *said* th
apartment was mine, mother.'

'Very well! It shall be so. I shall send my lawyer to this
oriental gentleman, if you will leave written instruction
on my writing-table. May I ask when you think of getting
married?'

'When do you think, Arnault?' said Virginia.

'Shall it be in two weeks?' he said, sitting erect, witl
his fists on his knees.

'In about a fortnight, mother,' said Virginia.

'I have heard? In two weeks! Very well! In two week
everything shall be at your disposal. And now, please ex
cuse me.' She rose, made a slight general bow, and move
calmly and dimly from the room. It was killing her, tha
she could not shriek aloud and beat that Levantine out o
the house. But she couldn't. She had imposed the restrain
on herself.

Arnault stood and looked with glistening eyes round th
room. It would be his. When his sons came to England
here he would receive them.

He looked at Virginia. She too was white and haggard
now. And she flung away from him, as if in resentment. She
resented the defeat of her mother. She was still capable o
dismissing him for ever, and going back to her mother.

'Your mother is a wonderful lady,' he said, going to
Virginia and taking her hand. 'But she has no husband to
shelter her, she is unfortunate. I am sorry she will be alone
I should be happy if she would like to stay here with us.

The sly old fox knew what he was about.

'I'm afraid there's no hope of that,' said Virginia, with a
return to her old irony.

She sat on the couch, and he caressed her softly and aternally, and the very incongruity of it, there in her mother's drawing-room, amused her. And because he saw that the things in the drawing-room were handsome and valuable, and now they were his, his blood flushed and he caressed the thin girl at his side with passion, because she represented these valuable surroundings, and brought them to his possession. And he said: 'And with me you will be very comfortable, very content, oh, I shall make you content, not like madame your mother. And you will get fatter, and bloom like the rose. I shall make you bloom like the rose. And shall we say next week, hein? Shall it be next week, next Wednesday, that we marry? Wednesday is good day. Shall it be then?'

'Very well!' said Virginia, caressed again into a luxurious sense of destiny, reposing on fate, having to make no effort, no more effort, all her life.

Mrs Bodoin moved into an hotel next day, and came into the apartment to pack up and extricate herself and her immediate personal belongings only when Virginia was necessarily absent. She and her daughter communicated by letter, as far as was necessary.

And in five days' time Mrs Bodoin was clear. All business that could be settled was settled, all her trunks were removed. She had five trunks, and that was all. Denuded and outcast, she would depart to Paris, to live out the rest of her days.

The last day she waited in the drawing-room till Virginia should come home. She sat there in her hat and street things, like a stranger.

'I just waited to say good-bye,' she said. 'I leave in the morning for Paris. This is my address. I think everything is settled; if not, let me know and I'll attend to it. Well, good-bye! – and I hope you'll be *very happy*!'

She dragged out the last words sinisterly; which restored Virginia, who was beginning to lose her head.

'Why, I think I may be,' said Virginia, with the twist of a smile.

'I shouldn't wonder,' said Mrs Bodoin pointedly and grimly. 'I think the Armenian grandpapa knows very well what he's about. You're just the harem type, after all.' The words came slowly, dropping, each with a plop! of deep contempt.

'I suppose I am! Rather fun!' said Virginia. 'But I wonder where I got it? Not from you, mother –' she drawled mischievously.

'I should say *not*.'

'Perhaps daughters go by contraries, like dreams,' mused Virginia wickedly. 'All the harem was left out of you, so perhaps it all had to be put back into me.'

Mrs Bodoin flashed a look at her.

'You have *all* my *pity*!' she said.

'Thank you, dear. You have just a bit of mine.'

MORE ABOUT PENGUINS

Penguinews, which appears every month, contains details of all the new books issued by Penguins as they are published. From time to time it is supplemented by *Penguins in Print,* which is a complete list of all books published by Penguins which are in print. (There are well over three thousand of these.)

A specimen copy of *Penguinews* will be sent to you free on request, and you can become a subscriber for the price of the postage. For a year's issues (including the complete lists) please send 30p if you live in the United Kingdom, or 60p if you live elsewhere. Just write to Dept EP, Penguin Books Ltd, Harmondsworth, Middlesex, enclosing a cheque or postal order, and your name will be added to the mailing list.

Some other books published by Penguins are described on the following pages.

Note: *Penguinews* and *Penguins in Print* are not available in the U.S.A. or Canada

D. H. LAWRENCE

The Mortal Coil and Other Stories

Fourteen stories through which can be traced D. H. Lawrence's development in his twenties. Among these stories: *A Prelude*, his first published work, was written for a newspaper competition.

The Old Adam and *Witch a la Mode* reflect the years of intense sexual frustration Lawrence endured while a schoolmaster in Croydon.

A Chapel and *A Hay Hut Among the Mountains* records a happier period – the first months of his life with Frieda.

The Thimble and *The Mortal Coil* ('a first-class story, one of my purest creations') take us to the years of the First World War, years of Lawrence's maturity and growing sense of tragedy.

Not for sale in the U.S.A.

LAURIE LEE

As I Walked Out One Midsummer Morning

It was 1935. The young man walked to London from the
security of the Cotswolds to make his fortune. He was to live
by playing the violin and by a year's labouring on a London
building site. Then, knowing one Spanish phrase, he decided
to see Spain. For a year he tramped through a country in
which the signs of impending civil war were clearly visible.

Thirty years later Laurie Lee has captured the atmosphere
of the Spain he saw with all the freshness and beauty of a
young man's vision, creating a lyrical and lucid picture of the
beautiful and violent country that was to inextricably involve
him.

'A marvellous book' – Kenneth Allsop, BBC, *The World of
Books*

'A beautiful piece of writing' – John Raymond, *Observer*

Also available
CIDER WITH ROSIE
A ROSE FOR WINTER

Not for sale in the U.S.A.

MELVYN BRAGG

The Second Inheritance

When his father dies, Arthur Langley comes out of the army to run the estate. But his good intentions soon evaporate and he becomes a dilettante recluse . . . only seeking the company of young John Foster, the shy but clever son of an ambitious tenant-farmer.

Then Arthur's beautiful sister Pat gets tired of persuading Arthur to resume their too-intimate teenage relationship . . . and turns her attentions to John.

In *The Second Inheritance* Melvyn Bragg writes with truth, power and simplicity: the interplay between the Langleys and the Fosters – and the odd, tense triangle of Arthur, Pat and John – is unforgettably described.

For Want of a Nail

Clever, shy and a victim of his fantasies, Tom Graham is disturbed by his mother's harsh indifference; tortured by doubts about who his father is; confused and enraged by the ambiguous patronage of the vicar . . .

Set amongst the wild Cumberland fells, *For Want of a Nail* takes us right inside Tom as he tries to resolve the furtive secrets around him, and arrive at some sort of truce with his background, his family . . . and himself.

Also available
WITHOUT A CITY WALL

Not for sale in the U.S.A.

BARRY HINES

Kes

Billy Casper is a boy with nowhere to go and nothing to say; part of the limbo generation of school leavers too old for lessons and too young to know anything about the outside world. He hates and he is hated. His family and friends are mean and tough and they're sure he's going to end up in big trouble. But Billy knows two things about his own world. He'll never work down the mines and he does know about animals. His only companion is his kestrel hawk, trained from the nest, and, like himself, trained but not tamed, with the will to destroy or be destroyed.

This is not just another book about growing up in the North. It's as real as a slap in the face to those who think that orange juice and comprehensive schools have taken the meanness out of life in the raw working towns.

The Blinder

'Hey up, Len! Where you been?'
'Celebrating.'
'Where?'
'In t'bushes.'
'Who with?'
'Jenny.'
'Again! You'll both get expelled if you're caught.'
'I know.'
'It's not work the risk.'
'There's no risk at half past eight in the morning. What's the first lesson?'
'Art appreciation.'
So Lennie Hawk begins his day in the sixth form. The star of the school whom everyone adores or hates. The best young footballer anyone's ever seen. Every game he plays is a blinder and every manager in the First Division is after him. So is everyone else who ever loved or hated him. And most of them get him in the end.

Not for sale in the U.S.A.

RUDYARD KIPLING

A Sahibs' War and Other Stories
Friendly Brook and Other Stories

Of the two volumes, *A Sahibs' War and Other Stories* and *Friendly Brook and Other Stories*, Professor Rutherford who selected the contents of both volumes writes: 'There are fewer tales of Empire than the popular stereotype of Kipling might lead readers to expect. . . . Increasingly he was preoccupied by the condition of England herself, as he rebuked her blindness, folly and complacency, and sought reassurance in groups, types, or individuals who might still redeem her backslidings. Simultaneously, he found himself involved in a fascinating process of discovery, for the country-side, its people and traditions, came as a revelation to him once he settled in Sussex. . . . Public themes bulk large in *A Sahibs' War and Other Stories*, as his preoccupation with the Great War does in *Friendly Brook and Other Stories*; but these coexist with more personal, psychological, and more spiritual interests, especially in his later years . . . using a remarkable variety of settings and of *dramatis personae*, he offers stories on a characteristic range of themes – stories of revenge, seen sometimes as wild justice, sometimes as an almost pathological obsession; stories of forgiveness, human and divine; stories of the supernatural, to be taken now literally, now symbolically, but never trivially as mere spine-chilling entertainment; stories of hatred and cruelty, but stories also of compassion and of love; stories of work, of craftsmanship, of artistry; of comradeship and isolation; and stories of healing, sometimes physical, but more often moral, spiritual or psychological.

Not for sale in the U.S.A.

D. H. Lawrence

D. H. Lawrence is now acknowledged as one of the greatest writers of the twentieth century. Nearly all his works are available in Penguins:

Novels

AARON'S ROD*	LADY CHATTERLEY'S LOVER*
THE LOST GIRL*	THE PLUMED SERPENT
THE RAINBOW*	SONS AND LOVERS*
THE TRESPASSER	THE WHITE PEACOCK
WOMEN IN LOVE*	KANGAROO*

THE BOY IN THE BUSH (with M. L. Skinner)*
THE VIRGIN AND THE GIPSY

Short Stories

THE PRUSSIAN OFFICER*
ENGLAND, MY ENGLAND*
ST MAWR *and* THE VIRGIN AND THE GIPSY
LOVE AMONG THE HAYSTACKS
THE WOMAN WHO RODE AWAY
THREE NOVELLAS:
THE FOX, THE LADYBIRD, THE CAPTAIN'S DOLL*
SELECTED SHORT STORIES*

Travel Books and Other Works

MORNINGS IN MEXICO *and* ETRUSCAN PLACES
SEA AND SARDINIA*   TWILIGHT IN ITALY*
STUDIES IN CLASSIC AMERICAN LITERATURE*
FANTASIA OF THE UNCONSCIOUS*
A SELECTION FROM 'PHOENIX'*
SELECTED ESSAYS   SELECTED LETTERS
SELECTED POEMS*

* Not for sale in the U.S.A.
Remainder not for sale in the U.S.A. or Canada